ARTIFACT
A PETER GRANT MYSTERY

D. GRANT GEDDES

St. Crispin's Press
New York

Copyright © 2002 by Donald G. Geddes, III

Library of Congress Control Number: 2001090919
ISBN # Hardcover: 0-9710632-0-6

All rights reserved. No part of this book may be reproduced or transmitted in any form by any means, electronic or mechanical, including photocopying, recording, or by any information storage and retrieval system, without permission in writing from the copyright holder.

This is a work of fiction. Names, characters, places and incidents either are the product of the author's imagination or are used fictitiously, and any resemblance to any actual persons, living or dead, events, or locales is entirely coincidental.

This book is printed in the United States of America.

StC

St. Crispin's Press
244 Fifth Avenue
New York, NY 10001

StC

For My Children
and
My Grandchildren

"From the man I trust may God defend me.
From the man I trust not I will defend myself."

                Anonymous.
                Scratched on a dungeon wall
                in the Doge's Palace, Venice.

PREFACE

It has been my good fortune to have spent sufficient time in Venice to capture some of the fascination that this uniquely engineered city has long engendered among those who come to pay homage to its glorious past and to partake in its uncertain future. There is a decadent splendor about Venice unequaled in the modern world. Its melancholy character has evolved as a direct result of its fabled history and its constant struggle to survive the fickle whims of nature to which it is ever hostage. It is only through the courage, persistence, and resignation of its inhabitants and its benefactors worldwide that the beauty that is unique to *La Serenissima* is preserved.

Foremost, Venice is a city of facades, a carnival mask that disguises the true identity of its wearer. Like the pervasive fragrance of its wisteria, an aura of self-indulgence and intrigue wafts through the city. If you are curious, and those who come to Venice usually are, explore its maze of narrow streets, its meander of canals, and its complex of campos, and your eyes will feast on sensuality unrivaled anywhere on earth.

Many people generously lent their time, effort and suggestions to this novel. I am indebted to them all, especially Janis Martin, Venetian guide, muse, and fellow author; Marissa Rubinow, my writing coach; John Ed Bradley, an admired friend and gifted author; Harry Cipriani, who fed me too well, and Claudio, whose magic Montgomerys assuaged my worries.

The Author

ARTIFACT

Chapter 1

INSIDE Madrid's Prado Museum a Goya is slashed to ribbons; the perpetrator escapes. Later a Basque terrorist group claims responsibility. In the Netherlands a Vermeer vanishes from a museum in the Hague; the culprit is unknown. In South Beach, Miami a film star is murdered for a Salvadore Dali that once adorned his living room wall. Authorities in London confiscate fake Etruscan figurines from a London dealer's showroom; their origin is traced to a hastily abandoned workshop outside Florence. In Osaka a Japanese businessman pays twenty million dollars to a Canadian swindler for a skillful forgery of a Gauguin falsely documented as the original. Pre-Colombian jade offered for sale by a prestigious New York auction gallery is impounded by customs agents after a complaint filed by the Peruvian Government claims the jade has been looted from a Moche gravesite. Terrorism, theft, murder, forgery, greed and pillage! Welcome to the seamy underbelly of the art world where everything and everybody is fair game, a world that I'm a part of, except I'm one of the good guys.

My name is Peter Grant and I'm a New York-based fine arts expert. I sell my expertise to a highly select clientele including international auction houses, prestigious museums, major art dealers, and exceedingly rich collectors. Occasionally major corporations and insurance companies retain my services. My work mainly involves authentication, but sometimes I'm hired to find works of art *gone missing,* a discreet terminology that refers to rare paintings or masterful sculptures that have been stolen. These purloined objects are usually pricey works of art and, more often than not, priceless. I am known for my *good eye,* as they say in the trade, which means I'm usually able to spot things that aren't *quite right,* forgeries for example, some tediously blatant, others tantalizingly brilliant. The challenge, of course, is to recognize the handiwork of the forger and to expose him or her, as the case may be. Because of my *good eye,* my prowess with tools of the trade, x-rays, infrared and ultra-violet light scanners, spectroscopes and chemical analyzers and my inclination for discretion, I am generally in demand. Although I am technically an art detective, I personally prefer the term *art sleuth,* which has a more sophisticated ring to it, more Hercule Poirot let's say than, Sam Spade.

During the summer my clients scatter to posh retreats, socializing in Southampton, basking in Bermuda, or cruising off Cannes. Relaxing and entertaining are uppermost in their minds, not fine art. Thus after Independence Day I find myself in a nearly deserted city along with its eerily quiet museums and its shuttered auction houses and art galleries. When my wife, Claire, and I were together we always had summer plans, but after our separation I find I'm not terribly gung-ho about doing things alone. These days I feel a tad lonely, perhaps even a bit depressed. And unless something interesting crops up, I guess I'll just muddle through the summer malaise by myself, albeit at glacial speed.

Following my traditional Fourth of July rooftop bash for friends and clients, I wake up enervated from everyone bragging about their fabulous vacation plans, wilted from the oppressive heat and humidity and bowed but unbroken from an excess of champagne that I have consumed. I chase down two aspirin with a glass of ice water and resolve to settle into my summer torpor with breakfast and a good novel when I'm rudely interrupted by a most unexpected telephone call from London.

"Peter Grant here."

"Colin Marshall of Lloyd's, old chap. I'll get right to it, Peter. We need you in Venice, chop-chop, as they say. You must endeavor to recover several Renaissance oils, including a Bellini masterpiece, stolen from the palazzo of one of our clients, an Austrian Archduke. We're staring down the barrel of a loaded gun and should it go off it will blow an immense crater in our corporate wallet."

"I see." Colin is his usual dramatic self.

"I'm authorized to offer a generous retainer, thirty thousand quid and reasonable expenses, of course."

"Book it," I reply without hesitation.

"Lovely, Peter. My regards to your smashing, Claire."

"Of course." I reply. Colin hasn't a clue about my breakup with Claire, for which I'm thankful. The bloke, though married, has a roving eye and as I'm reliably informed, a rather remarkable bird to bed ratio. Anyway, the theft of pictures from an Austrian Archduke's palazzo sounds rather my cup of tea, which will spare me boredom and possible cremation in the "Baked Apple." While I'm not keen about the heat, the crowds and the fetid canals during the height of Venice's tourist season, I have nonetheless agreed to venture forth. In addition to a handsome fee, I have a most compelling personal urge to go. The trip provides me the excuse to see the stunning, husky voiced former fashion model who is my estranged wife. Claire, it so happens, resides in *La Serenissima's* melancholy splendor, except when she's cavorting about the continent with a bizarre assortment of male admirers.

In spite of our breakup and Claire's quirky, often outrageous behavior I'm still terribly in love with her. She's enchanting to look at, tall and slender with smooth golden skin and long blond air. She's curious and intelligent, affectionate and funny, direct and demanding, spontaneous, and as I mentioned, quite unpredictable. For six years we seemed the ideal couple, close friends and ardent lovers when without warning, she suddenly bolted. Despite her hasty exit, I'd like to try to convince her to come back.

Chapter 2

Seeking relief from a hazy Adriatic sun that wilts me on the choppy passage by water taxi from Marco Polo Airport to the fabled island Republic which looms mirage-like in the distance in pinkish splendor, I instruct the driver to deposit me at the vaporetto stop nearest Harry's Bar.

Motoring into the Canale di Cannaregio on the approach to the Grand Canal I experience my usual feeling of wonderment. I think the feeling has to do with the fact that Venice seems more fantasy than reality, an ancient, crumbling city out of place in a modern world. Hauntingly beautiful, it occupies a time warp of romantic decadence that has miraculously survived thirteen centuries of tumultuous conflicts and nature's caprices. Venice rests upon oak and larch poles that were long ago rammed into the sediments and clay of one hundred eighteen islets now segmented by one hundred seventy-seven serpentine canals and reconnected by more than four-hundred picturesque bridges each as individual as any member of the human race. Little wonder then that every visitor who walks this maze gets lost!

Cruising along the Grand Canal, I never cease to be awestruck as I gaze at the decaying splendor of the ornate *palazzi*. How those ancient waterlogged foundation posts continue to bear the massive weight of all that Istrian stone, brick, marble, terrazzo, wood, stucco, and tile is itself a mystery. The very thought staggers my imagination as does a guess at the sum required for annual maintenance, which no doubt accounts for the shabby appearance of many elegant *palazzi*. Grudgingly, many houses have been abdicated to wealthy foreigners who can best afford to keep them afloat, while attempting to restore them to their former magnificence.

Behind the opulent facades of the Grand Canal's architecture my mind recalls what my eyes cannot see, the dark labyrinth of narrow passageways and sunny campos with their unique and mysterious-looking wells upon which stray cats snooze on sun-drenched lids. Here and there ancient brick reveals itself, exposed by crumbling stucco. Gray-haired grand mothers peer from open windows their faces framed by peeling shutters, while inside TV sets blare incessantly. Above the narrow passageways flap the pigeons and the ubiquitous laundry. Strung out to dry, clothing and undergarments undulate suggestively in the breeze. And everywhere there are flowers, white roses cascade over brick walls, geraniums thrust brazen pink and red blossoms skyward from earthen pots and purple wisteria dangles in pungent profusion like a tangled arbor lush with grapes. Already I detect or perhaps I just imagine the familiar aromas, sewage, floral attar, fresh bread, dead fish, garlic, mildew and Gorgonzola, smells all tinged with salt air from the vast greenish colored lagoon.

Before I realize it I stand aboard a floating dock within a stone's throw of the Piazza San Marco with its Egyptian granite columns and brick Campanile and in the background the ornate, Moorish-looking Doge's Palace and the golden domes of the basilica of San Marco. The water taxi driver relieves me of a vast sum of lire, or so it seems. Then he whisks me and my luggage forty meters away to the frosted glass entry to *Harry's Bar* where now secure within its frigid Spartan interior I quickly forgive Venice her oppressive heat.

The bartender greets me with a vulpine grin and a roguish wink. To him I am known as *the other Mr. Grant*. Prior to my arrival at this idyllic oasis Claudio had been on intimate terms with a previous Mister Grant, Cary, who lived in Venice when married to the Woolworth heiress Barbara Hutton. Referring to me as *the other Mr. Grant,* is Claudio's way of flattering me, but in the same breath, reminding me of my slightly inferior status. Not that I'm offended, mind you. Quite the contrary, I feel complimented by his casual acceptance of me as a *regular.*

In Harry's, I always feel a swelling of self-importance as Claudio, surrounded by his faithful clack, orchestrates cocktails the way Luciano Pavarotti sings arias. As I perch atop a barstool Claudio loudly exclaims, *"Ah, the other Mr. Grant . . . buon giorno . . . come stai?"*

Once, very briefly I was a Wall Street stockbroker. In New York Stock Exchangese, I respond, "Oh, a half to five eighths, Claudio, and you?"

"Molto bene," he grins, catching the gist of my reply. Claudio is perceptive, unusually so, a combination of Doppler radar and ESP. Seeing the weariness etched onto my face from the overnight flight from J. F. K. to Venice, he anticipates my need and effortlessly concocts a "Montgomery." This lethal cousin to a martini, fifteen parts gin to one part vermouth, gets its moniker from the feisty British Field Marshall of World War II who allegedly ordered his troops to advance only when they outnumbered the Axis enemy by that same ratio. Obdurate little Scotsman, that Monty!

Across the highly polished bar, Claudio slides a frosty tumbler toward my eager fingertips. Then, from his jacket pocket, he extracts a ring of keys, which smugly he dangles before my eyes. Plucking the keys to Claire's flat from his fingers I pocket them, raise my glass, and toast him, *"Grazie, Claudio . . . salute, amore, e ricchezze."* For an instant patrons and tourists alike stare at me in wonderment. I have spoken like a native son. I feel acclaimed. Since my separation from Claire, nearly a year now, it's the first time I've felt much of anything beside numbness. I presume Claudio assumes we're still together and I won't tell him otherwise. It's too painful.

When he has a moment, I anticipate Claudio will ask, "What brings you back to Venice?" I will fib, of course, for I'm not at liberty to reveal that Palazzo Aldrovani has been robbed of its priceless Bellini along with other art treasures. The police are keeping that information secret, at least for now. Nor, will I confide that Lloyd's has employed me to investigate the Archduke's theft. That's confidential. So when he asks, and eventually he does, I'm prepared. "I'm researching material at the Accademia for a coffee table book on Renaissance art," I tell him.

"*Va bene.*" Thinking my response vapid, he smiles politely and returns to his task, creating Harry's trademark "Bellini," the sparkling Italian white wine called prosecco that he artfully combines with white peach juice. I pause to wonder if there's any connection between the drink and the painter of the Archduke's purloined masterpiece. If there is it escapes me. I'm too exhausted to dwell on the possible coincidence. Instead, I focus on how pleasant it is to once again hang out at Harry's.

Like rice pudding, there's something comforting about old haunts and one's acceptance as an habitue, even though one appears sporadically or perhaps only after a long absence. It's reassuring to know what to expect, a bracing and friendly atmosphere with no surprises. A home away from home, home in my case being my two-bedroom Beekman Place Co-op, where prior to my departure, I had screwed up sufficient courage to telephone Claire.

"Claire, I've just accepted an assignment from Lloyd's. They've asked me to try to recover some paintings that were stolen from a Venetian palazzo several days ago. It's all very hush, hush, so please, not a word. I'm flying over day after tomorrow. I was hoping you might let me to stay with you."

"You may have my flat all to yourself, Peter. I'm leaving for Switzerland in the morning. No one in their right mind stays in Venice during July and August with this ghastly heat, the dreadful mosquitoes, and the hoards of tourists."

"Thanks, Claire, that's kind of you. I accept, but I'm crushed I won't get to see you.

"Well, if you're still here when I return in September, we'll get together."

"I doubt I'll be in Venice that long."

"Peter you sound down. Are you all right?"

"Yeah . . . just disappointed. By the way, Claire, how will I get the keys to the flat?"

"Suppose I leave them at Harry's . . . with Claudio."

"*Perfetto*," I reply in Italian, cheerfully, in an effort to mask my shattered expectations. I hope you enjoy your summer." I tell her. But I really don't mean it for I suspect she's going off with . . . *a friend*.

"Thanks. Oh, Peter, I'll leave you my real estate lady's number in case anything goes haywire at the flat or you need anything. Her name is Cinzia . . . and she's very attractive."

"Trying to fix me up, are you? Take my mind off you while you're gone, is that it?"

"No, I . . . Oh shit, Peter, I don't really know. You might like her, everyone does. She's your type, dependable, cultured, conservative, and elegant, not disorganized and flighty like me." I can't tell if she's really serious or if she's having a momentary lapse of self-esteem because she feels guilty about going off with . . . *a friend*.

"And one other thing, please don't disturb Franco."

"Franco! Jesus, Claire, who's Franco?" My mind conjures up some Italian stallion who shares the rent and certain other amenities on which I prefer not to dwell.

"Your first line of defense against mosquitoes, my pet house spider."

"Oh, that Franco! Uh, what's he look like? You know, so I'll recognize him when I run into him?"

"He's shiny black with long spindly legs and he lives in a lovely web in the corner of the salon ceiling over the bookcase. Make sure when you leave the apartment that the window's ajar so he's able to catch bugs."

Disbelieving, I shake my head and mutter to myself, "I hate spiders. God, I hope Franco hasn't got a red hour glass on his thorax!"

I locate Claire's flat in a five-story house in Campo Santa Stefano, a lovely square near the Accademia Bridge with its usual medieval cistern, marble statue of a patriot, the requisite parish churche and outdoor cafes. The house, sandwiched between others resembling it, has a seasoned Renaissance look about it, a charming tilt, stress cracks, patches of exposed brick, and crazed stucco that has weathered to a pale patina of canary yellow. Viewing the ancient structure, which I figure dates to the fifteenth century, causes my imagination to run amok. I envision the richly robed Marco Polo standing on its threshold as he regales a throng with his adventures. What an imagination! No more "Montgomery's" for me after an all night flight from the Big Apple.

Dragging my weary bones and suitcases, I stagger up worn marble stairs, concave from centuries of use. When I'm able to breathe normally again, I realize the staircase has taken its toll. Without the least thought of unpacking, seeking out Franco, or brushing my teeth, I stumble into the bedroom and collapse onto the bed. As I think about Colin's request, to telephone the Questura in the morning, I fall into an exhausted sleep fully clothed.

Chapter 3

IN THE GRAY DAWN, Commissario Luca Moretti has been jolted out of a sound sleep by the jangle of the telephone that squats beside his ear. The call from a cell phone patched through the Questura, comes from his deputy Roberto Chiari

"We've fished a body out of the Rio dei Gesuiti, Commissario. We need you here right away."

"Who is the victim?" asks Luca, rubbing a thick hand across his eyes, trying to help them swim into focus.

"A Benedictine monk. Your wife's cousin found his body floating beside his gondola."

"*Madonna!* You're certain?"

"Absolutely. He's dressed in a hooded, dark brown robe with a braided cord around his waist and he's wearing leather sandals. There's a seminary ring on his left hand and a crucifix hanging around his neck."

Covering the phone's mouthpiece, the Commissario reaches out and gently shakes his wife by a shoulder. "Carla, wake up." Rolling over, she squints up at him, "What's wrong, Luca?"

"I've got an emergency. Would you please fix me a *caffè?*"

"*Subito,*" she replies, getting out of bed.

"Does it look like an accident, Roberto?" Silently, he prays it is, otherwise, he can expect public outrage.

"I don't know." It appears he drowned, but there's an ugly

head wound. It's either an accident or somebody assaulted him."

"Wake the Coroner. I want him to meet me there. Keep the press out of it. That's an order, *avete capito*?"

"Yes sir, I understand."

"And send the launch for me."

"San Toma?"

"*Esattamente.*" Hanging up the phone, Luca extricates his large frame from the tangle of covers and climbs out of bed. As he heads for the bathroom, he notices Carla standing motionless in the bedroom doorway. Her face bears a troubled expression.

"Caro, is it serious?" she asks.

"It couldn't be worse', he replies, hiking up his pajama bottoms. "Your cousin, Alfonso, found the body of a Benedictine monk floating alongside his gondola near the Church of the Gesuiti. It's possible there's been foul play."

"How dreadful," she exclaims, while making the sign of the cross. "What kind of person would harm a humble brother?"

"I don't know, but if we don't get some answers in a hurry, the media will crucify us. Carla, *mi caffé*?"

"I'm going, Luca." Gathering her nightgown about her ample bosom so she won't step on the hem and trip, she dutifully pads down the chilly terrazzo hallway toward the kitchen.

The Commissario's launch arrives at six-twenty a.m., joining two other boats moored alongside the *fondamenta*, a police launch that duplicates his own and the Coroner's boat, painted a depressing chartreuse-gray, which always reminds him of bile. Several uniformed officers, the Coroner, his two assistants, and Luca's deputy, Roberto, stand in a circle, surrounding the body. Atop a widening stain of canal water, the corpse lies on the *fondamenta's* concrete apron where it's covered with a bright orange tarpaulin.

Bathed in the pink glow of dawn, Luca notices that the men's faces looked strangely radiant as he searches for Alfonso who is not among them. Making a mental note to ask his whereabouts, he feels his stomach rumble. Indigestion! He wishes now that he'd eaten the two slices of buttered *pane* that Clara had offered. He'd refused them. Knowing better, he'd gulped down two black coffees on an empty stomach.

Despite his bulk, Luca steps off the boat and onto the *fondamenta* as nimbly as a ballet dancer. The bright orange hue of the tarpaulin covering the monk's body offends him. It's an ignominious color for a man of the faith. Conjuring up in his mind the appropriate shade of ecclesiastical purple, he joins the circle of men.

"What have we got here, Bruno?" says the Commissario, pumping the sallow, puffy-eyed Coroner's hand.

"Severe trauma to the right temporal area of the skull, Luca. Without an X-ray, I'd wager the skull's fractured. The blow came either from a fall or a heavy blunt instrument. Here, I'll show you." He bends over the body and lifts up one end of the plastic tarpaulin.

Luca cranes over the Coroner's shoulder. He notices the soggy cowl of the monk's habit bunched up under the victim's head. The skin has turned a bluish-gray and the victim's lips are purple. Between his ear and his eyebrow protrudes a large purple and black edema with spacklings of dark red where the capillaries have burst. "Nasty sight," he comments. "Cause of death, Bruno?"

"We have to do an autopsy, Luca. Offhand, I'm pretty certain he drowned." He pulls the tarp over the corpse's head and stands erect.

"Then it's possible it's an accident? We don't need a high profile murder case on our hands during the height of tourist season."

"Possible, but not likely," Bruno responds.

"Why?"

"Mostly a gut reaction, but when you see as many dead people as I have, you sense when there's been an accident."

"Well, in this case, Bruno, I hope you're wrong. Neither Venice nor the Questura wants the Italian press swarming all over us like bloodthirsty mosquitoes."

"The gondolier who found the body also found this," interrupts Roberto. He hands Luca a ticket folder. "This may have belonged to the victim."

"Where's Alfonso?" asks Luca.

"I took his statement and let him go. He had an appointment to take his gondola to the San Trovaso boat yard for repairs." "Where did he find this folder?"

"At the base of that mooring over there." Roberto points out an old iron cannon, painted black, whose muzzle and part of its barrel has been long buried in the *fondamenta's* concrete coping. Luca remembers seeing other cannon lining the canal and he reflects on the vast number of them he's passed each day. They're formidable reminders of Venice's golden era, when for centuries its navy and its guns ruled the Mediterranean.

Opening the folder, Luca sees a time stamped and punched first class ticket from Rome to Venice and an unused first class return ticket to Rome. "Alvise," exclaims Luca, reading aloud the ticket holder's name. "At least we know who he is."

"It was for last night's express train," says Roberto, pointing to the unused ticket."

"So I see. What's this?" Luca holds up a stub. "This came from the Murano boat," he exclaims. "Let's have a look at that mooring, shall we?"

On the way over to it, Luca asks Bruno, "How long has the victim been dead?"

"Eight to twelve hours. With a body submerged in tepid water, It's hard to be more exact."

Between six and ten last night, muses Luca.

When they reach the inverted cannon, Luca bends over and peers at the bulbous iron ball known as the cascabel, which protrudes from the breech end of the cannon. The cascabel, he knew, provided the means to "warp" the gun into firing position by adjusting ropes looped around it. "This looks like dried blood. What do you think Bruno?" *Madonna!* he swears under his breath. How could all of them miss this?

One of Bruno's assistants pulls a magnifying glass out of his lab coat pocket. He hands it to the Coroner who examines the cascabel. "I agree with you, Luca. We'll take a scraping. Bring the lab kit over here, Mario," he calls to his other assistant.

Shoving the ticket folder into his jacket pocket, Luca says to Roberto, "I want you to take the launch to Murano. Find out what Brother Alvise was doing there. Check the church first. If he didn't go there, ascertain if he visited any of the glass factories." In a loud voice Luca asks, "Can anyone tell me if a monk's habit has pockets?"

"Monk's aren't allowed pockets," says Mario, wearing a cocky smirk, which implies some kind of inside joke.

"Something you want to share with us, Mario?" asks Luca, challenging him.

Mario can tell by the Commissario's glare that he's not amused. "Oh, well . . ." he says, dancing around the Commissario's question as his face flushes red. "They don't have pockets . . . so they can't be tempted to . . . you know?" he says, making a lewd up and down motion with his closed fist.

I've noticed the monks usually carry a cloth bag slung over one shoulder," volunteers an officer.

"Did we find one of those?" asks Luca, examining each man's blank expression.

"You men," snaps Luca, glaring at the idle uniformed officers, "take my launch and drag the canal for evidence. There's equipment on board and the driver's name is Alberto. Roberto, you get going. I'm not reporting this to the Questore until I have a full explanation of exactly what happened here. Bruno, your autopsy report, I need it yesterday."

Closeting himself in his office at the Questura, Luca waits impatiently for Roberto's call from Murano. The grapples and nets recover only trash that indolent tourists have pitched into the canal. There's no sign of the monk's pouch, which isn't a good omen.

Finally, around ten-thirty, Roberto phones in with his report. "Commissario, the victim is definitely Brother Alvise. He brought an object to Gino Cenedese, the glass-maker, and asked him to encase it in a cylinder of Murano crystal."

"What kind of object?"

"The glass-maker said it was a wrought iron nail that resembled a ship's hull spike. He said it was very old and before encasing it, he had to remove surface oxidation."

"What do you suppose it was?"

"I have no idea. According to Cenedese, Brother Alvise didn't volunteer any information about it, but he hovered over him the entire time he worked on it. In the early evening, when he finished the job, the monk paid him in cash, put the object in a gold tooled, red leather case, slipped it into his canvas pouch, and left. That's it."

"Roberto, stop by the Coroner's on the way back and pick up Brother Alvise's autopsy report. See you shortly. *Ciao*."

Hanging up the phone, Luca rocks back in his chair and utters an audible sigh. The pouch and the leather case are both missing. Had Alfonso found them, he would have turned them over to Roberto. Before calling his superior, the Questore, Luca decides to first speak with the Vatican.

His conversation with the Papal Secretary is terse. He learns that the Vatican has ordered *Dottore* Umberto Ferculi, the Director General of the Vatican Museum, to Venice to oversee the recovery of the object the dead Brother Alvise had in his possession. "The most precious religious artifact in all of Christendom," declares the Papal Secretary.

Chapter 4

Awakening with "jet lag," my mind is foggy. Initially, I'm confused as to my whereabouts. Nothing looks familiar. I hear the enchanting high pitched squeals of children playing tag, the animated voices that echo from the campo, and the strains of Mozart and Vivaldi drifting in the window from the neighboring Conservatory of Music where students play classical music with varying degrees of accomplishment. There are no bleating horns, roaring motors, screeching tires, shrill sirens, or grinding garbage.

"Ahhhhh, Venice!"

Plumping up the pillows, I lie back and enjoy the sounds. While trying to orient myself to a different environment, my mind wanders.

I think about Claire and how we first met. I had been working long hours at the Metropolitan Museum of Art and as a result I had virtually stopped dating. Also, at the time, it seemed to me that the female population of New York City had changed for the worse. Woman seemed more cynical, tough, and a lot more aggressive. My perceived waning of femininity could easily have been blamed on the feminists, but they were not at the root of these attitudes. Financial problems and emotional baggage were. Owing to the City's cutthroat competitive forces and its escalating inflation, many single women were barely surviving. Others were experiencing emotional scarring as the result of abusive relationships with predatory men who later escaped by passing them along to like-minded acquaintances. The result was a large pool of jaded women all seeking "Mr. Wonderful." While generally sympathetic, I felt imposed upon. I didn't like listening to a date's monologue of her problems. And if I introduced intimacy into the equation it implied that I was going to help resolve them. Under these circumstances I found dating to be a cynical exercise. Where had spontaneity, fun, and romance gone? And whatever happened to the concept of friends and lovers?

I made a conscience decision to find an unencumbered fresh face, an innocent not yet part of the landscape of New York City. I knew that in order to find such a person I couldn't rely on the usual networking with friends and acquaintances. I had to take an entirely new approach, something I had never tried before. "It pays to advertise," some smart person had once said. So I took out a *personal* ad in *New York Magazine,* which I hoped might attract the attention of a woman who was not only new to the city but unspoiled. The ad read as follows:

Handsome SWPM, Native N.Y.- N\S – Age 45, 5'-11," 170 lbs., ath. bld., premature gray hair, blue eyes, romantic, affectionate, sensitive, humorous, intelligent, curious, honest, and secure ISO tall, attractive, fit SWPF, 30-45 with similar qualities, brand new to N.Y. who enjoys art, theatre, opera, music, movies, fine dining, dancing, travel, adventure, participates in sports and plays backgammon, all for possible LTR. Ad # 6269.

Ten days later, over cocktails at Le Cirque, I stare approvingly at the woman who has answered my ad. "Out of sheer curiosity," she responds to my question, "because I'm a tournament backgammon player who'd like to see how good *you* are." She's a tall blond with green eyes and has the loveliest face imaginable. She's a former fashion model, an actress from Atlanta, Georgia who has just moved to New York to work in Soaps. I guess that she's in her mid-thirties. I'm enchanted for she speaks with a husky voice and sounds like Lauren

Bacall. *Here's looking at you, kid!* I silently toast as we clink our wineglasses together.

Within a year Claire McConnell and I marry.

My thoughts shift to Harry's and Ernest Hemingway, who are both woven into the fabric of Venice. Harry's was the writer's favorite watering hole and he was known and envied there for his great capacity for drink and his wondrous tales about his adventures. A revered fixture, Hemingway vividly embodied his own characters: the macho big game hunter, Francis Macomber, who met an untimely demise in the African bush and the gruff, hard drinking and impotent American Army Colonel Cantwell, who cut his own swath of pathos through the heart of Venice.

I think about Hemingway as a boy, particularly his upbringing. Although he was of a different era, I identify with him. The second son of an admired family that was outwardly prosperous, educated, and morally and politically staid, young Ernest grew up lonely. His parents were self-absorbed, what we now refer to as dysfunctional. Ernest found his happiness using his restless curiosity to pursue the adventuresome literature of Theodore Roosevelt's exploits, to participate in nature's sports, and to master the fundamentals of creative writing. That he never penned a word about his parents and his siblings speaks volumes. It was as though they had never existed, but of course they had. Like chalk on a blackboard he had erased his family, as suddenly and completely as the plane crash that had obliterated mine.

When my parents died, I was too young to remember anything about them. My father's parents raised me. They were much like Hemingway's parents, wealthy conservative Republicans, socially prominent, well-educated, and devoted to church and community. I grew up in an immense forty-four room Tudor mansion on thirty-five manicured acres replete with an English butler, a Scottish chauffeur, and twenty-three other servants, not a single one among them under age forty. I'm not complaining mind you, for I realize I was extremely fortunate to have a privileged upbringing and a first rate education.

Though I dearly loved both my grandparents, they were

busy and distant. Grandfather managed the family firm on Wall Street, while grandmother was preoccupied with an active social life. Left pretty much to my own devices, I sated my curiosity with books from their library and paintings from their large art collection. Like most boys my age I collected things, stamps and coins and birds eggs. I even practiced the ancient art of falconry with a Coopers Hawk I had retrieved at six weeks from its nest. On occasions when my grandfather had spare time I joined him in trout fishing or shooting skeet, activities Hemingway would likely have approved.

"Ahhhh, Venice!"

There's nothing more delightful and rewarding than traveling all over the world on behalf of collectors, museums, auctioneers, and insurance companies, though it sometimes requires putting up with the likes of Colin Marshall. He's not only an insufferable bore and tighter with money than bark on a beech tree, but he's a lecher. I believe the only reason he's hired me is to find a way to get into Claire's knickers.

Getting out of bed, I explore the salon. It's large and airy with high ceilings and it's appointed with tasteful Venetian antiques. Four tall windows with Juliet balconies face west and overlook the campo and the red roof-tiles of the deconsecrated church of San Vidal, which, no longer dedicated to God, is the home of mediocre and overpriced art. Most evenings at sunset, the azure sky over the rooftops becomes tinted with a glorious wash of pink that is streaked with the darting black silhouettes of chimney swifts and swallows.

Claire's apartment has three drawbacks; the exhausting climb up four flights of worn and patched marble stairs, the blood thirsty mosquitoes that have relieved me of a pint of blood, and the archaic water pipes that shudder ominously when I turn on the faucet, plumbing that probably predates Pompeii. Filling the bathtub only half-full takes a dismaying two hours so I decide the best course is to take evening baths. This allows me sufficient time to stroll the campo, consume a brace of *spremuti con amero* at Caffe' Paolin, and admire the parade of lovely leggy titian-haired women as they return home from work. The finest legs in the world, I assure you. It's all that walking and climbing steps on Venice's four hundred-fifty humped bridges.

Dimly, I recall in my jet-lagged mind that I had postponed my introduction to Franco. Stepping over to the bookcase, I look up at the ceiling. A web! Ah ha, there's the little bugger, only he's not so little. He's big! Much bigger than I imagined. Cautiously, I maneuver under the web to examine his thorax for a red hourglass. Ominously, he rises up in the center of his web and waves two spindly forelegs at me. Franco and web begin to vibrate as one. Appearing angry and poised to leap on me, I back off, then flee into the entry where I consider relocating to the arachnid-free Gritti Palace Hotel. However, once I think about the cost of an indefinite stay and picture Colin Marshall's reaction to my hotel bill, I pass. How silly, I reassure myself, a grown man frightened by a mere spider. Screwing up my courage, I creep back into the salon where I throw open the window to the insect world. "There, Franco," I exclaim, "soon you'll be so gorged with juicy bugs, you'll forget I exist."

Triumphantly exiting the salon, I begin my desperate search for caffeine.

Before leaving New York, I had received a fax from Colin Marshall listing the paintings stolen from Palazzo Aldrovani, the Archduke's home. The first one on the list astounds me: Giovanni Bellini's masterpiece, "Madonna of the Columbine," painted in 1504. Its image flashes through my mind. The Bellini portrays an intimate scene of the Madonna gazing with adoration at her infant son while an illuminated dove flutters overhead and a multitude of worshippers look on with expressions both pious and melancholy. The other stolen pictures include a colored Tiepolo cartoon for a ceiling mural, and two oils by "Tiziano," better known as Titian. Unfortunately, Colin Marshall's typically brusque communication has omitted both detailed descriptions and photocopies, so I have no idea what the Tiepolo or Titians look like. Fortunately, I had studied their work and knew their techniques. Tiepolo painted in the Rococo style of the 18th century, creating ethereal religious themes that featured brilliant skies filled with religious figures, puffy clouds, and cherubic angels. Epic Biblical subjects painted in a traditional manner, using light and shadows to heighten drama and action, is the hallmark of Titian.

Emboldened now by coffee, I unpack my suitcases and settle into my new digs. Finding the telephone directory, I locate the number for the Questura, Venice's police station. I ring up their number.

"Questura," answers a bored female.

"May I speak to the official in charge of the Palazzo Aldrovani case?" I hear a mumbled response, some crackling sounds, and an unusually long pause as I press the lifeless phone to my ear. Next thing, I muse, they'll automate 911. For a murder — press one, for a rape — press two, for an armed robbery — press three, and so on.

A male voice interrupts my thoughts. "Commissario Moretti, how may I help you?"

"Oh, yes . . . Peter Grant here, Commissario."

"I've been expecting your call, Signor Grant. Mr. Marshall at Lloyd's sent us a fax requesting we assist you."

That's the bloody least he could have done, I silently rail at my employer. "I appreciate that, Commissario. When will it be convenient to meet with you? Any chance this afternoon?"

"I'm afraid today is out of the question. I'm fully engaged in a murder investigation."

"That's a rather rare event in Venice, is it not?" I ask without thinking.

"Yes, and this one is particularly offensive." I detect stress in his voice. "I can see you tomorrow morning, around eleven o'clock," he says. He also sounds weary.

"That's fine, Commissario. Will you give me directions to your office?"

"The Questura? It's impossible to find. I'll come to you. I presume you'd like to view the crime scene?"

"I would indeed. That's considerate of you."

"*Prego*. I'll pick you up in a police launch at Rio San Vidal by the Accademia Bridge, eleven o'clock."

"You know where I live?"

"That's my job. *Buon Giorno*, Signor Grant."

I'm awestruck. I haven't been in Venice twenty-four hours and already the Commissario knows where I'm staying. "Of course," I mutter, Immigration has my Venice address from my landing card. But how has the Commissario obtained it so quickly? He must have accessed data from Immigration's computers. These Italians are more skilled at high-tech communications than I imagined. If I decide to take a spin on the information highway, I better be on the lookout so I don't get pulled over by a cop.

If the Commissario's all wrapped up in a murder investigation why would he be interested in knowing where I live? Perhaps I'd better talk to my friend, Princess Irena about this. "Oops," I exclaim, picking up the phone. She never takes phone calls until after two p.m.

I walk to the other side of the Rialto Bridge, where one shops for fish and meat, vegetables and fruit, and cheese and bread. The market is crowded, bustling with customers gesturing and pointing, calling out their choices under tented stalls that permit soft sunlight to illuminate tiers of luscious produce and briny seafood enticingly arranged. It's more a food show than commerce. I stare in open-mouthed wonder at ropes of fat green eels, shimmering sardines, flat mottled brown and white soles with little bulging eyes, black edged slabs of snowy swordfish, baskets of lively crab, netted bags filled with dark clams, gray oysters, and shiny ebony mussels. There are so many fish varieties I hardly recognize their names except for my favorite, *branzino*, or sea bass. The vegetable stalls are festooned with braids of garlic, bunches of herbs, and garlands of tiny bright red and yellow peppers, the kind that burn like fire. Each stall is a graduated terrace of shades of green, pale cabbages and leaf lettuces, glossy green arugula, parsley and spinach. Interspersed among them, as if to lend symmetry to the vender's art, are deep purple egg plants, glossy yellow, red, and green peppers, deep orange carrots, white onions, and fiery red tomatoes. It's at once overwhelming and confusing. I buy six succulent pears, a wedge of ripe

Gorgonzola, and a loaf of thick crusted bread in the shape of a large Frisbee. My Italian's rusty, so I point a lot and resist the temptation to touch, for nothing incurs a vendor's wrath quicker than handling his produce.

On the way back to the flat I pass several news kiosks where I scan the newspapers for screaming headlines concerning a murder, but there are none. I'm puzzled that the papers haven't reported it, especially Venice's *Il Gazzettino*.

At the flat I put everything away, pour myself a glass of Tocai, and ring up Princess Irena Dashikova, the former prima ballerina of the Moscow Ballet during the nineteen-thirties and forties.

The Princess had been a great beauty in her youth. I know because she had once showed me her photographs, more than a hundred. They were from her childhood, her apex as a ballerina, and the waning days of a cabaret career that followed her retirement from dance. She had the most exquisite face, large expressive dark brown eyes like Garbo and lustrous black hair, shiny as anthracite. Small in stature, like most ballerinas, she stood only five feet-three. Unlike most dancers who appear to be anorexic, Irena had a strong and sensual-looking figure, a veritable vest pocket Venus. I remember from her photographs how her expressions vary, ranging from innocent vulnerability to head strong confidence, from melancholy to elation, emotions one might expect from a stunning, enigmatic Russian princess. These days, in spite of her afflictions, she's observant, intense, childishly demanding, amusing, and at once, stimulating and exhausting.

"Irena, Peter Grant. How are you?"

"Peter, caro," she exclaims. "I'm fine. I knew you'd be calling me this afternoon."

"You did?" Puzzled, I take a sip of wine.

"Of course, you know I'm a clairvoyant?"

"All right, Irena who tipped you off?" I say it in a teasing way so she won't be offended.

"No one. You're here because of the theft at the Palazzo Aldrovani, aren't you?"

"Good grief, Irena," I gasp. "How do know about that?"

"My dear boy, this is Venice."

"But no one, except the Questura and the Archduke's gardener, knows anything about the theft," I protest.

"Well, I do! A little bird told me." Her laughter sounds like the trill of a schoolgirl.

"Irena, you're toying with me. She tries unsuccessfully to suppress another high-pitched laugh. It's infectious. She makes me laugh too.

When we stop, she says, "Peter, I'm so sorry about you and Claire. You must be quite upset and terribly hurt."

"Yes, but I'll get over it, not to worry."

"Can you be at Harry's tomorrow about one o'clock? We'll have a long lunch and talk."

"I'd love to, but isn't that a bit early in the day for you?" I ask.

"For certain people, I make exceptions."

"I'm flattered. Thank you."

"*Prego.*"

"Irena, let me ask you something. Have you heard anything about a murder?"

"I knew something terrible must have happened. Last night, around eight-thirty I had a premonition. It was dreadful, about someone from the Holy See."

"But there's nothing in the papers."

"It's being suppressed, I assure you."

"Several hours ago, Commissario Moretti told me he can't see me today because he's busy with a murder. For some odd reason, he seems to have taken an interest in my whereabouts."

"You're staying at Claire's while she's off with the Prince."

Good heavens, how does she know that? Who told her? It must have been Claire. "Who's the Prince?" I ask.

"I'm sorry, that's insensitive. I never should have mentioned it."

"Since you did, who is he."

"Prince Hans Augustus Bernard Frederick von Haffenberg, pretender to a throne, which for all practical purposes doesn't exist anymore."

"God, what a name. It's longer than most Chinese menus. I suppose I ought to be jealous."

"About Hans? He's Euro trash, Peter. Very tightfisted,

watches every pfennig like a raptor eyes a rabbit. I assure you Claire will quickly tire of his boorish ways."

"Have you spoken to her recently?"

"Not for at least a month. Anyway, while you're here there's someone I want you to meet."

Irena didn't find out where I was staying from Claire. Hmmmm! "Sorry, you want me to meet someone, a woman?"

"Yes, a woman."

"I'm really not very good company right now."

"Caro, I understand completely. You two will enjoy each other. You'll become best friends, I promise you. I'll tell you more tomorrow when we meet at Harry's. Oh, and Peter, please be careful. Lately, I've been having these ghastly headaches. They usually forewarn of trouble."

Chapter 5

Leaving Claire's apartment building, I feel a blast of July heat. With the humidity, it's like a sauna. Just from the short walk to the *fondamenta* of Rio San Vidal my shirt is splotched with perspiration. Waiting for the police launch, I walk a few paces away and hang out in the shade of the Accademia Bridge. Idly, I watch people clomp up and down its wooden stairs and reflect on Irena's comment about Claire going off to Switzerland with the Prince. Thinking about it gives me a sinking feeling in the pit of my stomach, which I attribute more to jealousy than to annoyance. I have to stop letting these thoughts eat away at me. What I probably need is a wanton fling with a lusty Venetian bombshell. Sweet revenge! I can see it now. The news of my escapade reaches Claire and in a jealous rage, she races back to Venice and snatches me from the arms of the voluptuous titian-haired seductress. Then, we walk off into a magenta sunset, arm in arm, just like in the movies. Cut and print that!

My reverie is shattered by a bullhorn, "Mr. Grant, over here!" I'm so lost in my thoughts I haven't taken notice of the police launch that's cruised past me, turned into the Rio San Vidal and is idling beside the *fondamenta*. Walking over to the launch, I accept the Commissario's helping hand and step aboard. "Luca Moretti, at your service, *Signor* Grant," announces the balding, heavyset Commissario wearing a wrinkled brown suit. He hangs up his bullhorn on a hook on the side of the cabin.

"Thank you, Commissario. It's nice to meet you."

The helmsman backs the launch out into the Grand Canal, swings the bow around in the direction of the Rialto Bridge, and we cruise along The Grand Canal. I stand in the stern, legs apart, knees bent slightly in an effort to maintain my balance in the launch, which rocks in the rough chop caused by the boat traffic. The Commissario notices my uncertainty and smiles. "*Motto ondoso*," he comments, referring to the water's turbulence.

While enjoying a refreshing breeze on the Grand Canal, I admire the stately *palazzi*, all quietly crumbling behind their florid facades. The Commissario walks off to give instructions to the helmsman who deftly pilots us through the boat congestion. Just before a sharp right bend in the Grand Canal we swing hard to port and enter the Rio di Ca' Foscari, a sparsely used backway between the sestieri of Dorsoduro and San Polo, then through *sestiere* Santa Croce to the *ferrovia*, or railway station. Water taxi drivers prefer the longer route to the *ferrovia* along the Grand Canal for they can extract more money from their passengers. However, unlike the haughty cab drivers of Paris and the sneering chauffeurs of Athens, they are pleasant and smile broadly as they reap a harvest of lire from the tourists.

Proceeding along the Rio di Ca' Foscari, the Commissario leaves the helmsman and rejoins me. With a smug smile he hands me a large manila envelope. "Photographs of the stolen paintings," he says."

I thank him and silently reproach Colin Marshall for his cavalier treatment. He should have sent me these pictures before I left for Venice. As I am about to examine them, the Commissario interrupts. He takes my arm and points out the Palazzo Aldrovani. It stands at the intersection of the Rio di Ca' Foscari and a smaller canal, the Rio di Santa Margharita. It dawns on me that the palazzo is off the usual tourist route. Undoubtedly, its quiet location worked to the thieves' advantage. Then, as if he's read my mind, the Commissario comments, "this area is particularly vulnerable to burglars as there's not much traffic here."

"You're right," I reply. "For seven months I had an apartment in Dorsoduro not far from here. I'm familiar with this area."

"When was that?" he asks.

"In nineteen ninety-four. By the way, has anyone made a ransom demand for the paintings?" I ask, examining the photographs to assuage my curiosity about the Tiepolo and the Titians.

"Not that I'm aware of," he replies.

The launch slows, crosses the canal, and glides toward a row of black and gold striped gondola poles that stand opposite the palazzo's water entrance. Putting the photographs back in the envelope, I look up at the palazzo's flamboyant gothic front, which consists of three tiers of bay windows with colored marbles set into brickwork. At canal level an arched water entrance, as dark and foreboding as a cave, gapes at me. Its marble maw appears ready to ingest us. Although I haven't left the launch, already I imagine my footsteps echoing off dank, slimy walls.

"Fabulous looking building," I exclaim, trying to ward off a spectral chill.

"Designed by Antonio Raffaele and Franco Cavalletto," he says, absently watching the helmsman secure the launch to the striped gondola poles.

I'm impressed. The Commissario knows his architecture. "Unfortunately it's in foreign hands," he remarks.

I note his caustic tone.

He motions for me to disembark.

Carefully I step from the launch onto a marble entryway. There are patches of algae, which I avoid. I'm not ready for a dip in the canal's aromatic green water, which is particularly rank during summer. The Commissario's sarcasm is directed at the owner of the palazzo, the Austrian Archduke. Even after two hundred years, Venice's former conquerors enjoy little popularity among native Venetians. I picture the Commissario as a Caffé Florian devotee. I see him sipping his Campari in the Piazza San Marco as he peers down his patrician nose, his contemptuous sneer directed at Quadri, the rival Austrian restaurant across the square, while in the background their respective orchestras duel loudly with one another for musical supremacy.

Following the Commissario through the eerie passageway, dimly lit by reflected sunlight, I notice flaking plaster walls are discolored from oozing moisture and *acqua alta* marks have left indelible reminders of past flooding. As we climb the worn marble steps, the Commissario touches the uppermost stripe. He makes the sign of the cross, a symbolic gesture meant to engender hope that there will never be a repeat of the 1966 flooding that inundated the entire city and caused heart-breaking damage.

After climbing to the third story the Commissario pauses at the top. "The theft was" . . . he pants . . . "here on the *piano nobile*." He points to a pair of immense, floor to ceiling, carved wood and polychrome doors, . . . "in there . . . in the grand salon."

"Was the house protected?" I ask.

He hesitates, drawing a breath, "Only the alarm system. The thieves bypassed it," he puffs.

"Was there no one in the house?"

"Not a soul." He grimaces, displaying irritation that the Archduke left the palazzo unoccupied. "The Archduke's gardener found the palazzo broken into and the paintings gone. He was the one who summoned us." Motioning for me to follow him, he takes hold of a large brass ring and tugs open one of the tall doors. We step inside. The Murano chandelier, the Venini wall-sconces, and the exquisite Venetian and French antiques cause me to suck in my breath. Immediately, I wonder why the thieves had passed up the antiques, which alone are worth a fortune.

"They took only the paintings?" I exclaim.

He sees my amazement. "Apparently, they only came for those."

On the faded coral-colored walls I see ghostly rectangles where the painting's once hung. Imbedded in plaster are heavy brass hooks, now glaringly bare, and below them dangle alarm wires that have been neatly severed. I'm stunned by the size of the outline where the Bellini once hung. I estimate it to be five meters tall by four meters wide. "How the devil did the thieves ever remove a painting that size from this room?" I inquire.

"Through the front windows," replies the Commissario, jingling coins in his trouser pocket. Pointing to the parquet floor, he says, "There was an enormous Oriental carpet that lay here. They probably wrapped the carpet around the Bellini and trussed it up with rope. After pushing it through the front window they lowered it onto the barge with the vessel's crane."

"And all this took place in broad daylight?"

Giving me a wary glance, he jingles his change again.

"Didn't anyone notice them?" I ask.

"We interviewed water taxi drivers and area residents. We found only two people who admitted seeing the robbers. Both witnesses confirmed there were three men, but neither one of them paid the men any heed, assuming they were movers hired by the palazzo's owner. As a result, we don't have an accurate descriptions of these men."

"I don't suppose they left any fingerprints?"

"None. They wore gloves. There's not a clue anywhere," he says with a nonchalant motion with his hands.

"So, what do we do now?" I ask.

"We wait." He jingles his pocket change.

"For what?" I ask, finding myself distracted by his annoying habit.

"*Allora*," He looks at me as only a Venetian can, tolerant yet condescending. He makes me feel like a small child. One who has asked a foolish question. "For the ransom demand, of course."

"But you said there hasn't been one."

"That's correct."

"Well, how long are you prepared to wait?" It's really not my nature to be curt, but the Commissario's responses are vague and they are beginning to irritate me.

"At the moment, I can't say."

I stare at him in disbelief.

Aloof, he says, "At the moment we're working on a more pressing matter."

"The murder investigation of which you spoke?"

"Yes."

"A matter involving the Church, I gather?" The Commissario's glares at me, his eyes narrowing slightly. Other than that he remains impassive, but clearly I've struck a nerve.

"I'm unable to comment," he replies curtly.

So Irena's right. The murder does have something to do with The Holy See. She's also right about the fact that the authorities are suppressing news of the crime. I wonder what's really going on?

Turning his back on me, the Commissario walks over to the window. He stands, hands clasped behind his back, staring out at the canal. I can't wait around for a ransom demand that may never occur. I have to make something happen. I've got Lloyd's approval to offer a reward for the return of the artwork and I now wonder if the Commissario is prepared to cooperate or does he plan to put everything on the back burner until they solve this murder. I'm bothered by the Commissario's attitude. He's entirely too cavalier about the theft. Is it because he figures the Archduke's an idiot for leaving his house unguarded and has simply gotten what he deserved? Or is it because he figures the Archduke's loss is insured and there's little justification to pursue the crime? Or what if the Commissario's in on the theft? Maybe he's just going through the formalities of an investigation which he's intending to let ebb away? According to the newspapers, there's been an epidemic of corruption among Italian law enforcement officials, bribery, extortion, kickbacks, you name it. Payoffs have become an acceptable way of life. A few million lire might be enough of an inducement for a Commissario to turn a blind eye to an art theft, especially where the victim is a wealthy foreigner whose loss is insured. Like who cares?

Lloyd's does and so do I.

The Commissario seems friendly enough, helpful even, considering he offered to escort me to the palazzo. Also, he provided me with photographs of the stolen paintings. He didn't have to do that. Clearly he's intelligent and I need someone like him on my side. I'd like to think I can trust him. Perhaps I'd better talk to the Princess about him. Meanwhile, I'm going to see how he reacts when I tell him about Lloyd's willingness to post a reward. If he rejects the idea or he's uncooperative, then I'd guess that I've got real problems with him.

Walking over to the window, I join him. "Commissario, I have a proposal. Lloyd's has authorized me to advertise a reward of one hundred thousand pounds for the return of the Archduke's paintings. How do you feel about that?"

"*Va bene*," he shrugs. "It's worth a try. Who knows, maybe one of the thieves will get greedy and attempt to collect the reward for himself."

"I was hoping you'd be in favor of it," I smile, greatly relieved by his answer. "But first, I need the Archduke's permission to offer such a reward?"

"He's not in Venice."

"Not in Venice? Where is he?"

"Switzerland."

"Switzerland?" I'm aghast! "Look at this place, Commissario, it's practically a museum. These antiques are worth a bloody fortune. Why isn't the Archduke here? Doesn't he care what happens to his possessions?" The more I think about the absentee Archduke, the more agitated I become. "Commissario, doesn't the Archduke realize his absence makes him a possible suspect?

"*Allora*, the Archduke maintains he's a victim."

"Listen," I snap, "If I were you, I wouldn't rule out the possibility the Archduke may have perpetrated an insurance fraud."

"*Piano, piano, Signor* Grant." He says, motioning with his hands like the conductor of a symphony who is slowing down the orchestra's tempo. "I understand your concern, but I'm afraid there's nothing further to be gained by speculation."

He's right of course. I'm wasting time, venting my frustration over the Archduke's absence. "Sorry, Commissario, I didn't mean to get carried away."

Retracing our steps down the stairs, we walk through the passageway, and climb back aboard the police launch. As the boat pulls away from the palazzo, the Commissario remarks to me, "Very frustrating people these Austrians. I don't like dealing with them, but in my position I have to put personal feelings aside and just get on with the job." The Commissario fishes a business card out of his jacket pocket and hands it to me. On it, scrawled in his handwriting, is a phone number in Switzerland.

"Perhaps you'll be more successful getting the Archduke to return to Venice than I. He refuses to come back, saying his family was threatened and someone stalked his children."

"I'll get in touch with him, Commissario."

"When you do, suggest that he cooperate with us. Now, I have to return to the Questura. May I drop you off somewhere?"

"San Marco, please."

As the Palazzo Aldrovani fades from view we enter the Grand Canal and encounter a swarm of traffic; barges and water taxis, vaporettos and traghettos, private speedboats and gondolas that have churned the waterway to frothy turbulence. Laughing, the Commissario points out a flotilla of bobbing gondolas carrying well-dressed Japanese tourists. Looking woefully out of place in business suits in the midst of Venice's churning water and its miasma of heat and humidity, they appear impassive as they listen to the singing of hired balladeers. Their body language however denotes fear as they cling fiercely to the gunwales of their rocking gondolas, rigid and unseeing, unaware that traditionally gondolas always have the right of way in heavy traffic.

"Can this be their idea of a romantic boat ride?" I ask.

Rolling his eyes to the heavens, the Commissario exclaims, "*Mama mia*! And *they* think Venetians are strange!"

I laugh, mentally chalking up one for the observant Commissario. It's difficult not to trust a man with a sense of humor.

At the San Marco vaporetto stop, I thank Commissario Moretti. Extending him a warm handshake, I disembark.

"Are you going to Harry's?" he asks.

It seems everyone in Venice reads my mind. "Absolutely," I reply, looking forward to an icy "Montgomery."

"If you should see Arrigo Cipriani, kindly give him my regards. *Buon giorno*," Mr. Grant.

"With pleasure, Commissario, *Buon giorno*."

Seeing me step off the police launch, the people waiting

for the next vaporetto fall back to make a path. Walking through the midst of the crowd, I think about the Commissario's request. If he's a friend of Harry's, he has to be a stand-up guy, but it won't hurt to double check. I'll still ask the Princess about him. Glancing at my watch, I see it's twelve fifteen. Perfect timing. Before Harry's turns into a babbling zoo I'll have a quiet drink at the bar, converse with Claudio and catch up on the local gossip.

Walking through the smoked glass doors, I'm surprised to see a stranger standing behind the bar in Claudio's place.

"Where's Claudio?" I ask, climbing on a stool.

"He's off today. I'm Dominico. I substitute for him on his day off."

"I see. Well, I'll have a "Montgomery" then, with a lemon twist."

"Very good, sir. Have you a lunch reservation?"

"Only Indians have reservations."

Dominico stares at me, uncertain what to say.

Actually, I do have a reservation, but I'm a bit early."

Indulging me with a smile, Dominico slides a plate of tempting chicken croquettes within my reach. Placing a small stack of paper napkins next to the plate, he says, "Have one while they're hot?"

"*Grazie.*" I take a napkin, pick up one and take a bite. It melts in my mouth and tastes delicious.

"*Prego,*" He pours an icy Montgomery, wipes the frosty rim with lemon peel, drops in the rind, and sets the tumbler in front of me. "Enjoy," he says.

"Enjoy? That's a New York expression."

"I lived and worked in New York in the nineteen-seventies and eighties. For ten years I tended bar at Nanni's Il Valletto.

"I know the place well, I reply. The name Irwin Shaw, one of Nanni's famous customers, comes to my mind. He was a friend of a friend and he had once asked me to join him for lunch. Afterward I read his novels. I recall a quotation, 'There are cities that your soul recognizes at first glance.' That pretty accurately sums up my feelings about Venice."

The bartender extends a hand. "Call me Dom," he says.

"Pleasure, Dom, I'm Peter Grant."

"Glad to know you.

"Do you bartend regularly or just on Claudio's day off?"

"Usually on his day off, but sometimes it gets pretty hectic here and *Signor* Cipriani brings me in to help out. Mostly I bartend private functions." Turning abruptly, he takes two plates of finger sandwiches from one of the waiters who calls him by name. Setting the succulent egg and anchovy and chicken *tramezzini* on the bar, he remarks, "The Venetian version of the hero."

"Git-atta-hea," I kid him in a faux Brooklyn accent. An intuitive feeling tells me were going to be friends.

Chapter 6

Someone lays a hand on my shoulder. Spinning around, I come face to face with Arrigo Cipriani, the owner of Harry's Bar.

"Harry! I exclaim. "How are you?"

He smiles. "Fine, Peter. Nice to have you back." Of medium height and build, Harry has a countenance that all successful restaurateur's seem to have, that pleasant look of undivided attention that flatters a customer and makes him feel as welcome as if he was home in his own dining room. Harry wears an impeccably tailored light gray suit with a fabulous-looking flowered tie. On a previous occasion when I had praised a similar tie, he confided that he had bought the silk in New York City and had the fabric sewn into a tie in Venice. His casual remark stunned me, for Italy is regarded as the silk capital of the world.

"Great tie, Harry."

"*Grazie*," he says. Stepping aside he reveals the diminutive Princess who had been standing behind him. "I think you know the Princess?" he chuckles.

"Of course," I laugh, hopping off my barstool. "I'm happy to see you, Irena." Bending over, I kiss her cherubic, uplifted face, once on the right cheek, once on the left cheek, and again on the right cheek.

Her brown eyes sparkle as she titters in amusement, "You

remember." Turning to Harry, she exclaims in her excited, high pitched voice. "Peter acts more like a Russian than I, Arrigo."

We all laugh.

"How are you feeling, Irena?"

"Moving about, as you can see," she replies. Shuffling forward with the aid of her walker, she moves out of the entry ahead of patrons who now crowd the doorway. "Arrigo insisted on bringing me here in the Cipriani Hotel speedboat. He's such a thoughtful friend."

Looking embarrassed by the flattery, Harry gives the Princess a shy smile. "I suggest we seat you before it gets too crowded." he urges.

While I collect my drink at the bar, Harry escorts the Princess to a table beside the upstairs doorway where it's convenient for her to slide into the banquet and keep her walker close by. Ambling over, I join her.

"Irena, I'm so delighted to see you out and about."

"It's an exertion, you know? I'm so used to being a recluse." She adjusts her billowy caftan about her ample form. Catching me staring, she adds, "And to think I used to be such a peri. My, it seems so long ago."

Her comment makes me sad and I'm momentarily at a loss for words as I watch her case the room with her sharp eyes. She turns to me with a mischievous smirk on her face.

"What will you have to drink?" I ask quickly, sensing gossip is imminent.

"*Acqua minerale, per favore*," she replies, waving a hand in her typically Slavic gesture. From her ring finger glints a huge round diamond.

"*Subito*," interjects a passing waiter who overhears her request for bottled water.

I break out laughing. "I love Harry's. The waiters are so alert."

Returning almost instantly, the waiter sets down a glass and pours cold water from a liter bottle of San Pellegrino, which he leaves on the table.

"Why are you giving me that impish look?" I ask.

"Caro, don't turn around. Marchese Mochedon just walked

in. He's certain to come over to say hello, but before he does, I have to tell you the most amusing story. As you probably know, the Marchese is in his eighties, but he still thinks he's a young Casanova. Recently, while pursuing Claire, he nearly suffered a heart attack."

"My Claire?"

"Yes. The old rogue was romancing your wife. He took her to dinner several times and afterward found he couldn't handle the four flights up to her flat. On the ground floor he asked, `Quanta dista?` how far? On the second level he sighed, `Allora!` On the third landing he puffed, `Mama-mia!` On the final flight he gasped, `Madonna!` When he finally reached her apartment door he was so out of breath and wet with perspiration, that he was too spent to attempt seduction. Another time, after suffering heart palpitations, he gave up trying to negotiate her stairs and bid her *adieu* at the building's front door. After several more dinners he telephoned her and you won't believe what he proposed," tittered Irena.

"What?" I ask, eagerly.

"He told Claire he'd buy her an apartment in an elevator equipped building if she'd consent to be his mistress."

"Oh my God," I howl with laughter, nearly choking on a sip of my "Montgomery."

"Oh, dear, here he comes now," warns Irena.

I stifle my laughter as Marchese Mochedon arrives at our table.

"Irena, how nice to see you. You seem to be having a jolly time," he says, placing a kiss on the back of her outstretched hand, like a chicken pecking at corn.

"Thank you. We're having a delightful chat. You've met Peter Grant before . . . Claire's husband?"

"Ahhhhhh . . . Yes, indeed I have." He appears unsure of himself and backs off as I rise from my chair to shake his hand. "Gianni Mochedon," he announces, inclining his head slightly in a formal bow.

"Pleasure to see you again, Marchese," I smile. "How is your lovely wife, Lucia?"

Looking like a fox with its forepaw in a snare, he stammers, "Oh, . . . Lucia . . . yes, ahh . . . well, very well indeed as a matter of fact. What brings you to Venice?"

"I can't bear being away from Irena." I wink at her. She giggles like a schoolgirl and hides behind her hands. Peering over her finger tips, her eyes dance with amusement.

The Marchese glances at Irena, then eyes me suspiciously. Deciding I've made a joke after all, he smiles awkwardly. "Ah yes, I see," he says.

"Would you care to join us?" I offer.

"Thank you," he says, forcing another smile, "I'm expecting a friend, . . . any minute now. If you're still here this fall, Signor Grant, you must come join us on one of our famous duck shoots. It's not quite as exciting as the old days when I shot with Hemingway," he boasts. "Those were good old times. We'd shoot ducks until either we exhausted the ammunition or ran out of champagne and caviar."

"Thank you for the invitation, Marchese. I'm not much of a hunter, but I happen to be a great fan of Hemingway's books."

"Are you?" he smiles smugly. "As Irena will attest, my daughter was a close friend of the Contessa Renata, Hemingway's heroine in *Across the River and Into the Trees*."

"Really?" Condescending old braggart, I mutter to myself.

Glancing toward the entrance, the Marchese turns his attention to Irena. "If you'll excuse me?" he says, bowing slightly. "I see my friend has arrived. Always a great pleasure, my dear." Addressing me, he says, "You keep impeccable company, *Signor* Grant. *Buon giorno.*"

"*Buon Giorno*. My regards to Lucia." Wincing at my use of his wife's first name and my obvious barb, he turns and walks to the bar. A woman with wildly teased apricot hair awaits him. She wears a provocative dress that leaves very little of her anatomy to the imagination. I find it impossible not to stare. Everyone else is. "Irena, I don't believe I've ever seen such a wild looking creature. And that head of hair, why, it looks like an osprey's nest."

"Bah!" says Irena. "She's a notorious harlot, . . . preys on married men. She was once married to a French diplomat and she roamed Europe bedding her husband's wealthy friends. She lives with Count Ugo Benzoni and an entourage of debauched Venetians. Stay away from *that one*, caro."

"Thanks for the warning. She's so blatant, exposing her breasts like that, I'd be embarrassed to be seen with her."

"Defying gravity, you mean?"

Irena's remark tickles me and I howl with laughter. "Doesn't it ever upset Lucia that her husband is seen in Harry's with such a notorious femme-fatale?"

"Heavens no. Lucia knows her husband's a *cacciatore*. His pursuit of spring chickens bores her to tears. In spite of his foolishness, she keeps up pretenses, but she admits she's happy when he ignores her. Apparently the old roué is utterly hopeless in the bedroom."

"Do you think people are fooled into believing Lucia and the Marchese are happily married?"

"A facade, Peter dear, like everything in Venice." Unable to keep a straight face any longer, she bursts out laughing.

"Ahh, so that's why the Venetians are such proficient mask makers."

"They come by it naturally," she affirms. "Oh my, I nearly forgot, I meant to speak to you about my dear young friend, Cinzia Aliverti."

"Isn't she in real estate?"

"Yes. How did you know?" Irena looks puzzled.

"Claire mentioned her to me."

"Of course, Cinzia manages your wife's building. Well, with Claire away, I thought you should have someone you could enjoy while your here. She's from an old Venetian family, educated in England and extremely pretty."

"Irena, I really appreciate your thinking of me, but I think I'd feel awkward seeing someone right now."

"Caro, you can't go around like a turtle with its head in the sand."

"Ostrich, you mean." I'm so amused I nearly fall out of my chair.

"Yes, those too. Stop laughing and don't interrupt. You need companionship, Peter. You need a charming, intelligent young woman whose company you can enjoy." Irena reaches across the table and pats the back of my hand. "I'm suggesting a friend, not a lover."

"Okay, I understand. Let me think about it."

"What am I missing?" asks Harry, materializing in the doorway adjacent to our table.

"Nothing you don't already know, Arrigo," the Princess teases, merrily wagging her finger at him.

"Harry," I interject. "I happened to be with Commissario Moretti this morning. He sends you his regards."

"That's kind of him. As Irena knows, Luca's married to my cousin. I expect he's been busy. He and Carla haven't been in to see me in a while."

"He seems to be a nice chap," I reply.

"I'm fond of Luca," replies Harry. "He's a good family man and completely trustworthy."

"He's also my dear friend," interjects the Princess, giving me a charming wink.

Aha, so that's how Irena found out I was staying at Claire's flat.

Lunch at Harry's turns into a marathon repast. All through the afternoon and evening the Princess holds court. Finally, near midnight, I drag her majesty away from her weary subjects and escort her back to her flat on the Giudecca. She insists on pouring me a nightcap, which I need like a ham sandwich at a banquet, but one can't refuse royalty. In my stomach the fizzy prosecco embraces the gin of all the "Montgomerys" I've consumed and forms a lethal "French Seventy-Five," a cocktail named after the powerful French artillery piece of World War I. More than slightly impaired I leave Irena's flat and lurch onto a vaporetto going in the wrong direction. Well up along the Zattere, literally a staggering distance back to my flat, I collect my wits about me like a cloak and veer diagonally across Dorsoduro. Stumbling across the Accademia Bridge, I trumpet, "Aha, familiar territory at last." Lurching through Campo Santo Stefano I find Claire's building and drag my abused body up four flights. Once inside the apartment I call out to Franco, "*buona notte,*" then I crash.

Chapter 7

I AWAKE WITH a bad case of "bottle fatigue." My head throbs. Stumbling into the bathroom I search for and find Excedrin. "Damn these kid proof lids!" I shout, chasing the elusive tablets as they scatter across the bathroom tiles. I manage to capture three and wash them down with leftover Schweppes quinine, which I vaguely recall someone telling me wards off malaria. I look in the mirror. Major mistake. My eyes are a disaster! For the bags under them I need a skycap, plus a six pack of Visine to get the red out.

After splashing around in two inches of luke-warm bath water, I somehow manage to shave without cutting my throat. "*Miracolo!*" Then, I get dressed, sort of.

Stepping out the apartment door, I look down the stairwell. Bad move! Lurching, I grab for the railing like a sailor in heavy seas. My stomach objects, but mercifully I'm able to descend to the ground floor without heaving. With a sigh, partly of relief, but mostly of resignation, I tug open the dungeon-like front door and step out into blinding sunlight.

"God! What a shock . . . daylight!"

Shielding my tormented eyes, I stagger toward the nearby pharmacy and purchase sunglasses, the darkest pair of shades I can find.

Thus shielded from Aten's wrath and looking about as cool as a Blues Brother, I head across the campo toward the heady smell of espresso. Envisioning tiny little cups heaped full of sugar and topped off with a lemon peel, I accelerate my pace, but a news kiosk steps rudely into my path.

"*Buon giorno, ha Herald Tribune?*" I ask, hovering close to death's door.

"No . . . *finito*," comes a terse reply and a salutary wave off.

"*Il Gazzettino, per favore,*" I implore, holding out a handful of coins. The newsstand operator, observing my deplorable condition, reaps the required amount from my outstretched palm. Buying an Italian newspaper, I realize, is an act of sheer desperation, but I need a prop, something to hide behind. And even if the news escapes my dismal command of Italian, a rolled up *Gazzettino* will later make a formidable weapon in the unending war on mosquitoes. Then, from depth of memory, emerges the admonition of my former Venetian landlord. "Swatting insects on the white plaster walls is absolutely forbidden and will result in forfeiture of your deposit." I forget turning my newspaper into a weapon, entrusting my fate to Franco's appetite.

Outside Paolin, a cafe facing the Church of Santo Stefano, I slump into a white molded plastic chair and pray for divine intercession. The requested hangover cure appears to be elusive. Giving up hope, I order two espressos with extra sugar. Suddenly energized by a sucrose rush, I unfold *Il Gazzettino* and plunge into the news, understanding nothing save the headline: "*Corpo morto*" which I know means, a dead body, and "Rio dei Gesuiti" which I recognize as a canal in the Cannaregio district near the Jesuit Church.

I'm trying to determine exactly who has died and from what when all at once I become aware of the sensation of cool flesh. Directing my eyes toward the intrusion, I see a shapely tanned leg. Its bare flesh presses against the back of my hand. I look up to find a lovely inquisitive face, framed by lustrous honey-colored hair gazing into my bloodshot eyes. She smiles. In slow motion, I lower my newspaper. My plea has been answered after all, an intercession by Saint Stephen from across the way. He's sent me a divine angel to administer CPR, though the spirit's attire seems rather odd, tight white shorts and a luscious Ferrari red halter-top that matches lipstick, fingernail and toenail polish. But who am I to question such a holy offering... that is until I spot my English artist friend, Pomeroy, leering at me over my savior's supple shoulder. Like a zinc zeppelin, my soaring spirits plummet to earth. "Jesus, Pomeroy. I might have known you'd be behind this . . . if I weren't so damn hung over, that is."

"Say hello to Adriana, Peter."

"*Buon giorno*, Adriana."

"*Buon giorno, poverino.*" Leaning over, she purses her scarlet lips and kisses me on both cheeks. Her lips warmth and tenderness restore my flagging spirits, elevate my heart rate, and eradicate my pallor with flame-colored residue.

"Do sit down," I urge, struggling to get my feet underneath me in order to rise. "I'll buy you a coffee."

"Only for a moment," replies Pomeroy with his usual brusque air. "We were just passing by on our way to the gallery when I spotted you. Adriana's my newest figure model." He seats the deliciously perfumed girl beside me. "What are you doing with *Il Gazzettino*?" he asks. "You hardly speak a word of the language."

"Right you are," I reply, ignoring his question. I'm unable to tear my eyes away from Adriana, who looks to be about twenty years old and extremely well constructed. Aware of my interest, she strikes a provocative pose. Her affectation alerts Pomeroy whose eyes fill with suspicion as they home in on me like lasers.

"Peter, if you don't stop gawking at Adriana we're going to leave."

"Sorry, I had a rough night."

"Anyone I know," asked Pomeroy.

"Your neighbor, the Princess. We closed Harry's."

"So that's why you look like a pile of dog crap."

"That's tactful," I respond, in a tone laced with sarcasm. "How would you like your coffee, one teaspoon of strychnine or two?"

"Cappuccino will do fine, old boy. Cappuccino, Adriana?"

"*Per favore, uno doppio,*" she answers, fishing around in her shoulder bag for cigarettes and a lighter.

"Pomeroy, stop her," I protest. "Tell her if she lights up I'll likely barf on her pedicure."

"*Cara*," Pomeroy says, taking the lighter from her hand. "*Per favore, pui tarde*."

"Thanks." I sigh, grateful that Pomeroy has suggested she light up later.

As Pomeroy orders, "*Due cappuccini, uno doppio e due espressi, per favore*," the waiter hovers over Adriana. He peers down at the breathlessly tanned topography that respires beneath his pad. He has a breathless expression like a Meriwether Lewis when he first viewed the Rockies.

"Looking irked, Pomeroy barks at the leering waiter, "*Cameriere?*"

"*Subito signore*," replies the startled waiter. As he turns away to get our order, he smirks at me and bats his eyebrows like Groucho Marx.

"Since you're here, Pomeroy, would you mind telling me what happened to this person in the headline?" I pass him the newspaper.

"No need," he says, rejecting my offer with a curt hand wave. "I've already read about it. The poor chap was robbed, hit over the head and thrown in the canal. He drowned and was found by a gondolier in the Rio dei Gesuiti. The Questura identified the victim as a Benedictine monk from Rome. His murder has caused a media frenzy. Both the Italian Government and The Vatican are in a twit about it."

"I would think so!" I exclaim. "What sort of idiot would rob a monk who'd taken a vow of poverty?"

"The article hints he might have had something of value on his person. It quotes a witness who was on the boat from Murano with the monk, who says the Benedictine wore some sort of shoulder bag that police have been unable to locate."

"That's curious." I think about the Commissario. He must be taking a lot of heat. "I was under the impression homicides were practically nonexistent in Venice?"

"They are, except for the odd drug-related death. Either the monk was mixed up in drugs or he was transporting something valuable," speculated Pomeroy. "Who knows?"

My mind is too addled to speculate.

The waiter returns with our coffee. He bends over, sets down the cups, and again ogles Adriana.

Looking violated, she folds her arms and glares at him.

"*Porco!*" she exclaims, spitting out the swine epithet.

"Artistically speaking, Peter, her breasts really are perfect," Pomeroy whispers to me as Adriana shakes her fist at the waiter. She turns just in time to catch Pomeroy gesturing like a fruit peddler juggling melons in his hands. Icily, she stares at him.

Pomeroy turns crimson.

Suddenly, Adriana breaks out laughing, leans over, grabs Pomeroy's head and plants a loud kiss on his forehead. Seeing the scarlet imprint she's left, she dips into her purse, extracts a lipstick, and nonchalantly applies another layer of gloss.

"What are you up to this afternoon?" inquires Pomeroy, trying to remove Adriana's lip print with a paper napkin.

"I have to make a few phone calls. I'd sure love to get a massage and then take a nap. Adriana doesn't give massages, does she?" I ask hopefully.

Still fussing with her lipstick, Adriana glances at me. She grins.

"No, nor naps either," scowls Pomeroy. "For the next few weeks her time belongs to me."

"I get the picture . . . ahh, sorry, no pun intended," I say, giving Adriana a dejected look.

Putting her hand on my arm, she consoles me with a gentle squeeze.

In return, I gave her a winsome smile. "Thanks for the mini massage," I tell her.

Pomeroy bounds to his feet. Taking Adriana's hand he yanks her to her feet and announces, "Time to be off. Thanks for the coffee, old boy. If you're feeling up to it, come by for drinks later and I'll show you my newest work."

"*Ciao, bambino,*" says Adriana, grasping me by the forearm and squeezing hard. She stares into my eyes, her lips home in on my face and ever so gently she repaints both my cheeks.

"Mmmmmmmmm. At'sa nice," I exclaim in faux Italian.while Pomeroy glares daggers at me.

As he tows Adriana away, I admire the view from the rear. Who wouldn't? At the top of lovely long legs, she has a firm well-rounded derriere and shapely boyish hips. Serpentine strands of honey blonde hair cascade like Victoria Falls down her pretty, well tanned back. Wow!

I can't fault Pomeroy for acting territorial. She wasn't particularly subtle about flirting with me, but she probably does that to every man. Beside, what could she possible see in me? I look like death warmed over. Maybe it's only my imagination, but I thought I noticed a hint of lust in her eyes . . . and that squeeze. "Dream on, Peter," I sigh. Depositing a few hundred lire among the coffee cups, I struggle to my feet and leave.

At Claire's flat, I brush the cotton from my mouth and phone the Archduke's number in Zurich. The phone is picked up on the first ring.

"*Ja?*" answers a male voice.

"May I speak to the Archduke?"

"Who is zis calling?"

"Peter Grant, representing Lloyd's of London."

"Vun moment." During the pause I hear German being spoken. "Vood you be zo kind as to giff me your telephone number. His highness is not in. Vee call you beck zoon."

I give him my number.

"*Ja, das ist seargut. Guten tag*, Herr Grant." After hanging up, I feel a hunger pang. Going into the kitchen, I rummage through the refrigerator as I wait for my call to be returned. I find a ripe pear and a small wedge of Gorgonzola and barely have time to wolf them down before the phone rings.

"*Si pronto*," I answer, trying to sound like a native.

"Herr Grant?"

"Yes?"

"This is Heinrich Bernhard, the Archduke's solicitor. My apologies for keeping you waiting, but I had to verify your name with Lloyd's. They advised me that you are authorized to speak for them. How may I help you?"

"I need to speak with the Archduke."

"I'm sorry. It's impossible at the moment. He and his daughters are in seclusion."

"Oh, and why is that?"

"While in Venice the Archduke received phone calls threatening his children's safety. His youngest daughter told him two men had followed her home. After that the Archduke left."

I'm astounded to learn from the attorney that the Archduke discharged all his servants, except the gardener, whom he'd forgotten about, that he'd closed up the palazzo, and had left Venice without even reporting the threats to the Questura.

"Mr. Bernhard, I assume you are aware of the magnitude of this theft?"

"I am. My colleagues and I suspect these threats were a ruse by the thieves to get the Archduke to leave Venice so they could steal his paintings."

"Perhaps, but you must realize, as of now, we cannot rule out the Archduke as a suspect."

"Oh come now, Herr Grant. The Archduke is a man of impeccable character. He has no reason to steal his own paintings.

"For the insurance money?" I reply.

"I hardly think so."

"Then why isn't he cooperating with the Questura?"

"The Archduke is reluctant to return to Venice because of the threats to his family. Since Commissario Moretti is unable to assure the Archduke's safety, we have advised our client that he is under no legal obligation to return, unless of course, the authorities formally accuse him of an extraditable crime."

"Under the circumstances, Lloyd's will probably balk at paying the insurance claim, Mr. Bernhard."

"Perhaps, Herr Grant, but we consider our client's interests and the safety of his children to be of paramount importance. If Lloyd's or Interpol wishes to arrange for a solicitor to take sworn testimony in Zurich from the Archduke or his children, we will cooperate fully. Failing that, I can offer you nothing more."

"Fine, I'll pass on your comments to Colin Marshall at Lloyd's and recommend he contact you."

"Excellent, Herr Grant. It's been pleasant talking with you."

"Likewise," I reply. I say goodbye and after hanging up, I feel frustrated. Nothing has been resolved.

Next, I ring up Colin Marshall and report my conversation with Bernhard in Zurich. Colin tells me Lloyd's will send a letter to the Archduke's Zurich counsel. He doesn't sound like he's in any great rush. Who can blame him? I wouldn't be too anxious to pay a twelve million pounds sterling claim either? When I tell Colin I've been to the crime scene with Commissario Moretti and that there's been no new evidence, he groans. Though, when I advise him that the Commissario has voiced support for Lloyd's offer of a reward, he grunts his approval.

"Have you arranged for the police to follow up the leads?" he asks. "Every crackpot in Italy will try to claim our reward money."

"Damn! Sorry about that, Colin," I apologize, berating myself for forgetting such a simple detail.

"You're probably jet lagged," he says dryly.

"No doubt," I reply. "Look here, Colin, I'll telephone Moretti straight away and I'll advise you before I place any reward notices."

"Jolly good. My best to Claire." Abruptly, Colin hangs up. "I'll be in touch." I mutter into the silent receiver, then curse rude executives who end conversations without saying goodbye.

I try calling Commissario Moretti, but he's out. I think the girl said he went to lunch but my mind's hazy about the Italian word, *pranza*? Is it lunch or is it dinner?

"Lunch!" At once, the word sounds appealing. I must be staging a comeback. I have the munchies. I picture something spicy . . . arugula . . . pepperoni . . . Adriana. The trouble with hangovers is that they make you hungry. Randy too! Getting some food would be good. Getting laid would be even better. God, it seems as though it's been ages.

Snapping back to reality, I wander over the Accademia Bridge and stop in Trattoria San Trovaso where I devour an arugula salad, a pepperoni pizza, and a cold beer.

After a nap, I phone the Princess and invite myself to dinner at her flat. At first, she sounds reluctant, but when I suggest she call around the corner to Harry's Dolce and order in, she's all for it. Of course, I plan to stop by Pomeroy's studio first.

"My treat," I insist.

"Naturally," she replies.

Royalty never pays.

Now that the Benedictine's murder has hit the newspapers and has become Venice's hottest topic, I know Irena will be hooked into her information pipeline. No telling what she's learned about the Archduke's art theft or the monk's murder. She's relentless. Nothing escapes her.

"Peter," she taunts in a seductive tone of voice, "I can hardly wait to see you."

The air of intrigue is as pungent as ripe Gorgonzola! And, speaking of aromas, I better not forget to take Irena flowers.

Chapter 8

It's shortly before six when I arrive at Pomeroy's studio on the Giudecca's *fondamenta*. I ring his entrance bell. The door opens as if by an unseen hand. Entering into a stairwell, I see worn wooden stairs leading to the second floor of the loft building. As I ascend, I detect the scent of perfume and recall that Pomeroy had told me the building had formerly been used as a cosmetics warehouse.

Still puzzled about the door, I notice on the way upstairs a clever mechanical rope contraption that Pomeroy has rigged to allow him to open his front door from the second floor. Aha! the spooky unseen hand. At least he doesn't have to worry about power failures I muse, reaching the second floor.

"In here," comes Pomeroy's clipped voice from the loft's front room, a north lighted studio. It's littered with paints, brushes, and canvases. Some canvasses are hung on the walls. Others are on easels or stacked against the walls. Pomeroy sits on a stool before a wooden easel that holds a large oil portrait of an alluring dark-haired woman. She's nude from the waist up. "I'll be right with you, Peter," he says, concentrating on his brush strokes. "Have a look around," he adds. "I need to touch up the background before I lose the light."

Walking across the studio, I take in the view outside the studio's floor to ceiling windows. Across the broad Giudecca Canal lies a breathtaking panorama. My eyes pan west to east, along Dorsoduro's Fondamenta della Zattere where various Venetian landmarks stand out, the Churches of St. Agnese and Espirito Santo, and Santa Maria della Salute, looking very much like a domed wedding cake. At the tip of the peninsula, the Dogana di Mari, or customs house, pokes its nose into the harbor like a crouched lion that's poised to vault across the inner harbor and pounce on a formidable morsel, the red brick fortress-like Church of St. Georgio Maggiore. Beyond these buildings, rise the towering campanile, the golden domes of Saint Mark's Basilica, the columns of the Piazzetta, and the Moorish looking Doge's Palace. Too bad I forgot to bring my camera.

"How about a glass of wine?" Pomeroy wipes paint from his hands with a grungy looking towel.

"Fine, if it's decent," I remember his British penchant for serving cheap wine. Where's Adriana?"

Pomeroy smirks, "She left about an hour ago. Why? Did you just come by to salivate over her like this morning."

"Give me a break, Pomeroy. I wasn't my usual self his morning. I was terribly hung over and I haven't a clue how I behaved. If you were offended, I apologize."

"Accepted. I must compliment you on your recovery. You look almost human."

"I suppose a backhanded compliment is better than none at all," I reply.

He ignores my comment. "If you'd like to see the luscious Adriana in all her unadorned glory, follow me." He grins like a feline from Cheshire. We walk past a small room, its walls hung, floor to ceiling, with paintings. Its only furniture is a large day bed. I eye it suspiciously. It's chaotic looking, as if it has only just been occupied. My imagination runs away with me. Pomeroy catches me staring. He lets out a loud guffaw. "I know what you're thinking."

Pointing at the bed, I exclaim. "*Che casino!* I swear there's steam rising from the sheets."

"Really?" he shrugs, wandering into the next room as I follow him. The room is immense and its walls are lined with tables. Other tables stand in two long rows in the center. On top of each are piles of drawings, mostly sketches of nudes.

Six to seven hundred, I estimate. Many are already matted, ready for framing.

"There's Adriana's stack." He directs me to it and walks toward the kitchen at the rear of the loft. "I'll be right back with the wine. "Cheese?" he asks.

"Not for me, thanks," I reply, eager to see the drawings of Adriana.

"God, what a body," I gasp, looking at the first sketch. She's lying across a sofa, naked. She arches her back and stretches as though awaking from a nap. I feel heat rise up in my face as I go through the pile of drawings. Halfway through, I find a lovely sketch. Adriana stands in a meditative pose wearing a loose Oriental robe that's casually open and reveals a voluptuous torso, culminating in a dark pubic triangle between slender, shapely legs. Partially covering her large breasts with folded arms, she pensively holds her chin in one hand. Her thumb rests lightly against her full, slightly parted, lower lip. Her head is inclined and her gaze is cast downward, making her look child-like and vulnerable. Streamers of long blond hair cascade about her face and tumble around her shoulders.

I put the drawing aside, knowing I have to own it.

"Your wine?" Pomeroy's voice startles me. I'm so absorbed that I'm unaware he's walked up behind me.

"Yes, thanks," I say, turning to take the glass from his outstretched hand.

"I see you've set one aside. I rather fancy that one myself."

Tasting the cold white wine, I tell him, "I have to have it. It's stunning."

"It is, isn't it?"

Modesty is not one's of Pomeroy's virtues. "Was this done before or after?" I ask.

"Back to the steaming sheets, are we?" He sounds like a barrister answering a question with a question. "Don't be a crashing bore, Peter, I don't discuss my sex life, but if it makes you feel any better I'll tell you this. She's not the least bit as innocent as my sketches may make her out to be. She's a smashing-looking strumpet with a delicious body and the morals of a vacuum cleaner. I can't say I blame you for being smitten by her. Everyone is and that includes me. In a few weeks I'm sure I'll get tired of her and some other girl who's panting to show me her body will take her place. If you still fancy her, then have at it, but one caution. She runs with a very fast crowd."

"What's fast in your view?"

"Drugs, orgies. Surely you must know how decadent some of the Venetians are. Though you've met quite a few, you've probably no idea who the players are."

"Who, for instance?"

"Ask the Princess that question. I make a living here, painting portraits and sketching nudes. Some of these people are my clients. I can't afford to *rock the boat* as they say."

"Yeah, I understand." I could appreciate Pomeroy's apprehension. There are a few very wealthy descendants of old Venetian families, who along with a small cadre of nouveau-riche foreigners, behave with impunity. Hidden behind the walls of their palazzi they engage in all form of debauchery and if challenged they can be as ruthless as a Borgia or a Medici. Unwilling to confront these degenerates, the Venetians simply turn away and act as though they don't exist.

"I'm really sorry to hear about you and Claire, Peter. I mean that."

"Thanks. It's been rough."

"I understand. I hope you get her back, if that's what you want. In the meantime don't get obsessed with Adriana. She's mouth-watering to look at, but eventually, she'll cut your *you know what* off."

"Okay," I laugh, thinking he'd better pay attention to his own advice before he ends up singing soprano as a *castrato*.

I glance at my watch. "Damn, Pomeroy, I've got to run. I promised to buy the Princess dinner this evening."

"Didn't you have enough excitement last night?" he chortles.

"I guess not," I reply and take a final swallow of wine. "I want that picture," I remind him as we walk to the stairway.

"I'll wrap it and bring it over to my gallery. You can pick it up tomorrow or whenever. Bring me a check. Seven hundred-fifty, U.S."

"Deal." We shake hands. I pick up Irena's flowers.

"For the Princess?" he asks, peeking inside the wrapper.
"Yes."

"Definitely her color," he comments. "Peter, if you get tangled up in the sheets with Adriana, don't ever say I didn't warn you."

"Okay, Pomeroy. *Ciao* for now."

It's a five-minute walk along the Giudecca Canal to the Princess' apartment complex, where I feel like I'm about to enter a fortress. A narrow footbridge crosses a moat-like canal, tall iron gates with spear points protect the enclosure and a uniformed guard stands watch, cradling an Uzi sub-machine gun in his arms. Except for the submachine gun the scene is positively medieval. I suppose royalty is used to a siege mentality, but then so are most New Yorkers.

Waiting for the elevator, I'm joined by two waiter dressed in white jackets, from Harry's Dolce. They carry large round trays with covered dishes that emit salivating aromas. We do an awkward dance trying to arrange ourselves in the tiny elevator.

Emerging from the lift, I resemble a hunter on safari with his retinue of porters strung out behind. I ring the Princess' doorbell. She opens it wearing a sparkling smile, a leopard silk caftan, and an eye-catching necklace of cabochon emeralds the size of kiwis. "Oh my, you're all here," she exclaims.

I utter the customary, "*Permesso*," and step inside. "Irena, you look stunning." Going through the Russian kiss ritual, I hand her the bouquet of lavender tulips.

"*Permesso*," the waiters chorus as they edge past us and enter her minuscule kitchen.

"Thank you, Peter," she beams. "My favorite color. Come. Sit down." With a regal hand wave she ushers me into her small salon while she maneuvers her walker into the kitchen to put her tulips in water.

The room looks like an exotic *zenana* with its red Persian carpet and tiger covered *lit-de-repos* strewn with Oriental silk and leopard pillows. The antique Russian furniture is bathed in soft light from scented candles and several Oriental lamps. I ease into a silver gilt side chair. Awaiting Irena's return, I study a collection of Russian icons and crucifixes hanging on the wall above the sofa. On the opposite wall a portrait and framed photographs catch my attention. The Princess in her prime.

"Do you approve?" she asks, seeing me staring at her treasures.

"Yes, Everything's wonderful. I don't know what to look at first," I reply.

"It's eclectic I know, but each *objet* has its own story." With the aid of her walker, she shuffles over to the *lit-de-repos* and sits down heavily. Her spotted caftan blends in with the fabrics and makes her look like an exotic figure out of a jungle painting by Rousseau.

"Tell me about your icons, Irena? They look old."

With a sweeping gesture, she answers, "They belonged to my ancestors, the Dashikovas. Long before the Romanov's became Tsars, our family was one of the city's principal landholders."

"I had no idea."

"For generations our family and the Romanov's were very close. And during the Revolution, when we lost our land and estates, my great uncle was executed for trying to help Czar Nicholas and his family escape."

"I read about it, a grisly affair, those poor children." If everything was confiscated how did your family manage to get these icons out of Russia?"

"Fortunately, they were already in Paris, in my parent's apartment."

"Prior to the revolution?"

"Yes. When Tsar Nicholas lost control of the people after the October massacre my parents decided to flee Russia. They left carrying a few small mementos and my mother's jewelry," she says, fingering her emerald necklace. They barely made it to Paris, which was where I was born."

"Really." I wasn't about to ask when, for I had been taught never to ask a woman her age and Harry Cipriani had once told me no one in Venice knows the Princess' age. "She never discusses her age with anyone," he had warned me.

Mentally, I calculate she's close to eighty. Irena wears a

curious expression. She senses what I'm doing.

"Excuse me," I blurt out, "I'd best see to it that the waiters are paid." Jumping up from my chair, I head for the kitchen.

"Peter," she calls, "there's prosecco in the freezer for you. I'll have a glass of peach juice."

Whew, narrow escape. She reads me like a tarot card. After settling up with the waiters, I show them out.

"Would you mind bringing me the flowers," she asks.

"Of course not," I reply. She has them arranged in a silver samovar, which I set in front of her on the coffee table. Returning to the kitchen, I pour Irena a virgin Bellini, and open the chilled split of Nino Franco prosecco. As I pour some into a fluted glass, my hung over mind conjures up a bizarre fantasy about Nino Franco being the liquid offspring of Claire's house spider.

"Cheers," I toast the Princess.

"*Na sdrovia*," she responds in Russian.

We touch glasses and drink. The prosecco tastes good. A little hair of the dog, as they say. Immediately, I feel better and I'm relieved not to see spiders wiggling before my eyes.

I sink back into my chair. "Now tell me, Irena, what have you found out today."

She smiles. "Luca Moretti phoned. He often does. He uses me as a back-board."

Her expression startles me.

She reads my reaction on my face. "Did I say something wrong?"

"I think you meant to say sounding board," I laugh.

"I did. Thank you. I've been away from the United States too long," she explains. "Anyway, Luca values my thoughts."

"Your advice or your intuition?"

"Actually, both. We've been friends for many, many years. He wanted to know what I knew about you and I told him."

"Why would he be asking about me?"

"He wanted to know if you could be trusted."

Laughing, I nearly spill my prosecco. "I was going to ask you the very same question about him. When we went to the Archduke's palazzo together, I felt uneasy about him, but after what Harry said, I felt reassured."

"He wants to ask a favor of you. He wouldn't tell me exactly what, but he did mention that the Vatican had called him concerning the Benedictine monk's murder. They have sent an official to Venice. He's here to help Luca with the case and to try to enlist your help in the investigation."

"My help! Irena, but I'm already working for Lloyd's."

"Peter, Luca believes the two crimes may be related."

"What? That doesn't make sense. I'm investigating an art theft and he's involved in a murder investigation. Did the Commissario tell the Vatican I was here?"

"I'm sure he must have."

"I wonder why?"

Speaking in a near whisper, she says, "You may want to keep an open mind when I tell you this."

"Tell me what?" Intrigued, I move to the edge of my chair.

"I promised Luca you wouldn't tell a soul."

"Cross my heart, and hope to die."

The Princess titters. "What a quaint expression."

"Schoolboy talk," I grin. "I was about six years old when I learned it."

Irena rearranges herself on the lit-de-repos in a more comfortable position. "The Vatican told Luca that the monk was on a secret mission for them. They wouldn't say what he was doing, but Luca knows that the monk carried an iron spike to Murano to be encased in glass. He was returning it to the Vatican when he was accosted."

"An iron spike? What do you suppose it's from?"

"Luca thinks its something with important religious significance, a hull spike from Noah's ark or a fastener from St. Peter's Galilee boat, or perhaps a nail from the Crucifixion."

"Good heavens, what makes him think that?"

"It's speculation based on the pressure being brought to bear by the Vatican over the murder and the loss of this object. The Questore's taken Luca off all his other cases and he's been ordered to concentrate his efforts on solving the Vatican's case.

"Damn, that must mean he's been taken off the Archduke's theft."

"Yes, that's correct. When I told Luca you were coming

here for dinner this evening, he asked me to convey a message to you. He would like you to join him for lunch tomorrow at Montin's, at one o'clock."

"Sure. I'll be happy to have lunch with him. I just don't know what I can possibly contribute though."

"If you decide to help Luca, Peter, I want to warn you to be very careful. Whoever murdered that monk was ruthless. I can't explain why I say this, but lately, as I've mentioned, I've had the most dreadful headaches and premonitions. I sense they involve you somehow." She shudders as though seized by a sudden chill.

"Are you all right?"

"Yes, it's just something that happens."

"When you're being clairvoyant?"

"I suppose so."

"I'm famished, how about you?"

"Peter, you're not taking me seriously. Reaching behind her, Irena plucks an eight-inch long, Byzantine silver crucifix off the wall. "Here," she say handing it to me. "Swear to me that you will carry this with you at all times."

I take it from her. It's heavy. I feel like I'm holding a gun. I can tell from Irena's expression that she's serious. I raise my right hand and say, "I swear."

Sitting up straight, Irena assumes a regal pose. She makes a dramatic wave with her hand, and says. "Shall we dine?" Letting out a merry high-pitched laugh, she pushes off the lit-de-repos, grasps the rails of her walker, and trundles into the kitchen. Slipping the hefty crucifix in my jacket pocket, I follow her, hungrier than a Doberman Pinscher.

Chapter 9

COMMISSARIO MORETTI'S restaurant choice, Antica Locanda Montin in Dorsoduro, delights me. It's one of my favorites, the perfect setting for an al fresco lunch within a lovely brick walled garden filled with terra cotta pots of hydrangeas and shaded by a canopy of grape vines that entwine a high, barrel vaulted, latticework of iron. Surprisingly, in this picturesque setting, the food rivals the ambience.

As I walk through the restaurant filled with the works of local artists competing with one another for space and recognition, I spot two of Pomeroy's early oil paintings. They are bold abstractions of dismembered nude figures that suggest either a wild bacchanal or a massacre, which, I can't decide. If I dared ask Pomeroy, he'd say, "Make of it what you will, old boy, it's all in the eye of the beholder."

I enter the garden and find it teeming with tourists, mostly Scandinavians. After hearing their singsong manner of speaking I'm certain of their origin. I used to mimic a former Choate roommate who came from, "Copen-haaag-en."

Toward the back, beside the tall brick wall that encloses the garden's rear, I see a fleshy hand waving in the air. Commissario Moretti beckons me to his table. Seated with him is a slender, well-dressed older man with silver hair whom I immediately recognize, Doctor Umberto Ferculi, Director General of the Vatican Museum.

Smiling, I hasten to the table. "Dottore what a surprise!" He leaps to his feet and we embrace. "Commissario," I nod over Umberto's shoulder, not wanting him to feel slighted by our effusive greeting.

"Peter! How's the great art detective?"

"Very well, Dottore, and you?"

"I could be better. Everyone at the Vatican is mourning Brother Alvise's untimely death."

"Most unfortunate, I'm sorry."

"Thank you. Before I forget, Peter, how is your charming wife?"

"I hate to admit it, but Claire and I recently separated."

"Sorry, I didn't know?"

"On the bright side, there's a chance we might get back together."

"Good, I hope so. Before you arrived, Peter, I told the Commissario how much I enjoyed having you at the museum when you were studying Renaissance art with us. Best eye in your class. I mentioned how gifted you were, able to spot a bogus work of art before the forger's paint dried."

I laugh, embarrassed, not knowing quite how to respond to his flattery. I sit down opposite the two men.

Prior to joining the Metropolitan Museum I had spent a year in Rome studying Renaissance art at the Vatican Museum under Umberto Ferculi. He was a brilliant scholar, but somewhat difficult to fathom. Sometimes he was gregarious and outgoing and at other times reclusive and withdrawn. In spite of his important position within the Vatican he left me with the impression that he aspired to greater recognition and fulfillment. At any rate, it's not often one gets compliments from one of the world's recognized authorities on religious art of the Renaissance. "That's kind of you, Dottore, but I'm sure you didn't come here just to sing my praises."

"When I learned from the Commissario that you were in Venice working on an investigation, I decided, rather than send my deputy, I'd come myself. Isn't that so, Commissario?"

"Yes," agreed the Commissario, shaking out a napkin, which he dropped into his lap.

"Peter, I'm going to perfectly frank. We need your assistance. I know that you are committed to another case, but it so happens the Commissario and I believe your matter may be linked to ours. He'll gladly share his thoughts with us, won't you Commissario?"

"As you wish, Dottore. First, you might enlighten us about the purpose of Brother Alvise's trip to Venice."

"*Scusi*," interrupts the waiter. He rattles off the specials of the day in Italian, *zuppa de pesce*, fish soup, *cape sante con carciofi*, scallops with artichokes, and *vitello al funghetto con riso pilaf*, veal with mushrooms and rice pilaf. I opt for the veal dish, preceded by a tangy *ensalada rucola*, arugula salad, something I never tire of eating. Umberto and the Commissario order *granceola*, spider crab with olive oil and lemon, spaghetti Montin, a house specialty, and for the main course, scallops, which I love, but can't eat. Some enzyme inside a scallop poisons my system and for several days I'm a total basket case. We decide to share a liter of *vino della casa bianco*, the house's white wine, along with the mandatory *litro di acqua minerale naturale*.

When the waiter leaves, Umberto looks at the Commissario and then at me. He appears tense. "Brother Alvise's mission is going to require a lengthy explanation, but before I begin, I must have your assurance of complete discretion."

I glance at the Commissario. He nods in agreement.

"*Certo*, Dottore, I reply, looking into Umberto's dark eyes. "Peter, I presume you're familiar with the details of Brother Alvise's death?"

"Yes. I read about his murder in *Il Gazzettino*." Some of my information had come from the Princess, but I see no reason to introduce her into the conversation. The Commissario takes notice of my meditation and reacts with a faint and knowing smile.

"*Va bene*," says Umberto. "I won't repeat the details of his death. Brother Alvise was sent to Venice by order of the Pontiff. He carried with him the most precious artifact in all of Christendom. His mission was to take it to Murano and have it imbedded in crystal. The purpose of this was to preserve it for all times. Afterward, he was to—"

"What kind of artifact?" I interrupt, unable to stand the

suspense, as I recall the Commissario's speculation with the Princess about what he thought it might be.

Startled, Umberto looks at me. "You might contain your impulsiveness until I've finished," he snaps, irritated by my intrusion.

"Sorry," I reply, noticing the Commissario's unbroken concentration as he awaits Umberto's next words.

"As I was about to say, Brother Alvise was returning the artifact to the Vatican when he was accosted. His refusal to surrender the nail from Christ's Crucifixion cost him his life."

"I knew it," murmurs the Commissario.

"Incredible," I exclaim.

"Where did it come from?" asks the Commissario.

"I'll tell you after the waiter leaves," says Umberto,

The waiter sets a carafe of white wine and a bottle of mineral water on the table. Handing me a basket of crusty rolls, he fills our glasses. "Care for one?" I ask the Commissario, passing him the basket.

"*Grazie*," he answers. Taking the basket from me, he selects a roll.

"Commissario, the other day I neglected to ask you if the Questura will screen people who call in about the reward?"

"I've already spoken to my secretary about handling the calls. She'll take them, but she's not enthusiastic about dealing with a bunch of crazies. You might offer her a modest gratuity to encourage her effort. I'll leave that up to you."

"Thanks," I reply, "I'll phone her."

"*Salute!*" says Umberto. We lift our glasses and drink to health, as the waiter returns to the kitchen to bring out the *antipasti*. "The nail was found in 1954," continues Umberto. "One of the first mandates of Pope Pius XII was to resume the archaeological investigations under Saint Peter's Basilica that had been undertaken in 1940. Interrupted by World War II, those excavations had unearthed a number of pagan and early Christian tombs. When the excavations were resumed, the archaeologists found a small sarcophagus carved from stone that contained the remains of a Roman Centurion, named Marcus Orsini. He had evidently converted to Christianity as his remains were found in a Christian vault. In addition to his bones, his sarcophagus contained a lead pipe with both ends sealed with wax. The exterior of the pipe was badly corroded, but underneath the oxidation our conservators found a Latin inscription which read:

From the cross of Jesus of Nazareth.

"And inside the pipe was the nail?"

"Yes," he replies," but the minute the nail was removed from the lead pipe and air got to it, it began to deteriorate."

So intent is he on Umberto's words, the Commissario looks as though he's fallen into a trance. Turning to Umberto, I ask, "Then what did you do?"

"After removing some fragments for examination, we sealed the nail in a stainless steel tube from which we removed the air. It was the same tube Brother Alvise carried to Murano."

"If it was found in 1954, why did the Vatican wait all this time before having it preserved," asks the Commissario.

"An excellent question, Commissario, which I'll answer after we're served." Umberto glances past my head. I turn to see the waiter approach us carrying a tray. He sets the tray on a stand and serves plates of crab to Umberto and the Commissario. Placing the arugula salad in front of me, he asks, "*pepi, signore?*" Under one arm he carries a tall wooden pepper mill.

"*Per favore.*" I encourage him to grind away until my salad is covered with a blanket of black specks. He leaves, shaking his head, certain I'm demented.

"I see you like pepper," teases the bemused Commissario.

Before I can reply, Umberto quips, "Like Venice's own Marco Polo, he's cornered the spice trade."

They laugh. Picking up their forks, they dig out succulent chunks of crabmeat from the crustacean's rosy-colored shell and exchange glances of approval.

"As I was about to say," Umberto takes a drink of wine and continues, "the Holy See is a skeptic when it comes to religious relics. To avoid embarrassment and ridicule, authenticity has to be established beyond any doubt. Thus, Pope Pius XII assigned the Vatican Museum the job of proving that the artifact came from Jesus' Crucifixion. This was of course before my time, but ultimately I became involved."

"This is fascinating," I comment. "How did the Museum go about this task?"

"The historical part was tedious, but relatively easy. Our historians proved beyond question that Marcus Orsini was present at Jesus' Crucifixion. He was the Roman Centurion in charge of the soldiers who carried out Pontius Pilate's order to crucify Jesus. Also, Marcus Orsini officiated during the disposal of Jesus body to Joseph of Arimathea. And, we know from St. Matthew's gospel that the Roman Centurion who commanded the soldier's at the Crucifixion was so moved by Jesus' courage that he proclaimed on the spot his belief that Jesus must truly have been the son of God."

"So Dottore, the Centurion took a nail from Jesus' cross as a keepsake?"

"*Precisamente.* In order to conduct the scientific part of our investigation, we took the small samples that we had and subjected them to various testing methods. The carbon dating, metallurgical, and spectrographic analysis took some time, but ultimately, all proved to be positive. They confirmed that the nail dated to between 15 and 55 A.D., that the metal content of the nail was commensurate with raw material of that era and that the nail was hand wrought by a method in use at that time. After the Vatican Council was given the museum's findings it took them nearly thirty years to declare the artifact a holy relic of The Church. Now, having said all that, I'm going to finish my *granceola*. Commissario your turn."

"*Allora*, Over the past five years a number of major art thefts have occurred in Europe all of which remain unsolved. They share three things in common. All the stolen property had religious significance, all the thefts occurred at times when their owners were away, and finally, none of the stolen articles have ever surfaced nor have any legitimate attempts ever been made to collect the rewards offered."

"I think I'm familiar with most of the cases you refer to, Commissario. I accept your reasoning as it applies to the Archduke's theft, but I fail to see a similar *modus operandi* in the death of Brother Alvise, except for the stolen article's religious significance."

"The Commissario has an interesting theory," interjects Umberto.

"Okay," I reply, "I'm all ears."

"Let's suppose for the sake of conjecture that Brother Alvise's death was an accident?"

"What?" I exclaim.

"Peter, the Coroner's report indicates Brother Alvise's head wound may have been self-inflicted, meaning he may have slipped and fallen against the object that caused his head wound."

"And afterward, he fell into the canal and drowned?" Askance, I look at the Commissario and then at Umberto who returns my gaze with a slightly raised eyebrow.

"Personally," replies the Commissario, I think Brother Alvise was accosted by a person or persons who knew what he was carrying was extremely valuable. When he was ordered to surrender the artifact, he tried to run, tripped on the hem of his robe, fell against the mooring and was knocked unconscious. The fact that the blow was to right side of his temple indicates he was running away from, not toward, the canal's edge. The blood and tissue we collected on the *fondamenta's* side of the inverted cannon supports this conclusion, which means that Brother Alvise fell to the side of the mooring that faces *away* from the canal. That being the case, Brother Alvise could not possibly have fallen and rolled into the canal. The mooring post stood in his way. So, whoever took his bag thought he was either mortally wounded or dead and pushed his body into the canal. The point I'm making is that Brother Alvise's attackers never expected a monk to offer resistance. They expected a quick and easy score. In my opinion that's the similarity to the other thefts and the fact that something unexpected may have occurred is, therefore, irrelevant."

"I think you're stretching the point, Commissario, but you could be right." I glance at Umberto. He looks uncomfortable. Clearly, he's taken the Commissario's comment to heart, about someone knowing what the monk carried. "And another thing," I add, "it's too early for us to know if anyone will come forward to claim the reward for the Archduke's property."

"I grant you that," responds the Commissario, "however, I'm convinced we shall end up with the same result, no one comes forward to claim the reward."

"I share that opinion," agrees Umberto. "Commissario, I must take exception to something you inferred. I cannot conceive of anyone in the Vatican betraying his Holiness' sacred trust by providing information about the artifact to Brother Alvise attackers."

The Commissario gives Umberto a steely-eyed glance. Just as he appears ready to challenge Umberto, he pauses.

I jump in. "Dottore, how can anyone be certain there wasn't a leak from inside the Vatican?"

"I guess we can't be one hundred percent certain," replies Umberto. His face pales and he takes on a gloomy expression.

"I'm sure of one thing," growls the Commissario, jabbing the air with his fork. "It's inconceivable that Brother Alvise's death was a random act of violence. Only an idiot or a madman would attack a monk for his purse. As far as I'm concerned, that means the Vatican remains suspect until proven otherwise."

Offended by the Commissario's tone of voice, Umberto glances at me. It's clear he's withdrawn from the conversation, tuned out and so immersed in his own thoughts he won't speak up. To relieve the tension, I offer, "Gentlemen, why don't we move on. We're not accomplishing anything with disagreement."

"Fine," replies the Commissario, drinking down half a glass of mineral water. "Suppose we examine the cases individually, shall we? The first theft involved a rare early Christian ivory diptych that had been carved by the Carolinians. It was stolen from a collector's town-house in London while the owner was in Paris."

"Is that the one with the iconography that portrays the various miracles of Christ?" asks Umberto.

"Yes. It's unique. It's the only one of its kind in existence," I reply.

"And priceless," the Commissario reminds us.

Reverting to small talk, we chat as the waiter returns to clear the plates, serve the entrees, and refill our glasses. Lifting a tray of dirty dishes to his shoulder, he departs and leaves us to continue our discussion.

"Less than a year later," resumes the Commissario, "a large Catalan crucifix and a carved wooden altar from the thirteenth century was taken from a private chapel in Madrid. The owner, a banker, was in Switzerland during the theft. Then, fourteen months later, outside Wiesbaden, Germany, a Lucas Cranach painting of a Madonna and Child, a set of Albrecht Durer's engravings of the Stations of the Cross, and a tenth century golden chalice were looted from the private museum at Baron von Hesse's estate. At the time of the theft, the Baron was hunting boar in the Black Forest.

"I'm familiar with the Cranach," I break in. "I was at Christie's when the painting was sold to the Baron. It brought a record price."

"Only eight months after the German robbery, fourteen important religious paintings were looted from the castle of an Austrian industrialist near Vienna. They included works by Benvenuto Cellini, Titian, Paolo Veneziano, Giovani Bellini, Veronese, Tintoretto, Sandro Botticelli and others. The Austrian was in Rome at the time and his servants abandoned the castle to fight a fire purposely set in the stables. As they were busy extinguishing the blaze, thieves removed the paintings. The value of that theft alone exceeds seventy million dollars."

"The entire world heard about that one, Commissario. And now we have the Archduke's robbery. So where are we going with all this?" I ask.

Umberto lays down his knife and fork. "Wouldn't you both agree that the reason we have not seen any of this stolen property is because it's too well known and it can never ever be sold anywhere?"

"Without question," I respond.

With his mouth full of food, the Commissario nods his head up and down in agreement.

"Then who are we looking for?" asks Umberto. "What kind of person or persons takes some of the world's most valuable art? Assuming they're not interested in the ransom, which seems to be the case, what do they plan to do with their spoils?"

"In my experience," I offer, "An art thief fits one of three profiles. There's the fanatic who wants to deprive the world of these objects. Let's call him an art terrorist. Then there's the mentally warped individual, an art kleptomaniac, who derives exquisite pleasure from successfully stealing objects of great value. And finally, there's the deranged collector who gets his gratification from having these objects in his exclusive possession. The former is likely to destroy what he's stolen while the latter two will most likely keep their spoils as souvenirs of their sickness. Nevertheless, I sense it's going to be very difficult to get the stolen articles back unless we either catch the perpetrator in the act or someone comes forward and exposes him."

"Precisely, my boy," exclaims Umberto, spearing a scallop with his fork. "Therefore I'm of the opinion that we should set a trap for him and see if he rises to the bait?"

"What's the bait, I ask."

"It's *who's* the bait," corrects the Commissario.

"All right then, who?" I ask.

"*You!*" Umberto thrusts a speared scallop at me. Realizing what he's done, he immediately lays down his fork. "*Scusi*," he says.

"*Me!*" I exclaim. Heads turn. "Oops," I mumble. "Look, I don't think this is something I'm comfortable doing. If you're right about the monk's death being a part of this whole picture then I'm likely to be the next victim. No offense, gentlemen, but I just don't . . . "

Umberto interrupts. "Peter, the Vatican is in turmoil over Brother Alvise's death and the loss of this holy artifact. If we don't find his murderer and recover the artifact heads will roll. Look what the press is already doing to us."

"They're relentless. They've reduced us to carrion," interrupts the Commissario. "Next come the vultures!" He winces, as though one has landed on him and torn off a piece of his flesh.

"I'll probably lose my job at the Vatican Museum," bemoans Umberto.

"Surely you can't be serious." All at once, I feel sorry for

Umberto. The Commissario, too. They must be under terrific pressure. I think back to my days in Rome. Although we were not all that close, Umberto was certainly there for me when I needed his advice and guidance. And the Commissario, he's a good guy. He doesn't deserve to be a "scrapgoat" as the Princess would say in her fractured English, when she means, "scapegoat." I owe Umberto a favor, maybe the Commissario too. What the hell!

"Commissario, no doubt you're reeling under pressure from the Government?" asks Umberto.

"Everyone's demanding answers, Dottore, but we haven't any to give."

"Okay you two, *basta*, I'll help you."

"You see," Umberto said, turning to the Commissario with a look that said, "I told you so. Didn't I tell you he was a generous person and he'd offer us his help?"

The Commissario laughs. Reaching over the table, he pats my hand, "*Grazie mille*. We accept your kind offer."

"No problem," I say, knowing I've been had. I still have plenty of reservations. What in God's name am I getting myself into? I must be daft. Laying my knife and fork across my untouched food, I realize my appetite has vanished.

Over cappuccini, Umberto, the Commissario, and I discuss a plan designed to lure the perpetrators of the thefts into the open. It's based on the Commissario's information that Italian men speaking in the Venetian dialect were involved in the theft of the paintings from the Archduke's palazzo.

Taking advantage of the Venetian penchant for intrigue and gossip, we decide that I will assume the role of an art appraiser who is in actuality an art thief. I will disseminate false information, which questions the authenticity of the Archduke's Giovani Bellini. Since there's been no public announcement about the theft, only the perpetrators will know that the Archduke's masterpiece, *Madonna of the Columbine* has been stolen. We hope my public comments, labeling the painting a fake, will reach them and cause them sufficient anxiety to force them to come looking for me. "But how and where am I supposed to plant these seeds of doubt?" I inquire.

"With the help of a friend's daughter, I have arranged for you to attend a number of social gatherings. They involve Venice's arty set, where rumors tend to spread like brush fires,"

"Fine." I reply. "Who's this social guide you're referring to?"

"Cinzia Aliverti," the Commissario responds.

"I don't believe this," I exclaim.

"You know this woman?" asks Umberto, seeing the surprised look on my face.

"No, but Princess Irena, among others, suggested we meet."

"Now you will," laughs the Commissario, looking a bit sheepish. "I must warn you not to compromise the young lady by telling her what we're doing."

"Okay." I detect the subtle Machiavellian art of manipulation at work.

"Gentlemen," says Umberto, "if you'll pardon me. Nature calls."

"Certainly, Dottore," replies the Commissario.

"What *have* you told her?" I ask.

"Only that I would consider it a great personal favor if she would introduce you around."

"Okay. Then I don't have to make up any stories about myself?"

"Not really," he says. "Just don't reveal that you're employed by Lloyd's, unless you're forced to. I've taken the liberty of giving her your telephone number and she's agreed to call you. Normally, a Venetian woman would never dream of telephoning a strange man. However, after living in England, Cinzia's become less conventional. You'll like her, Peter. She's from a very old and prominent Venetian family, not Dogel, but the Aliverti's certainly qualify.

"Commissario, I believe you mentioned her father is a friend of yours?"

"Yes. Antonio is a dashing fellow, a lady-killer as you American's say and quite unpretentious in spite of great wealth. He's been separated from Cinzia's mother, oh, twenty years now. They'll never divorce, of course. She's a stunning looking woman, but sadly an eccentric and now virtually a recluse. Antonio's quite the opposite, very gregarious though he's a bit of a *vitelloni*."

"*Vitelloni?*" I knew the expression had something to do with veal.

"*Scusi.* Literally that's a person who enjoys baby veal, in Antonio's case young ladies in their late teens and early twenties. Under the circumstances who can blame him. Nevertheless, he's been a decent father and a responsible provider. The day I picked you up in the launch, do you recall seeing an ocher colored palazzo that faces the Grand Canal on the opposite side of the Rio San Vidal.

"You mean the palazzo with the little arched bridge that crosses over the canal?"

"Yes, that's Antonio's family home. He allows his wife to live there. Can you imagine the *Signora* rattling around in that huge palazzo all by herself."

"No, I can't. Where does Cinzia live?"

"She has her own apartment near the Gritti Hotel, but she's always at the palazzo, looking after her mother."

"Is she an only child?"

"Oh, no. She has an older sister who's married and lives in Verona. Cinzia also has a younger brother who has an apartment in Dorsoduro. He works with his father looking after the family investments.

"Well, I look forward to her call, Commissario."

"I guarantee you'll enjoy her."

Mmmmm, that's the same thing Claire and the Princess said to me. This woman's beginning to arouse my interest.

"Peter, you must not forget that these thieves are dangerous."

"Here." He hands me a dog-eared card with a telephone number scrawled across the front. "In case of emergency," he says. "Memorize the number, then destroy the card."

I look at the number on his card and pocket it just as Umberto rejoins us. Why in God's name am I sticking my neck out like this?

Chapter 10

As I begin to realize I've agreed to become the decoy in a scheme to entrap perpetrators of a half dozen major thefts and a brutal murder, I get a bad case of the jitters.

Leaving Montin's, I try to settle my fears by taking a leisurely stroll to the offices of *Il Gazzettino*. In an alley near the Church of San Barnaba a pot of geraniums narrowly misses me and smashes to the pavement at my feet. Startled, I jump. Some students passing by think I look like a space shuttle during lift-off and laugh uproariously. After re-entry my heart pounds, as I try to regain my composure. Looking up, I discover one of the ubiquitous Venetian cats is the culprit. His inscrutable stare greets me from an empty space on the windowsill where the smashed flowerpot formerly resided. Warily examining all window ledges for cats or flapping laundry that might dislodge another missile, I make my way to the newspaper's offices where I pay for a week's publication of a reward announcement. The reward promises one hundred thousand pounds for the safe return of four Renaissance paintings with no questions asked. The telephone number specified in the announcement belongs to Maria Rossi, the Commissario's secretary. If a caller identifies the paintings she knows to get in touch with me. A long shot to be sure, but perhaps worth the effort.

The minute I walk into Claire's flat and bid Franco, "*buona sera*," I notice he too has enjoyed a hearty repast. Four shiny translucent wings and the hollow carapace of a bumblebee litter the floor beneath his web. He appears to be sleeping off his feast. Now's my chance. I stare up at him, looking for the telltale red hourglass, but the phone rings, interrupting my quest.

"*Pronto*," I answer with a sigh.

"Peter, is that you? Cinzia Aliverti here."

"My goodness. Less than an hour ago, the Commissario told me you'd be calling."

"Oh, am I catching you at a bad time?"

"No, I was just trying to identify a spider."

"A spider?"

"Franco, Claire's pet spider."

"Really? I didn't know she had a pet spider."

"I don't mean she's had it for a long time or anything like that. I think she sort of inherited it." Oh, God, what am I saying. "Franco was already here when she moved in. I mean, I never laid eyes on him until I got here." This woman must think I'm a nut case, rambling on like this.

"Is this Franco poisonous?"

"I really don't know. That's what I was trying to find out when you called." Lord, how did I get myself into this mess?

"It's not one of those hairy South American tarantulas, is it? If it is, the building's owner will be terribly upset. Under the provisions of her lease Claire's not allowed to have pets."

Oh, boy. I've done it now. "Cinzia, it's just a little Venetian spider that took up residence in the salon. Claire can't bear to mistreat or kill any living thing, so she just gave the spider a name."

"I see. Well, in that case I suppose I shouldn't concern myself about Franco."

"No and he does eat a lot of mosquitoes."

"That's good," she laughs.

Her laugh sounds slightly nervous. "I hope I haven't upset you with this spider business? I apologize if I have."

"No, it's not that. I can't ever remember having such a bizarre conversation."

"My fault entirely. Suppose we start over, shall we?"

"Lovely."

I can hear her trying to suppress her amusement. At least she has a sense of humor. "Cinzia, I'm delighted to hear from you. I've been expecting your call."

"Have you, now? The Commissario, . . . he . . ." she begins laughing. "This is too funny . . . this entire conversation is so weird . . . Peter . . . I can't stop."

"Take your time." Her laugh is infectious. She gets me started and together we laugh like small children.

"Peter . . ." she pauses to pull her self together. "The Commissario asked me to introduce you to my Venetian friends and it will be my pleasure."

"Thank you, Cinzia. Practically everyone I know in Venice has told me about you, especially the Princess."

"Irena's such a dear. Peter, I know it's rather last minute, but are you free this evening?"

"I am."

"Would you like to escort me to a party? Antonio Verdi, an artist friend, is having some people over to look at his new work and listen to him play jazz. He's a fine painter and an excellent guitarist."

"That sounds like fun, Cinzia. I'd love to go."

"Dress casually, sports jacket, slacks, open shirt, no tie. Suppose you pick me up at my mother's home at eight o'clock? It's the palazzo facing the Grand Canal just the other side of Rio San Vidal. Cross over the small arched bridge and ring the bell."

"I know exactly where it is. Eight it is. I look forward to meeting you."

"And I you, Piero. *Ciao.*"

"Piero?" I repeat the name. Must be Italian for Peter. It's a more complimentary label than, "DOG Three," which is what Claire often calls me. She bastardized my birth name, Douglas Osgood Grant, the Third and on my fortieth birthday presented me with special New York license plates initialed, "DOG III." She thought it hysterically funny. I was not amused. Hah! She can't get away with that in Venice. No automobiles! Perhaps she could call me, "DOGE Three." That at least sounds dignified and it goes with the territory for Doges were selected from the most important Venetian families and they wielded immense power. Admittedly there were a few squirrelly ones, the first Doge for example. He sent a couple of merchants to Alexandria to kidnap Saint Mark's ossified remains and bring them back to Venice. Hardly what one would call, "a good neighbor policy." On second thought, "DOGE Three," may not be such a great moniker after all.

"Piero." I like the sound of it.

"Peter," is my nickname actually. It was my Scottish great grandfather's first name and my grandparent's household called me, Peter, to avoid confusing me with Douglas Osgood Grant, Senior, my grandfather and guardian.

"Piero," I like the way Cinzia pronounces it too. I'm big on women's voices. It was what first attracted me to Claire. I must admit though, I'm a sucker for a British accent. Cinzia's English mixed with her Venetian accent is charming. I like the cultured warmth of her voice.

"Piero," my favorite new name.

Endeavoring to emulate Franco, I try to nap but it's no use. I'm too keyed up. Turning up the temperature on the hot water heater, I start a bath. Knowing how long the tub takes to fill, I leave the apartment and venture into the square.

The campo teems with children romping after soccer balls, playing tag, flying gliders, and riding bicycles while gaggles of mothers stand beside baby strollers and prams, gesturing and prattling on. Paolin's is packed to overflow. I make my way through a maze of tables looking for an empty spot. I see a couple leaving and slide into a white plastic chair that's still warm from its previous occupant. Ordering a gin and tonic, I engage in every red-blooded Italian male's favorite hobby, girl watching. "When in Rome!" as they say.

Nursing my second drink, I begin to feel slightly mellow. Laser-like, my eyes lock onto an elegant-looking Venetian woman with exceptional long legs who strides toward me. She notices me staring. Her faint smile evaporates as she realizes I'm not the familiar face she first thought. Thrusting her patrician nose skyward, she gives her cascading titian mane a haughty toss and prances off. As my eyes follow, I suddenly feel someone's arms encircle my neck. Warm lips nuzzle my ear. "*Ciao, Bambino.*" whispers a sexy voice.

"Adriana!" I exclaim, turning toward her.

"You like-a that?" she asks, pointing to the tall beauty I had been stalking with my eyes. Adriana's eyes narrow and in an accusatory manner, she glares at me.

"No, just looking." Having no reason to apologize for any visual infidelity, I await her reaction.

She breaks into a smile, slides into my lap, and drapes her arms around my neck. Gazing into my eyes, she remarks, "You gonna like-a me lots more than her, I show you." Like a heat-seeking missile, she locks on to my lips. All of that osculation and torso contact has its intended effect. Before I embarrass myself before the citizenry of Venice, I force her to get up from my lap.

Flashing me a mischievous grin, she grabs my hand, drags me from my chair, and tows me past amused onlookers into the campo. "Where-a you live?" she asks.

"Over there," I point to a row of rose and yellow colored buildings among which is Claire's flat. My heart pulses. My breath comes in short gasps. I can't believe this is happening. Tugging on my arm, she asks, "You want to be with me, yes?"

My mouth's suddenly so dry I can hardly reply. "*Si,*" I say, grinning at her like a kid about to board a roller coaster, both happy and terrified, all at once. Wow, it's been a while. What if I've forgotten how? What if I can't rise to the occasion?

Walking toward the apartment, I notice people stopping to stare at us. Some of their expressions are disapproving, others lecherous. I don't understand why. But on the stairway up to the flat I discover the reason. Silhouetted against a stairway window, Adriana's flowered dress is virtually transparent. *Mama mia*! She's not wearing any undergarments. No worries now, Sagittarius rising!

At the door to the apartment, as I fumble to get the key in the lock, Adriana notices my aroused state. Laughing, she gathers up the hem of her dress and strips it off over her head.

"You like-a me?" she asks. Dazzlingly naked except for her black pumps, she poses, one hand resting on her hip, the other holding the dress which puddles to the terrazzo floor.

"Not out here," I gasp, desperately trying to turn the key in the lock. As she tries to embrace me, the door flies open. Laughing, she darts inside the apartment, turns, and playfully drags me inside. As I close the door, she backs me against it, presses into me, whispers sexy Italian words in my ear, and tears at my shirt buttons and belt. Hearing the sound of running water, she breaks away and glances into the bathroom. "*Bello!*" she cries out, discovering the nearly filled bathtub.

Kicking off her pumps Adriana looks at me with a quizzical smile and a tilted head that asks, "Are you joining me?"

What a silly question!

I haven't had such fun in a bathtub since my childhood when I used to play with my battery-operated submarine. Pretty soon Adriana gets torpedoed and there's an indescribable explosion.

Wrapping a towel around my waist, I enter the kitchen and take from the fridge a bottle of wine and two glasses that I keep iced for auspicious occasions. Well, you never know.

Leaving her inhibitions and her see through dress on a hook on the bathroom door, Adriana joins me in the salon.

"I no like to wear nothing." she purrs, hugging me from behind. I feel cool damp breasts press into my back and the sensation nearly causes me to spill the wine.

"Here," I say, offering her a glass of wine. She lets go of me and takes the glass.

"*Chin, Chin,*" she toasts and casually strolls around the salon, sipping her wine while examining Claire's possessions. What a voluptuous body she has. She's an exhibitionist. I can't take my eyes off her. Now I'm really happy I bought Pomeroy's sketch of her. Speaking of Pomeroy, he'll draw and quarter me if he ever finds out about this. Wait a minute, what am I worrying about? I didn't initiate this tryst. She came on to me. Of course, I hardly offered any resistance, but who can blame me? After all I've suffered a very long drought.

In the bookcase Adriana spots a framed photograph of Claire and me.

"You wife?" she asks.

"Yes. We're separated." I realize as I say it, she probably doesn't understand what I mean. "We don't live together anymore?" I explain, recalling my pain the morning that Claire bolted out of our Gritti Palace Hotel suite after telling me during breakfast, "I need to get away. I have to find myself." Then, sheepishly she had mentioned her astrologer.

"Your astrologer!" I shouted. What's *she* got to do with any of this."

"Hilda said our astrological charts were totally compatible and we were meant for each other."

"You and me?" I asked.

"No, Peter, me and Hilda."

"Jesus, you're having a fling with your astrologer?" I said, buttering my best Hermés tie instead of the roll I had in my hand. "You're leaving *me* for a *woman*?"

While I barfed up breakfast in the toilet, Claire split. Unable to find her, I left Venice in despair, flew back to New York, and like a real "DOG III" licked my wounds. Months later I received an apologetic letter from her. She explained that Hilda, influenced by Jupiter in Taurus, had skipped off to Florence with Claire's family silver and a streetwise Senegalese handbag peddler who dealt exclusively in Vuitton knockoffs and cannabis. Little consolation, I must say.

"*Magnifica!*" comments Adriana staring at Claire's photograph.

"*Si, grazie,*" I reply, not knowing what else to say. Claire always looks sensational. Models know how to pose and play to the camera. Watching the lusty Venetian bombshell study Claire's tall slender figure, her lovely face, and her lustrous champagne colored hair makes me feel strange, awkward and, yes, even a bit guilty.

"*Prego,*" she shrugs. Putting the picture back on the shelf, she walks over to the sofa and curls up on one end. Setting her wine on the coffee table, she looks up at me. "This-a not where-a you live?"

I can tell she suddenly feels ill at ease, realizing that she's in Claire's apartment. I walk to the sofa and sit next to her. "I live in America, in New York. Right now she's in Switzerland with someone else. It's all right for you to be here with me, you understand? It's okay." I'm speaking with my hands like an Italian and I'm looking and sounding frightfully serious. Adriana puts a hand to her mouth. She looks at me wide eyed. Her eyes crinkle at the corners, a smile washes over her face and she breaks into laughter. Reaching out with her arms, she embraces me. "*Adorable*," she whispers in my ear, then kisses me passionately on the lips. Under my towel, I feel her fingers snake across my thigh.

"*Andiamo*," she says and I obey. Following Adriana into the bedroom I prepare to engage in the twilight half of a double header that goes into extra innings.

"Pomeroy's going to kill me if he finds out about this," I protest, but not very much.

"Don't-a you worry bout-a Pomeroy," she smiles, stripping off my towel. "I take-a good care-a Pomeroy."

I'll just bet you will. Sinking into Adriana's edacious embrace, I imagine how Franco must have enveloped the bumblebee he ate for lunch.

Adriana leaves the apartment at seven-thirty for the Giudecca. Presumably when she gets there, she'll "take-a good care-a Pomeroy." Checking my face in the bathroom mirror for lipstick smears, I nervously glance at my watch. I have only thirty minutes to get my act together before I'm to collect Cinzia.

Amazingly I ring Cinzia's doorbell right on time. I don't really expect her to be ready for I'm aware Venetians aren't known for punctuality, ever.

Surprise!

Cinzia opens the door. She's ready and waiting. Chalk it up to English schooling and good manners.

"*Buona sera*, Cinzia," I lean in and plant air kisses on each cheek. Her perfume and freshly washed hair smell delicious.

She responds with two air kisses and "*Ciao*, Piero. Ready to go?"

She's tall and slender with shoulder length black hair, large, wide set brown eyes, and an oval face with a narrow nose and full sensual lips. She's casually dressed, yet stylish, in a black pleated skirt, a black silk blouse, and a colorful red, gold, and black Gucci scarf, loosely knotted around her neck. An expensive Prada bag is draped over one shoulder, definitely not a knock off.

While I close the door, Cinzia strolls part way across the narrow bridge spanning the Rio San Vidal. When I turn to catch up with her, I have an opportunity to admire her long, shapely Venetian legs. I'm tempted to emit a wolf whistle, something I've seen Manhattan construction workers do when they see a really pretty woman, but I suppress the urge. Following in her perfumed wake, I catch up to her and take her gently by the arm. "You smell absolutely wonderful. What scent is that you're wearing?"

"Thank you," she smiles. "It's Jardins de Bagatelle, by Guerlain."

"It's intoxicating."

She laughs. "I'm glad you like it. It's my favorite fragrance. Do you mind walking to Antonio's?"

"Not in the least. It's a lovely night for a stroll," I reply. Ahead of us, I notice my neighborhood flower stand. The owner is standing out front, locking it up for the night. He waves to us. We wave back and walk up the wide wooden steps of Accademia Bridge.

"You're sure? Antonio's apartment is in the middle of San Giacomo dell Orio in San Polo. It's a long way if you're not Venetian."

"I'm positive, I answer. "I love walking the streets of Venice at night, especially with such a pretty woman."

"Thank you, what a nice thing to say." Putting her arm through mine, she climbs the Accademia Bridge beside me. We cross over the Grand Canal and descend into Dorsoduro. Walking through a narrow street we reach the Rio San Trovaso where Cinzia calls my attention to Trattoria San Trovaso. "That's my favorite pizza restaurant."

"Mine too," I grin at her.

Walking past the area near Montin's, where I had lunch with the Commissario and Umberto Ferculi, I remark, "I'm happy you called and asked me to accompany you tonight. After the flattering things everyone's had to say about you, I was anxious to meet you."

Cinzia laughs. Clinging to my arm, she swings her hip against me and bumps me off stride. "The Commissario warned me about you. He said you were a charming *lobo* and I'd better watch out. What do you say to that?"

"Look's like he's got my number." I put on a serious face. "I only fell in love three times today, two girls who passed by Paolin's and now you."

She looks at me with both eyebrows raised. "How many times a day do you usually fall in love," she inquires.

"Oh, six or seven times. Less and it's a lousy day," I tease.

"The Commissario's wrong. You're not a wolf. You're a *cacciatore!* Before we take another step, you need to go in there, and repent, you womanizer." She points at the Church of St. Barnaba and fights back a smile, while trying to maintain a stern countenance.

Watching her struggle to suppress her amusement, I reply, "I prefer the Frari, if you don't mind. It's my favorite church. It's on the way and it's not that far from here."

"All right," she relents, faking a petulant look, "You can repent there, but I'll not accompany you one step beyond the entrance until you . . ." Cinzia gets the giggles and we both break up laughing.

Passers by stare at us. Some seemed amused. Others appear condescending. Venetian's can be a bit lofty at times.

Cinzia yanks on my arm, leans her head on my shoulder, and exclaims happily, "Piero, I think I like you!"

"Ditto," I say."

"Ditto. What's that mean?" She gives me a puzzled look.

"Sorry, It's American slang for, me too." Taking her by the hand, I accelerated my pace. "Unless we get moving, the party's going to be over before we get there."

"Slow up, Piero. I can't walk fast in these heels. Besides, nobody in Venice ever arrives at a party on time."

I glance down at her pumps. "You have the best looking legs."

"Piero! she exclaims. "You never make comments like that to a Venetian woman."

Even though darkness had enveloped us I could tell she was blushing.

"I stand by my compliment."

"All right then, be a bounder. See if I come to your rescue when you say that to someone and she smacks you in the face with her handbag." She covers her mouth with her hands and starts laughing. "Piero, whatever shall I do with you?"

"As Tarzan said, when confronted by a nine hundred pound gorilla, whatever you want."

"Oh dear, we'll pass on sending you inside the Frari. I fear you're beyond redemption."

Walking into Campo San Giacomo dell Orio, Cinzia steers me under a *sotto portego*, a tunnel-like passageway erected over the street between two buildings. Underneath, she stops me and points to a small square opening in the ceiling between beams. "Do you know what that's for?" she asks.

"It looks like a hole."

"Of course it's a hole, but what is its purpose?"

I see that the aperture is over a boarded up entrance into the building, but it doesn't make any sense to me. Completely mystified, I shrug. "I give up."

Cinzia laughs, "This was once a house of prostitution, a *Casino*. That hole enabled the madam to look down into the street and make certain that it was client at the door and not the police."

"Really?"

"Yes, and at one time there were nearly twelve thousand prostitutes living in this section of Venice."

"When was that?" I gaze up and around for more peepholes.

"At the end of the sixteenth century. The total population of Venice was then about a hundred thousand people."

"My God! Twelve percent of Venice's population were ladies of the evening?"

"That's right. Think of all the legs you could have admired then, *Signore Cacciatore*."

"Touche!" I laugh.

Cinzia snatches me by the sleeve of my jacket. "Come on." She hustles me along the cobbles to a three-story, ocher-colored house that's set back from the street behind a wrought iron gate.

"Here we are." She presses the doorbell.

When the lock buzzes, I push in the gate and we enter. We walk across a patio to an arched entryway leading to a staircase. Standing next to the entry is a squat heavyset man wearing a gaudy sport-shirt. He smokes a cigarette. Cinzia comments, "Count Benzoni's here."

Incredulous, I ask, "That chap, dressed like a laborer, is a Count?"

"No, no," she laughs, "He's the Count's speedboat driver. I'll tell you about the Count when we're alone."

"*Buona sera, signorina e signore,*" says the man with the cigarette. His voice is surly and he rakes Cinzia from head to toe with his eyes.

"*Buona sera,*" she responds icily.

We climb the steps, following an ever-increasing cacophony of music to the third floor. Upon entering, a lanky dark haired fellow in a Polo sport shirt and blue jeans shouts, "*Ciao, cara,*" and gives Cinzia an enthusiastic hug.

"Peter," Cinzia says, breaking away, "our host, Antonio Verdi."

Sticking out his hand, he says with a southern drawl, "Hey, man glad to meet you."

"Peter Grant," I reply shaking his hand. "Nice to meet you, too."

"Make yourselves at home. Look around. There's wine on a table in the salon along with bread and cheese. Maria's made a big pot of shrimp Creole, which we'll be serving when everyone's here, meanwhile we're hanging out the roof deck."

"Where are you from, Antonio?" I ask.

"New Orleans. Y'all excuse me while I tune my guitar," he replies and ambles into a nearby bedroom where a sultry looking girl with a mass of black curly hair leans against the doorframe. She wears a long multicolored native skirt and a white scoop neck blouse with lace trim. She notice's us and waves.

"That's Maria, Antonio's girlfriend," says Cinzia. "She's wearing her native Honduran dress."

"She's really pretty."

"And very nice. I like her a lot."

Carrying our glasses of Pinot Grigio we follow the sound of voices and go upstairs to the *altane*, a covered wooden roof deck. Cinzia tells me the altane was where the noble ladies of Venice used to sit while drying their tresses they had just washed and tinted with henna.

The first person I recognize is the sultry looking woman with the wild nest of apricot hair that I saw with Marchese Mochedon at Harry's. She catches me staring at her and gives me a thorough once over, head to foot. She ignores Cinzia. After scoping me out, she turns back to her companion, a gaunt, yet handsome, fifty year old man, whose expensive clothes hang from his thin frame like limp laundry. He has raptor-like eyes that are rimmed with dark circles and a sallow complexion. I can't decide if he's sick or addicted to drugs. He has the look of someone who hasn't slept in about a decade. A coke head perhaps? I decide to refer to him as, "Count Dracula," not to his face, of course. When I share my thoughts with Cinzia, she pales. Taking me aside, she whispers "Piero, you can't joke about Count Benzoni. It's very dangerous. Don't look around, but the two big men standing behind him are his bodyguards. He's never without them. I'm told they'll gladly kill for him."

"Oh!"

"Ugo Benzoni is a notorious degenerate. It's rumored he has AIDS. He's into drugs, kinky sex, orgies, you name it. He's extremely rich. All his money is inherited. The Venetians are afraid to offend him so, despite his unsavory reputation, he's invited everywhere. That awful woman he's with is Lili Poirel. She was formerly married to a French diplomat. For a time we were friends until I learned she was cheating on her husband. They divorced and she took up with the Count. She lives with him in his palazzo on the Grand Canal doing God only knows what. I never speak to her."

"I saw her the other day having lunch with Marchese Mochedon at Harry's."

"A harmless infatuation I assure you. Gianni's a silly old *vitelloni*, who gets his jollies being seen with young tarts. Benzoni's the one you want to watch out for. Be careful, around him, won't you, Piero?"

"You make him sound worse than the Borgias, but I promise to watch out." Damn, everybody wants me to be careful. First the Princess, then the Commissario, now Cinzia. Danger and intrigue suffuse the air of Venice like ragweed pollen.

"Cinzia!" exclaims a woman behind me. I step aside as a slender blond of medium height rushes to embrace Cinzia. After the customary air kisses, Cinzia introduces us. "Moira Dunn meet Peter Grant."

"Hello." She looks casually at me through pale blue eyes.

"Hi," I reply, studying her face. Surgery has made her appear younger than she is. Her sharp features and her streaked blonde hair remind me of actress Morgan Fairchild's. She seems oddly familiar to me. "Are you by any chance from New York?" I ask.

"Yes, I used to live there," she replies, scanning her own mug book for *my* picture.

"Did you have a beautiful antique black and yellow Bentley that was garaged under One Beekman Place?"

"I did, but it wasn't my car. It belonged to my lover."

Nothing shy about this woman, I muse.

"He was a well known television entertainer," she continues. "We lived together at the United Nations Towers until six years ago. He had a massive coronary and died."

"I'm sorry." I reply, trying to sound sympathetic, but she's so cold and matter of fact about him that I wonder if *she's* got an hour glass tattooed on *her* tummy. I recall a silver haired man my garage man said was one of the first late night talk show hosts who had made a bundle investing in Atlantic City Casinos. It was probably the same guy. According to *The Post's* gossip column, I had read that he'd left his wife and taken up with, "a certain blond from a leading soap opera."

Judging from her clothes, the diamonds in her ear lobes, and the square emerald rock on one slim and impeccably manicured finger, she looks as if she's been left well off. Finding death an awkward topic, I ask her, "Do you remember the two big black 1949 Cadillac limousines parked in the same garage. The ones with wide whitewall tires, lots of chrome, and running boards?"

"Were those yours?" Her eyes light up with reassessment. The only things missing from the cornea are tabs with dollar signs on them, the kind on top of those old-fashioned cash registers, "ca-ching!"

"Yes, they were mine and I would gladly have traded both of them for your friend's Bentley."

Cinzia's eyes dart back and forth between us like she's at a tennis match. "How fascinating," she interjects. Both of you come all the way to Venice to discover you're old neighbors."

"New York's a big impersonal city," responds Moira. "Most people don't even know who their next door neighbors are."

"Strange, but true," I agree. "How long have you lived in Venice, Moira?"

"Five years. I was formerly involved with an archduke who lives here. We lived together and traveled extensively, but we broke up six months ago. I live in Rome now."

The Archduke? The one whose art was stolen? This is too good to be true.

"What brings you to Venice?" inquires Moira.

"I'm an art authenticator and appraiser." I reply, getting ready to drop a bomb. "I was hired to examine Bellini's, *Madonna of the Columbine*. It's—- "

Moira interrupts, "My former boy friend owns it."

"Unfortunately, it turns out to have been painted by someone other than Bellini. As you probably know, the Renaissance period is rife with 'schools of,' attributions and forgeries."

Moira looks taken aback. Her face turns rigid. Her sharp tone of voice confirms it. "Absurd," she snaps. "Of course it's a genuine Bellini. What in God's name could possibly make you think otherwise?" Glancing over my shoulder, she makes eye contact with someone.

Before I can respond, she turns quickly toward Cinzia and gives her a hug. "You must excuse me, Cinzia. Phone me when you have a moment." Flashing me a flight attendant's smile, she mutters, "Nice meeting you," and abruptly walks away.

"Likewise," I say, addressing her backside.

Cinzia wears a puzzled look. "What was that about?"

"I don't know," I lie.

"Have you met the Archduke?"

"No, never. The Archduke's solicitor was the one who arranged for me to examine his client's painting."

"All at once, Moira got furious with you when you questioned the painting's authenticity. Personally, I don't think she's gotten over her breakup with him. You have to understand the social strata in Venice to understand her predicament. The title of Archduke takes precedence over Venice's most illustrious titles. After he ended their relationship it would have been a dreadful social comedown for Moira to become involved with lesser Venetian royalty. That's the real reason she left Venice and moved to Rome."

"Where her prospects are better," I remark. "Why do you suppose the Archduke ended their relationship?"

"In a word, *money*. She has a good bit that her former lover left her and she's very comfortable, but it's hardly enough to induce the Archduke to marry her."

"So he's impoverished royalty looking for someone with megabucks."

"He's not exactly desperate, just cash poor. He owns valuable family properties, but I hear that they're all tied up and can't be sold so he's scouting for ready cash."

"I suppose his dumping her explains her fit of pique?"

"I wouldn't worry about it, Peter. I'm sure her behavior has nothing to do with you."

It did, but I was under oath not to divulge anything to Cinzia. What I said to Moira had the desired effect. It raised doubt about the Archduke's painting. I noticed she went straight away to join the Count's group, where hopefully, she would repeat what I said to her.

I wonder about the possibility Moira may have exacted her own revenge by stealing the Archduke's paintings. "Hell hath no fury," and all that. Maybe she tipped off someone else who stole the paintings. I really should have the Commissario check her movements over the past few years. Her passport will tell all. Who knows? She could be involved in the other thefts, especially if she was moving around Europe with the Archduke. He's probably got relatives and properties in most of the countries where the thefts occurred. Then again, she could be completely innocent and is simply outraged that I would dare cast doubt on the authenticity of the Archduke's Bellini.

The familiar mournful strains of "St James Infirmary" drift outside from Antonio's house. "Shall we watch Antonio and his group play?" I suggest to Cinzia.

"*Si*," she replies, leading the way.

As we approach the doorway to the stairs, I notice the people preceding us duck to avoid bumping their heads on the top of the doorsill. I tap Cinzia on the shoulder. She turns around.

"Watch-a you head," I caution, "Lollobrigida!"

She hesitates for a second, smiles, then leans back and kisses me on the cheek. "You're cute, Peter."

Chapter 11

I'M GLAD I trust my instincts. When Cinzia and I leave Antonio's party, I sense we're being followed. I only catch a fleeting glimpse of the man, but he looks like the burly guy smoking a cigarette we first encountered next to Antonio's staircase. Cinzia doesn't notice the Count's speedboat driver and I don't want to alarm her, so I keep it to myself. I guess the Count knows how to drive himself home, assuming he's not too stoned or too ill. One of those big goons of his will probably do the honors.

As we cross the tiny stone bridge that spans the Rio San Vidal to the palazzo, Cinzia tells me she plans to spend the night so she and her mother can attend Sunday mass together. "It's customary," she says, "I've accompanied her all my life, except when I was little and when I was away at school in London."

"Do you realize it's already Sunday?" I show her my watch. "One-thirty a.m."

She laughs, "I really had a nice time, Peter. Thank you." She gives me a friendly hug and turns to open the door.

"Let me do that," I insist.

She smiles at me and steps aside. I open the door and let her in. She turns, takes her keys, and blows me a kiss. "I'll ring you after church, all right?"

"Fine," I reply. Walking across the deserted campo, I see a

figure lurking in the shadows beside the flower stall. Whoever is there has an unobstructed view of me walking to my apartment building. Feeling apprehensive, I quicken my pace to my front door. As I enter, I scan the campo again. It's empty. It occurs to me that my pursuer only wants to know where I live. I decide, when I get upstairs, to test my theory.

Entering the apartment, I purposely omit turning on the lights. Going to the far window in the salon, I cautiously peek out from behind Burano lace curtains. Sure enough, half hidden in the dimly lighted entrance to the Church of San Vidal stands a man. He's smoking a cigarette and staring up at my building.

I walk to the salon's entrance and flip on the light switch. The wall sconces and Murano chandelier illuminate, sending Franco scampering into the corner of his web. "Sorry, Franco. I didn't mean to wake you."

I must be losing it, talking to a spider at two o'clock in the morning.

After getting ready for bed, I return to the salon and turn out the lights. Easing over to the window, I look out. I try to find my pursuer, but he's not in the church doorway or anywhere else in the deserted campo. He's left. It's as I thought.

Walking back into the vestibule, I telephone the Commissario's answering machine and leave a brief message, telling him about what I said to Moira Dunn, her reaction, about being followed home by one of Count Benzoni's men and my invitation from the Count to view his art collection.

Climbing into bed, I reflect on my conversation with "Count Dracula." He had crept up behind me while I admired a large oil painting of the Zattere that Antonio had painted for his guest bedroom.

"He certainly captures the colors and the mood of the city, doesn't he?" said a suavely accented male voice.

"Yes," I replied, momentarily startled. Turning around, I found myself face to face with "Count Dracula."

"We haven't been introduced," he said, extending a slender, effeminate hand, "Ugo Benzoni."

"Peter Grant," I replied, grasping his limp, clammy hand.

"Nice meeting you." It was a lie. *It wasn't nice at all.* I felt as though I had just shaken the hand of a cadaver.

"You're a friend of Cinzia's?"

"Yes."

"What bring you to *La Serenissima*?"

"Business. I authenticate and appraise art, mostly Renaissance paintings."

"Moira Dunn told me she knew you from New York. I expect you enjoy your work, traveling to fascinating cities like Venice."

"I do." Aha, so, Moira *had* aroused his curiosity. Wondering where he intended to take this inane conversation, I soon found out.

"Since you're here, you might enjoy seeing my art collection. No doubt, it's quite modest by your standards, however I do have several unusually good paintings. If you don't already have plans, say, tomorrow evening, about six. My card," he offered.

"Thank you," I took it from him. "Actually, I'm free tomorrow evening and I'd enjoy seeing your art, Count, ahh . . Benzoni." Damn! I almost slipped up and called him, "Dracula."

Sensing my near *faux pas* he stared at me with the concentration of a fencer. Then he smiled. "I see Cinzia has advised you of my title." *Parry*!

"Yes, she told me you're Venice's most notable aristocrat." *Thrust*! Hah, let him dwell on the meaning of that.

He smiled, condescendingly. "If you wish, feel free to bring Cinzia." He already knew she'd never set foot in his palazzo.

"Thank you. I'll extend your kind invitation."

"Until tomorrow evening then, Mr. Grant." He said, inclining his head in a perfunctory bow.

As he turned away I noticed his pronounced patrician nose. Head on he was much better looking, with full sensual lips and a narrow face framed by long curly black hair. I could see why women might be attracted to him. In spite of his fey demeanor, he had a certain arrogance that radiated an aura of high intensity energy. He'd make the perfect stand in for Mick Jagger. Cinzia's right, he's charming. Sharp, too. He jumped on my addressing him, "Count," like a terrier on a rat. I'd better watch what I say. He may be a drug addict, but he's certainly no fool.

Yawning I promptly fall into a deep sleep.

At eleven o'clock the Commissario calls. Having finished my second cup of *caffe latte*, I'm ready for him.

"*Buon giorno* Commissario."

"May we come over?" he asks.

"We?"

"The Dottore and I."

"Yes, of course."

"Is anyone watching your apartment?"

"Not that I'm aware of." Earlier, I had thoroughly scanned the campo. Anyone hanging about in the steady downpour would have been pretty conspicuous.

"Good, we'll be right over."

Twenty minutes later, I spot Umberto Ferculi and the Commissario. Huddling under large black umbrellas, they zigzag across the campo, two dark shapes maneuvering to avoid puddles. I notice that Umberto carries a large flat package wrapped in plastic. Aha, that must be the lure.

Shortly after they enter the apartment Umberto unwraps Sandro Botticelli's, *Judgement of Paris*. With a devilish grin on his face he holds it up for my inspection. "Magnificent, isn't it?"

"Superb. One of the best forgeries I've ever laid eyes on."

"So . . ." taunts Umberto.

"Terenzio da Urbino, without a doubt," I reply, mentioning the name of the foremost art forger of the seventeenth century. I had once unmasked one of his fakes, a Raphael that a museum client of mine had been offered for a small fortune. Naturally, they declined.

Leaning the painting against the wall, Umberto walks over and embraces me. "My boy, you make your old teacher proud." He thumps me on the back for good measure.

"Where did you get it?" I ask.

"It was part of a bequest to the Vatican from a Genoese merchant. It's one of the better forgeries we've been given. I thought it might prove useful in attracting our mysterious art thieves."

Looking on, with an amused expression on his face, the Commissario thrusts a hand in his trouser pocket. Idly, he jingles his pocket change.

From the kitchen I bring out three wine glasses and a bottle of Loredon red wine which I open and set it on the coffee table. "Something to lift the spirits on a nasty day?" I say, filling the glasses.

"*Perfetto*," the Commissario exclaims.

As we sit, sipping our wine, Umberto unveils his plan to smoke out the thieves. "Botticelli's original hangs in the Palazzo Cini which is presently closed for renovations. Last night, I removed the original and placed it in a storage vault in the Accademia Galleries. The directors of the Cini are allowing us to plant a story in tomorrow's *Il Gazzettino* that their Botticelli was stolen over the weekend. The Commissario asked Mario Cavallino, *Gazzettino's* crime reporter, to write the article. Before coming to see you the Commissario and I approved its content. Basically, Cavallino will report that a witness, fictitious of course, walking near St George's Church saw a lone male emerge from the Palazzo Cini carrying a large flat package. The witness describes the suspect's physical appearance, which happens to match yours, and quotes him as saying that, "judging from his clothing, he appeared to be an American.""

"Why didn't you just have *Il Gazzettino* print my passport photo," I remark.

The Commissario laughs, "We don't want you arrested!"

"Not just yet, anyway," laughs Umberto. He takes a sip of wine from his glass. Appearing to savor it, he comments, "Very nice, Peter. The Commissario tells me you were followed home last night. What do you suppose this person wanted?"

"Apparently, he wanted to know where I live."

"I think he's planning to break in here and check out Peter," says the Commissario.

"After my comment to Moira Dunn, about the Archduke's Bellini being a fake, I can't say I'm surprised. I'm sure she passed it on to the Count and his curiosity was aroused. Why else would he invite me to his palazzo?"

"Good point." Umberto looks at the Commissario. "You indicated that this Count has enormous wealth, do you think he's playing some kind of sick game, stealing art?"

"Considering his money, Dottore, I wouldn't think he'd be that reckless, but who knows what affect cocaine has had on him. If he's bold enough to flaunt our laws by providing drugs and prostitutes to his powerful friends, then I put nothing past him.

"Why can't you arrest him?" I ask.

"His vast wealth has made him virtually untouchable. He's bought and obligated too many important people. As long as he restricts his activities to the privacy of his palazzo I haven't a prayer of trying to get the Questore's approval to arrest him."

"I had no idea." I exclaim, noticing the Commissario's face flush with anger.

"If I find the Count or any of his associates had anything to do with Brother Alvise's murder, he's fair game." He says it in such a menacing way that I'm glad I'm not the Count. It's a side of the Commissario I haven't seen before.

"Take it easy, Commissario," says Umberto. "Anger isn't good for your blood pressure."

"Though red wine is," I counter. The Commissario cracks a smile. "As I mentioned on your recorder, I'm expected at the Count's palazzo this evening at six to view his art collection." "*Va bene*, but I suggest you exercise caution. In spite of his sickly look, the Count is clever. He's not to be trusted."

Another warning! Before long, I'm going to be paranoid. I watch Umberto pour himself a refill. "Wine anyone?" he asks.

The Commissario and I refuse.

"I take it then that the Count's invitation is really a ruse to get Peter away from here while one of his men has a look around?" Umberto looks expectantly at the Commissario.

"Let's hope so," replies the Commissario. He drains his glass and sets it down. "If the intruder finds the Botticelli he'll report it to the Count. When the Count sees Monday's *Gazzettino*, Peter, he's going to know that you stole the painting from Palazzo Cini. At that point he's faced with a choice, turn you over to the Questura or try to involve you with him in some way. Either way we'll see what he does."

"I'm ready," I respond.

"Good. I'll station two of my men in the campo this evening to see who enters or leaves your building. The Commissario glances at his wristwatch "Now, If you'll excuse me, I must get back to the Questura. *Buon giorno*, Dottore." The Commissario shakes Umberto's hand.

"Peter and I will continue our discussion, Luca, *Buon giorno*."

Handing the Commissario his umbrella, I let him out of the apartment.

"Is there more, Dottore?" I ask, sitting next to him on the sofa.

Umberto leans forward and gives me a fatherly pat on the knee. "There's something else we need to do. Peter." He hesitates, savoring the suspense filled look on my face. "We want you to steal the Pala d'Oro from St. Marks Basilica."

I gasp. "My God! You can't be serious? That's impossible."

Umberto looks at me, amusement washes over his face.

"That gold and jeweled altar panel is immense and heavily guarded. No one could possibly remove it from the Basilica? It must weigh nearly a ton."

"A thousand kilos," corrects Umberto. You're not really going to steal the Pala d'Oro. We just want whomever searches your flat *to think you're planning to steal it.*"

"How are they going to know that?"

"From the plans which you're going to leave for them. It's all right here in these notes," says Umberto, reaching into his jacket pocket and withdrawing two sheets of paper, which he hands me. "I want you to copy these in your own hand while I'm here. Then before you leave for the Count's palazzo this evening I want you to leave them where they can easily be found."

"Okay." Getting a pad of paper and a ballpoint pen, I copy Umberto's drawing and his notes. Handing Umberto back his papers, I tape my copies to the canvas backing of the Botticelli and stand the painting inside the foyer closet behind my raincoat. "How's that?"

"Excellent," comments Umberto. "Let's see if our fish rise to the bait." Pocketing his papers, Umberto reaches for his umbrella.

"You're leaving, Dottore?"

"I must. My train to Rome leaves in an hour and tomorrow's a workday. Be careful, my boy and good luck," he shakes my hand, and departs.

Left with my fourth warning, I glance at the time, ten minutes past two o'clock. Picking up the phone, I call the Princess.

"It's Peter, Irena." Listen, I need some information. Tell me what you know about Count Ugo Benzoni."

"An abomination! Trash!" she shouts angrily. "You must not have anything to do with that trouser snake."

"Sorry, Irena, I've obligated myself to visit him this evening at his palazzo. He invited me to see his art collection."

She calms down a bit. "Well, I suppose that's all right, though I've heard his collection is scandalous. If he's having an orgy," which she pronounces with a hard "g" and makes me snicker, "you must leave."

"Irena," I implore, "tell me what you know about him," "He's a horrid man, a shameless lecher, men, women, children, orgies, sexual circuses for the dissolute. I'm reliably informed that he's slowly dying of AIDS. I can't say I'm either surprised or sorry. Good riddance! When you go there be careful. Don't touch anything. Don't drink anything. He drugs and rapes his victims, I'm told. He's a perverted beast!" she shrieks.

"Gosh, Irena, I didn't mean to get you so upset."

"I'll be all right. I must sound like an old stick in the woods," she says.

Her malapropism amuses me. "Stick in the mud, Irena," I correct her.

"Whatever," she shouts. "I think I'll have some tea and try to calm my nerves. I'll speak with you later, Peter."

"Thanks, Irena. *Ciao* for now." I try to sound cheerful, but all I get in return is a deep sigh before she hangs up.

At two thirty Cinzia calls me.

"How was church," I ask?

"Fine, Piero. I lit a candle and said a prayer for you."

"Thank you. No one's ever done that for me before."

"*Prego*. I don't want any harm to befall you when you visit Count Benzoni."

"You wouldn't reconsider going with me would you?" I ask.

"No. Thank you for asking me, but I couldn't risk my reputation being seen at his palazzo."

"I understand."

"Now that the rain has stopped, I'd happily consider taking a stroll with you. Perhaps we could stop off somewhere for tea."

"Great idea, I'm anxious to see if you look as pretty in daylight as you do at night."

"*Grazie*, Casanova," she replies, sarcastically.

"Don't mention it," I tease.

"I won't, believe me," she remarks. "Pick me up at my mother's in twenty minutes."

"Okay."

Cinzia and I walk the Fondamenta Riva degli Schiavoni along the edge of the lagoon. We have such a good time, lost in our conversation, that we walk all the way to the end of Santa Elena, where we're able to look across the lagoon to the Lido. Turning back, we stop at the Hotel Danielle for tea.

I never really got to talk with Cinzia at Antonio's party. There was so much superficial bantering going on it reminded me of a typical New York cocktail party. They're the same the world over, I suppose.

I find I enjoy Cinzia. The Princess is right. She's not just another pretty face. She's beautiful, charming, well spoken, intelligent, and humorous. I feel happy being with her and I sense the feeling is mutual. She appears comfortable with me too.

"I'm having the best time," she says.

"So am I." Huddled together on a small settee in the Danielle's comfortably ornate lounge, we drink Earl Grey and munch on tiny sandwiches and delicate pastries.

"Tell me how you decided to become an art detective?"

I laugh, "Who told you that? The Princess, I wager."

"Yes, she made you sound like the Sherlock Holmes of the art world."

"That's flattering, but not entirely accurate. I'm really an art consultant. Most of what I do involves authentication through research and physical examination. Occasionally I'm asked to render an opinion about value."

"It's such an unusual business. How did you get interested in art?"

"Through my grandparents. They raised me after my parents died in a plane crash when I was a child."

"I'm sorry." She reaches out and takes my hand.

"Thanks. I was only three at the time. Anyway, my grandparents had a very large estate. It was full of art, mostly oil paintings. English portraits by Romney, Reynolds, and Gainsborough, French landscapes by Corot and Rousseau, and American Hudson River landscapes by Cropsy, Cole, and Church and Kensett, Bierstadt, and Moran just to mention a few. Their pictures fascinated me. I guess I fell in love with paintings and spent most of my spare time reading about artists and going to see their works in galleries and museums."

"Isn't that unusual? I thought all American children were only interested in sports."

Her generalization makes me laugh. "You're probably right," I reply, recalling that most of my school friends were sports nuts. "I played sports too, in prep school." I tell Cinzia how I had been raised in the English tradition, sent off to boarding school at age nine and as I got older had the freedom and encouragement to pursue a broad range of interests, which in my case turned out to be art.

"Where did you go to college?"

"Princeton."

"And afterward?"

"To please my Grandfather I went to work in the family firm, a brokerage house, but after a few years, I realized I was unhappy with the pressure of Wall Street. I left the firm and went to graduate school at Columbia University where I earned a doctorate in art history. It was during my internship at the Metropolitan Museum of Art that I found my real talent lay in 'authenticating' art, culling genuine works from bogus ones. Coupled with an ability to do archival research and physical and chemical analysis, I decided to set up my own consulting business."

"When did you and Claire get married?"

"While I was working at the Metropolitan."

"She's certainly beautiful. I don't know her all that well, but I like her. She's got the most unusual voice, slightly hoarse and very sexy."

"Lauren Bacall?" I reply.

She stares at me for a moment, thinking. "You're quite right," she says, laughing.

"Do you miss her?" she asks.

"Yes. I feel badly things didn't work out between us."

"But you've managed to stay friends and that's good," she says, giving my hand a squeeze.

"How about a glass of champagne? I don't know about you, but I've had enough tea."

"Splendid idea. I do hope you don't mind all these rather forward questions."

"Not at all, I appreciate your interest. Now, it's my turn."

"I suppose that's only fair."

"Everything, I want to know everything," I say, withdrawing my hand from hers and waving it in the air, trying to get a waiter's eye so I can order a bottle of champagne. "Come on, get started."

"Oh, dear. Can't I wait until I fortify myself with champers?"

Cinzia told me about her strict upbringing, her parent's separation, and her feelings of betrayal because her father had engaged in affairs, and had finally left her mother and moved out of their home. I got the impression that Cinzia's mother had become dependant on her and that she had schemed to estrange Cinzia from her father. She told me about her schooling in England and how she had felt freedom for the first time. She alluded to a number of relationships with men, nothing terribly serious, she had said, mostly casual. I got the impression she didn't trust the opposite sex and why not, betrayed by a philandering father and brainwashed by a self-pitying mother."

"No serious romances?" I ask.

"Once. There was this English chap I fancied. He was an insurance executive with Lloyd's. He led me a merry chase before I discovered the bastard had neglected to tell he was already married."

Oh no, I thought, it can't be. Dare I ask?

"Cinzia." I took her hand. "Was this fellow by any chance named Colin Marshall?"

She didn't have to answer. Her mouth fell agape and her face went ashen. "You know him?"

"Yes, I occasionally work for him. I can't say we're friends, because I've never really liked him. It's all rather personal as well."

The color came back in her face, but it was now the rosy tinge of embarrassment. "Claire?"

"Yes. He's been boringly persistent."

"Tell him to bugger off," she said, angrily. "God, I can't bear talking about that cad." She gulped her champagne.

"I'm sorry. I've upset you. I shouldn't have brought up his name."

"Not your fault. I wish I'd never laid eyes on that one. Made a damned fool out of me. He's the reason I came back to Venice. I felt humiliated. I couldn't bear being anywhere near him. May I have a bit more bubbly, please?"

"Certainly," I said, filling her glass. Looking like she might cry any second, she leaned her head against my shoulder. "Hold me."

I reach my arm around her shoulders and pull her close to me. Her hair smells lovely. Silently we hold each other like two wounded soldiers. Stiff upper lip and all that. Bearing up is a bit easier, when one's imbibing Tattinger, Blanc de Blanc.

"Thank you, Peter." Cinzia sits up and puts down her empty glass. Turning toward me, she gives me a tender kiss on the cheek. "You're terribly nice, Piero. Will you walk me back to my apartment now?"

Near her flat, a sudden impulse seizes Cinzia and she pushes me into a narrow alley abutting her building. Before I can react her arms are around my neck and she kisses me fiercely. She knows she's taken me totally by surprise. "It's only the champers," she laughs. Then she kisses me again, only this time, softly. I don't want her to stop, but she pulls back and reaches down the front of her blouse. I suck in my breath, not sure what she's doing. A heavy gold medallion, dangling from the end of a braided gold chain emerges. Reaching in back of her neck, under her mane of thick black hair, she unfastens the clasp, and takes it off.

"What are you . . . ?"

"Shhhh," she says, kissing me again. She puts the chain around my neck, secures it, and tucks the medal inside my shirt collar. Her lovely brown eyes fix on me and she whispers, "I don't want anything to happen to you, Piero. San Georgio will look after you."

I'm so touched all I can manage to say is, "Thank you."

Brushing her lips lightly against mine, she whispers, "Be careful, please." She breaks away and ducks around the corner. I follow her out of the alley and watch her walk briskly away. At the entrance to her apartment she turns and waves. She looks sad, like she might cry, but she manages a brave little smile.

"*Ciao*," I shout to her.

Turning toward Santa Stefano, I walk away with my emotions in a state of conflict, Cinzia and Claire. Adriana doesn't count, not really, she's just a fling. I can't dwell on this. I have an appointment with the Count. I need my wits about me. I could be dealing with a ruthless murderer. Let's see, I'm up to five warnings. I've got a crucifix and a Saint George's medal. That should be enough to ward off devils and dragons.

Chapter 12

CHURCH BELLS ring out all over Venice. It's six o'clock as I reach the Riva del Carbon, the *fondamenta* that parallels the Grand Canal from the Rialto Bridge toward the Palazzo Benzoni. I find the Count's home with little difficulty. The building's plain brick facade and it's columnar porticos with Byzantine capitals and dosserets that support stilted arches, identify it as late fourteenth century Venetian/Byzantine, precisely the way the Count had described his palazzo.

Entering the portico, I step up to the palazzo's immense wooden door fitted with iron hinge plates and studs. Mounted on the door is a large bronze lion's head with a ring in its mouth. I'm about to lift the knocker when I notice a strangely modern doorbell that's affixed to the doorway's archaic frame. I ring it. Soon, a servant responds. The massive door opens with an eerie creaking sound and I'm admitted into a large marbled floored and stucco walled foyer. The servant instructs me in his thick Venetian accent, "*sempre diretto*." He means for me to go straight ahead up a wide marble staircase that doubles back on itself to reach the second story *piano nobile*. I'm amused by his expression, for every tourist who has ever become lost in Venice's hopeless maze of streets receives the same ludicrous instruction when asking for directions, "straight ahead."

Count Benzoni, dressed in white linen slacks, a double

breasted navy blazer, a red silk shirt, and a colorful ascot waits for me at the top of the staircase. Peering down his patrician nose, he extends his hand in greeting. I'm momentarily shocked. His fingernails are painted a bizarre dark brownish-purple. He catches me staring at them. "Prune Danish," he exclaims, referring to their color. "Welcome to Palazzo Benzoni."

Forced to shake his extended hand, I try to mask my revulsion. It feels like a dead mullet.

"I trust you had no difficulty finding the palazzo?"

"No, no difficulty at all," I respond, quickly withdrawing my hand.

"Excellent. Come right this way"

I follow the Count into the grand salon, which has a superb view overlooking the Grand Canal. A spectacular multicolored Murano chandelier hangs from the eighteen foot ceiling, which is ornately decorated with ceiling murals. Desperately in need of restoration, they appear to be school of Tintoretto, rather than the master himself. They are spectacular in spite of their condition. Noticing my concern, the Count apologizes, "I'm afraid they're not in the best of condition. I'm planning to have them restored. Work on these old palazzi is unending."

"Nevertheless they're quite beautiful," I reply, sweeping the room with my eyes. The furniture is primarily Venetian, lacquered commodes and consoles, a tall Chinoiserie desk, and gilt armchairs. There is a sprinkling of French accents, sofas, settees, and chairs. All the pieces are fine antiques, undoubtedly inherited and very valuable especially a magnificent Gobelin tapestry, two immense gilded mirrors, and two large ancestor portraits that adorn the walls.

"The first Benzoni," the Count volunteers, seeing me fix my gaze on one of the portraits. "He missed becoming Doge by one vote." It was fortuitous. His victorious opponent was poisoned several months later by an aggrieved Ottoman Turk."

"Lucky fellow, your forebear."

"Yes, he was a survivor, died at age eighty six, an exceptionally long life in those days. I'm having a prosecco. Would you care for one before we have our tour?"

Remembering the Princess' warning I glance at the bottle

reposing in its silver wine cooler. It's unopened. "Yes, thank you," I reply. I watch closely as the Count opens the bottle. He pours the bubbly liquid into two elegant crystal flutes. Handing me one, he raises his glass, "To fine art and abiding friendship."

"To your health," I add, tipping my glass. It's, of course, a pointed remark. He accepts it graciously. I note the absence of his bodyguards. Where can they be, I wonder? Probably ransacking my flat?

"Shall we?" He extends his hand and with a foppish wave motions for me to follow him. Reentering the marbled hallway by the stairs, I see through glass French doors that the palazzo surrounds an inner courtyard, embracing it with two wings and enclosing it at the rear with what appears to be a separate building that abuts each wing.

Seeing my interest, the Count opens one of the French doors and we step outside onto a long narrow balcony with an ornamented balustrade. The smell of wisteria perfumes the air. Octopus-like it reaches up from the columns and roof of the cloister below and entwines the balustrade, its tentacles laden with a profusion of purple blooms.

Looking down I see a formal garden laid out in a geometric pattern that resembles a Celtic cross. Grassy areas, containing colorful rose beds, are separated and bisected by bricks paths, dark and green with age and dampness and they are lined with boxwood. The outer path is round. The other paths bisect it and converge on a sculpted Carrera marble fountain in the garden's center. The rippling pool of the fountain surrounds a huge statue of a winged lion, the symbol of Venice. Its bronze coat is weathered to a bluish-green patina and torrents of water spew from its snarling mouth.

As I admire the garden, a faint, but rank animal odor reaches my nostrils. Bounding out of the shadows of the cloister and startling me, are two enormous black mastiffs. They look up at us, bear their wicked-looking fangs, and growl menacingly.

The spell is broken. "Guard dogs?" I ask, backing away from the balustrade.

"To discourage intruders," replies the Count in a smug tone that makes my insides crawl.

"The building at the rear," I inquire, "it looks as though it may have once been a church?" It has bricked up stilted arches that suggest a house of worship's tall windows.

"Very discerning of you. It was formerly the palazzo's chapel. Sadly, my ancestors neglected the structure. Six years ago I saved it from collapse by having it shored up with steel and eliminating its doors and windows. It's rented out for storage. Come along, won't you?"

We bear off toward the left wing and enter a long corridor that extends its entire length. Stopping a few paces down the hall, the Count removes a key from his jacket pocket and unlocks an ornately carved wooden door. Reaching in, he flicks several light switches. Instantly, the room is illuminated by the glow from portrait lights affixed above two parallel rows of gilt-framed paintings. They hang against Chinese red lacquered walls and the effect is dramatic, all the more so, when I realize the subject matter is erotic art. So this was what the Princess referred to as, "scandalous." Stepping across the room, I examine the first three oil paintings. Two are by Fragonard, a third by Boucher. Each shows a woman lifting her garments to reveal herself to a man who lustfully gazes at her private parts. Four extremely graphic sex scenes follow the French paintings. All of them are by the English artist, John Rowlandson.

"What do you make of my beauties?" asks the Count referring to his pictures.

"They're exquisite," I reply. "How long have you been collecting erotic art."

"Forty years. My father started the collection. Let me show you the Degas I recently acquired." He motions for me to follow him to the center of the gallery where a large canvas portrays five prostitutes engaging in a sexual romp with a lone man.

"A bit outnumbered," I comment.

"Deliciously so, wouldn't you say?" He smiles at me in the most suggestive manner. "Most people think Degas painted only ballet dancers and race horses," he quips.

"Just like people only identify Millet with peasants working in their fields."

"Exactly. Now, If you'll just turn around."

I turn to see a charcoal of a woman. Her face contorts in ecstasy as she kneels, face down on a bed. Her lover has entered her from behind and from his facial expression, he appears to be in the throes of orgasm. "Unusually graphic," I comment. I don't want to insult the Count, but I can't ignore reality either. The picture is not by Millet. I try to be diplomatic. "You're certain this sketch is by Millet?" I ask."

"What tells you it's not?"

"The texture of the lines and the shadowing are wrong. Millet drew coarse lines with heavy shadows in keeping with the crude and earthy lives of the subjects he portrayed. This drawing is much too sophisticated to have been done by him. I hope you didn't purchase it as a genuine Millet?"

"Fortunately, I did not. I purchased it directly from the copier who is, as I'm sure you know, quite famous in his own right."

"Eric Hebborn," I laugh. I notice the Count refers to the well-known forger as *a copier*. The Count has obviously decided to use this forgery to test my skill. He's a tricky one all right. No wonder I've been given five warnings.

"Precisely, Mr. Grant. I compliment your eye. Now, you must see my Oriental pictures and my Netsuke collection. Walking to the far end of the room I pass five of Achille Deveria's paintings that are so pornographic that nothing whatsoever is left to the imagination. In one, a woman is copulating with a horse. Bizarre! Perhaps she's meant to be Catherine the Great who had many lovers and was rumored to have such an insatiable sexual appetite that she engaged in intercourse with animals to achieve sexual gratification. As I reach the first of the stylishly pornographic Oriental paintings that show a brightly robed couple engaged in coitus in the most fanciful position, I detect the scent of perfume. I turn around to see Moira Dunn embrace the Count. "My dear," he says to her, "our guest has the most impeccable eye."

Moira stares daggers at me. "We've already met," she says, icily. "Ugo, when you're finished you'll find me in the salon with the others." Abruptly, she turns and strides out of the room.

"Pity *Signorina* Dunn does not appreciate your talent. She feels you maligned her former lover. You must tell me your side of the story when we have time."

Well, well, well, he wants my opinion of the Bellini. The plot thickens.

After scanning the remainder of the Count's collection, which consist of over a hundred ivory carvings of couples engaged in a wide variety of tortuous-looking sexual acts, he escorts me back to the grand salon where a dozen people have gathered. The apricot haired temptress, Lili Poirel stands beside Moira Dunn. She has on another of her low cut dresses. This one's a skimpy black number that makes her look like a sausage about to burst from its casing. She vamps a group of well-dressed older men who appear enamoured with her provocative display of flesh. The men's common denominator appears to be the trappings of success, power, and money, not to mention their obvious interest in flesh. I don't recognize any of them.

Noticing me by myself, Lili excuses herself from the others. Wriggling in her tight dress like Bette Middler, she minces over to me. "I recognize you from Antonio Verdi's soirée," she says. "I'm Lili Poirel, Ugo's hostess."

"Peter Grant. It's nice to meet you." I'm polite, but saying she recognizes me is an outrageous understatement. At Antonio's, her eyes had stripped me to the buff.

"Ugo tells me you're an international art expert. Did you enjoy his collection? Her eyes flirt with me. She smiles, thrusts out her chest, and waits for my answer.

"Stimulating, to say the least."

Her eyes dart below my waist, then back to my face. "Ugo asked me to make certain that your visit with us this evening is pleasurable," she says, suggestively.

"You have something in mind?" I ask.

"Only your enjoyment," she taunts. Leaning into me, she whispers, "I'd gladly make myself available, but I must look after the gentlemen until my other guests arrive. After dinner, perhaps?"

"I'm afraid I won't be staying for dinner."

"How disappointing. Perhaps, you'll change your mind. I have some very beautiful young ladies joining us. They look forward to pleasing you, as do I."

"Like the gentleman in the Degas painting?"

She laughs. "I'd certainly encourage it if you'd care to try." Taking me by the arm, she leads me toward the men. "Come meet our other guests."

I recognize the name of a Spanish banker to whom I'm introduced. I know that he's extremely wealthy and that he owns several important El Greco's. I wonder if his inclusion in this impending bacchanal is merely a coincidence or if he's being set up for an art robbery? The banker and I exchange inane banter neither of us encouraged by our surroundings to engage in profundity.

Moira Dunn makes a point of avoiding me. Every time I get near her, she edges away. I hope no one discerns her behavior, otherwise they'll think I haven't bathed, or have halitosis, or something worse. Though, why should I care? She's the one who may have something to hide. If not, why is she here? She doesn't seem like the type to engage in orgies, but then, who knows?

Excusing myself, I leave the banker and walk over to a waiter in a white jacket. He stands with his back to me. He's pouring prosecco into flutes on a silver tray. He looks up at me and smiles. "Mr. Grant, nice to see you again."

"Dom. What a surprise."

"May I fill your glass?"

"Please. Do you work here often?"

"Yeah, It's kind of an interesting job. Pay's good and," . . . he looks around to see if anyone is close by, . . ."an occasional gratuity on the side, if you catch my drift."

"I do. I promise not to tell your wife."

"Geez! How did you know I was married?"

"Your gold wedding band gave you away." I drink down half my prosecco and hold out my glass for a refill.

"You don't miss much, do you Mr. Grant?"

"I try not to."

"Claudio says I can trust you. Something happened here I need to talk to you about." His eyes dart apprehensively about, making certain he can't be overheard. Forcing a smile, he takes my half-empty glass and exchanges it for a full one.

"When do—"

Cutting me off, he says, "Wow! Check out the action."

I turn to see four pretty young women enter the salon. They're dressed in slinky cocktail attire that provocatively reveals their physical attributes. The women, two brunettes, a red head, and a blond are all of medium height, but they appear taller owing to their high heels. As the red head passes, she takes a glass of champagne off Dom's tray and smiles at me. Her dark green dress has a plunging back that reveals two sexy dimples near the base of her spine. I feel my pulse rate quicken. Dom, mouth agape, nearly drops his tray.

At that moment a fifth woman walks into the salon escorted by the Count. She's blond and wears a daring red silk sheath that clings to her body like wet Kleenex. It's Adriana and her "gownless evening strap" sends my pulse racing. Seeing me, she does a double take, then waves.

"You know that doll, Mr. Grant?"

"Uh-huh." I reply, watching Adriana's quizzical expression, which begs the question, what are *you* doing here?

The Count pauses to introduce us. "Adriana, this is Mr. Peter Grant." She leans forward and gives me two air kisses. "*Buona sera, innamorato,*" she whispers in my ear.

Buona sera, Adriana."

"Ahh, you know one another," the Count remarks.

"We've been introduced. Adriana poses for an artist friend of mine."

"Who might that be?" he asks.

"Pomeroy, the English painter," she says.

"I've heard of him, he does portraits, if I'm not mistaken."

"And nudes, I add with a smile. In fact, I just bought a lovely one of Adriana."

"I not know you do that?" squeals Adriana. In her excitement she grabs my arm and spills some of my prosecco. "*Scusi!*" she apologizes.

"*Accidente.* Don't worry about it."

Dom, who is staring at Adriana, puts down his tray, walks over with a cloth napkin, and wipes off my jacket sleeve.

"Excuse us for a moment," says the Count.

"*Permesso*," says Adriana. Reluctant to leave, she shrugs her shoulders and follows the Count. She joins the other women whom Lili is introducing to the male guests.

That's the hottest skirt in Venice," comments Dom. "Some guys have all the luck."

Dom's envious. I grin at him. "With the right kind of information, Dom, I'd be happy to put in a good word for you."

Dom beams like a teenager who's just found a cure for acne. All at once, he turns serious. "I need to tell you something really important, but not here."

Pomeroy's right. I don't want to admit it, but after all he did give me fair warning. His voluptuous young model is playing dangerous games in powerful company. I watch the Spanish Banker hone in on her. Seeing her flirt with him and watching her touch him upsets me. I feel possessive and realize that's absurd. I need to get out of this bordello. Adriana catches me staring at her. Seeing my expression, she makes an excuse and walks away from the Spaniard. Heading toward the hallway, she appears to ignore me, but as she passes me, she whispers, "You want I come-a see you later?"

When Adriana returns from the powder room with a fresh coat of lip-gloss, she looks at me for an answer.

I shake my head side to side.

She looks stunned, stung by rejection. Turning away, she marches off in a huff to rejoin the Spaniard. Just as well, I'm in no mood to see her, especially after what I imagine she'll be doing to the banker.

Suddenly I become aware of the weight of Cinzia's Saint George's medal around my neck. It's as though Saint George is sending me a message, a reminder to stay out of trouble. Cinzia would approve. Taking my empty glass over to Dom, I set it on his tray.

"More prosecco, Mr. Grant?"

"No thanks, Dom. I'm leaving."

"Why not stick around?" he says. "You're going to miss all the action."

"I don't really care. Do me two favors, will you? Give Adriana a message for me. Tell her I must see her tomorrow,

Harry's Dolce, in the bar at five in the afternoon. Also quietly swipe me a glass with the hostesses fingerprints on it. Wrap it in a napkin, and keep it for me."

"You got it."

"Thanks. I'll get the glass from you when I see you."

"How about day after tomorrow, Harry's, around eleven in the morning?"

"Great! See you then, Dom."

Walking over to Count Benzoni, I thank him for his hospitality. He looks uneasy and tries to talk me out of leaving. He signals to Lili and she walks over to join us.

"Mr. Grant's leaving," he tells her.

"You must stay," she insists. "I'm so looking forward to spending some time with you." She undresses me again with her eyes, but all I can think about is having the Commissario run Lili's fingerprints through Interpol's files.

"I'm terribly sorry. I'm afraid I'm already late for a dinner party." It's a lie, of course. I wonder if the Count's discomfort with my leaving has something to do with the whereabouts of his bodyguards?

"We haven't had time to discuss the Bellini," he protests.

"Some other time perhaps," I tell him. "I really must be going."

"But the party's just beginning to get interesting." He sidles alongside me and drapes an arm over my shoulder like we're bosom buddies, which we're not. "Thank you for coming to see my collection," he says, poking his face into mine. I stiffen, noticing his glassy stare and the trace of fine white powder under one nostril. "We must get together, very soon," he grins.

"Certainly," I reply, trying to extricate myself from his grasp. For a second I fear he going to try kissing me.

Lili notices my expression of discomfort. "I'll see Mr. Grant out," she says, pulling the Count away from me.

"Thank you," I tell her. Giving the Count a slight nod, I bid him good night and turn toward Lili.

"I'm so disappointed," says Lili, walking beside me into the hallway. "Are you sure I can't convince you to stay?" she asks in a provocative tone. "I'm sure the others will excuse me for a while."

"It's tempting, but I can't. Some other time perhaps? Smiling hopefully, she takes my hand, places it on her breast, and leans in to kiss me.

I step back. "Sorry, but I'm already terribly late. Thanks for everything. Good night."

Leaving her stranded at the top of the staircase, I sense her icy glare as I descend. Why is everyone trying so hard to get me to stay. It must mean there's something going on at Claire's flat. I need to get back there now. No way I'm getting mixed up with Lili or her girls. Not that I wouldn't have fun, but I don't care to be indebted to the Count. Besides, his advances have convinced me that he's very anxious to introduce me to his, as the Princess aptly said, "trouser snake." I hate snakes. Maybe I need to carry a machete.

Chapter 13

On the way home, I worry. What if I surprise someone in the flat and what will happen to me if I do? I decide to stop in a *taverna* and telephone the flat first. When Claire's husky voice on the answering machine asks me to leave her a message, I say to an imaginary friend, "Enrico, If you arrive before me and I'm not there, wait for me. I'm on the way and I'll be there in ten minutes." The message, which the intruders will be able to hear, will give them time to clear out prior to my arrival.

My phone call turns out to be a smart move for when I arrive the apartment resembles a salad, "tossed," as a New York cop would say. Every room's been searched, all the drawers dumped, books pulled off the shelves, bed ripped apart, even the contents of the refrigerator are strewn across the floor. The Botticelli is in the hall closet, but it's been moved, probably examined, and put back. My plans to steal the Pala d'Oro are lying on the floor of the closet. They're wrinkled, obviously passed around and examined. In the bedroom I find the intruders have stolen Claire's color television set, probably to make the break-in look like a real burglary. I curse the crooks. I was planning to watch that popular Italian quiz show that Pomeroy raved to me about. For each wrong answer, the comely female contestants have to remove articles of clothing until they're down to their panties. *What a bummer!*

Checking to make sure my phone isn't bugged, I call the Commissario at the number he suggested I memorize.

"*Pronto.*"

"Commissario, Peter Grant here. You were right. The flat got burgled. They tore the place apart, looked everything over and then stole Claire's T.V. set."

The Commissario bursts out laughing.

"What's so funny?"

"The television?" he roars.

"Hey, It's not mine, it belongs to Claire. Now, I have to buy her a replacement."

When the Commissario stops laughing he tells me that he had two men stationed in the campo to watch my building. He says he hasn't heard a word from them.

"You won't," I exclaim. "The thieves entered and left through the kitchen window. They came across the roof of the adjoining building and down the fire escape."

Responding with a deep sigh, the Commmissario suggests sending over a crime lab technician to dust for fingerprints.

"Forget it," Commissario. "These guys are pro's." Anyone who goes to the trouble to steal a TV, to make their break-in look like a burglary, isn't going to leave fingerprints."

"Undoubtedly, you're right," he sighs again.

When I tell him about the note taped to Clare's front door, he again roars with laughter. My downstairs neighbor had left a note complaining about loud music. While the burglars tore up the flat they must have turned up the stereo to cover up the noise of their search.

"Peter," he advises, "When you disturb your Venetian neighbor with loud music or dancing, it's customary to send flowers." I hear him trying to suppress his mirth.

"Are you serious?" I'm being blamed for something I had nothing to do with. It's infuriating. "And what if I don't?"

"You're sure to be evicted." He says it in such a matter of fact way that I believe him. I can't allow Claire to be evicted, it's her flat, not mine.

"Sending flowers is an old Venetian tradition, I assure you. There may even be a provision in your wife's lease. There often is."

"Okay, Commissario, You've convinced me. In the morning, I'll send flowers." I inform the Commissario that I've arranged to get Lili Poirel's fingerprints and that I ran into several people I know at the Count's palazzo.

"Who?" he asks.

"Adriana, a model who poses for an artist friend. She's one of the Count's "call girls."

"Call girls?"

"You know, hookers, prostitutes."

"*Cosi*. And whom else?"

"Dominic, one of Harry's bartenders. There's something important he wants to tell me. I've arranged to meet with him. Moira Dunn, the Archduke's former girlfriend, was also there, though, for what reason I can't imagine? She avoided me like the Black Plague. I think you ought to check her out."

"In what way?"

"Her passport. It will tell us where she's traveled over the past four of five years. Don't you find it co-incidental that all the thefts occurred in places the Archduke frequents and during that time she was his lover and accompanied him everywhere?"

"How do you know that?"

"She told me, the first night I met her."

"You're suggesting she may have planned the thefts?"

"I'm saying it's possible. Remember, Commissario, the Archduke's still a suspect."

"Yes, you're right. I'll look into it. We've had our first responses to the reward, but I'm afraid they're all false leads. "Opportunists and nut cases, trying to claim the reward?"

"I'm afraid so."

After hanging up, I remember that I neglected to tell the Commissario about the Count challenging my art skills with his Millet forgery. It doesn't really matter. The Count's a suspect anyway.

I phone Cinzia to let her know I'm safe and to tell her about the break-in at the flat. She's elated to learn that Saint George had saved me from the temptations of the flesh.

"I've been told about the Count's sex parties. I'm glad you

left."

"Do I get a reward?"

"We'll see," she laughs. "Thank you for letting me know you got home safely. Ring me tomorrow, won't you? *Buona notte*, Piero."

Next, I phone the Princess. She's calmed down and she's delighted that I've escaped the Count's clutches. Irena's far more thorough than the Commissario. She expects a detailed report. Naturally, I have to tell her everything. She's ecstatic that I heeded her advice and left the palazzo soon after "the ladies" arrived. "Peter *caro*," she exclaims, "you're such a lovely pup!"

It's a good thing she never heard Claire call me, "DOG three."

The following morning I venture into the campo, looking for an espresso and a newspaper. At my local kiosk, I get the usual "*finito*" when I ask for *The International Herald Tribune*. My only fallback position is *Il Gazzettino* so I buy a copy. The story of the theft of the Botticelli from the Palazzo Cini is on the front page. There's even a picture of the painting. Whoever it was who ransacked Claire's flat and saw the painting knows, without a doubt, that I'm the culprit. Assuming they read my plans, they also know I'm highly ambitious, planning to steal the Pala d'Oro. I would give anything to have seen the look of surprise on their faces.

Cleaning up most of the burglar's mess takes me the better part of the day. I finish about three in the afternoon, shower, and dress to meet Adriana on the Giudecca. I have mixed feelings about seeing her. I'd rather neither Claire nor Cinzia know anything about her, nor Pomeroy, for that matter. I must find out what Adriana can tell me about the Count and what she knows about the goings on in his palazzo, beside drugs and sex.

In spite of the waning sun, It's still uncomfortably hot when I take the vaporetto over to the Giudecca. Harry's Dolce and its outdoor terrace teem with perspiring tourists. Under gaily-striped umbrellas they seek relief from the heat by sipping frosty Bellinis. They don't have a clue alcohol just makes them sweat more!

Entering the air-conditioned bar, I sit at a small table by the door and sip a kir royale while I wait for Adriana to show up. At five forty five she still hasn't arrived. I pay my tab and leave. I figure she's annoyed about my not letting her visit me last night.

Stopping by Pomeroy's studio I ring his bell. I'm hoping Adriana might be inside. Pomeroy's assistant, Iris, an attractive, ash blonde British girl answers the door. "Is he in?" I ask.

"Sorry, he's not. His model failed to show up for her session, he's gone off to look for her."

I picture Pomeroy, his nose twitching, tracking down Adriana like a bloodhound. I can tell from Iris' perplexed expression that she hasn't the foggiest idea why I'm here. "Tell Pomeroy, Peter Grant was in the neighborhood and stopped by to say hello. Tell him I'll be in touch. Cheerio."

Boarding the vaporetto, I cross the Giudecca Canal and head back to my flat. Alongside the Chiesa Gesuati, I hear a plaintiff cry, "Peter!" I turn toward the voice. At the side door to the Rococo church, half hidden in the shadow of the doorway stands Adriana. One glimpse is all I need to know why she hadn't turned up at Harry's Dolce. She's wearing dark glasses, but they can't hide her split lower lip, her swollen, discolored jaw and the dark edge of a shiner protruding from her right eye. As I edge through the doorway, Adriana falls into my arms, sobbing. I hold her and stroke her hair. "There, there, now. Who did this to you?" I ask, pushing the church's heavy wooden door closed.

"Count Benzoni's men," she cries, trembling all over. I lift up her chin, look into her tear stained face, and gently remove her dark glasses. She's a mess. Her right eye's badly swollen. She's barely able to see out of it. Her lower lip has split open again from all the crying. It's bleeding. Taking out my handkerchief I dab at it, trying to stanch the flow of blood, which stains the front of my shirt. She winces every time I touch her lip. Escorting her to the nearest pew, I sit down beside her. She holds my handkerchief against her lip and tries to calm down while I look around the church. Except for the two of us, it's empty, quiet, and cool. Soft light filters through lovely stained glass windows and combined with the flickering offering and altar candles creates a mosaic of light that illuminates a magnificent three paneled altarpiece painted by Tiepolo, portraying three saints whose identity I haven't time to make out.

"*Temo per la mia vita,*" she sniffles.

"You're afraid for you life?"

"*Si.*"

I feel sorry for her. "You're coming home with me," I tell her.

She begins crying again. I put my arm around her and hold her until she stops weeping. Handing her the dark glasses, she puts them on. "Is okay?" she asks. Her lip has stopped bleeding, but she needs reassurance in order to step outside into the street.

"You look fine, Adriana. Just don't smile, okay?"

Entering the salon, Adriana sees the empty bookcase and a pile of books stacked on the floor. She looks at me with surprise. "What happen?" she asks.

"The flat was broken into last night." No doubt, the same men who beat her up, but I refrain from mentioning it. "They stole a TV. Why did the Count's men beat you, Adriana?"

"The Count and Lili, they no like-a that I know you. When-a you leave, they get very angry with me, tell-a me stay away from you. The Count's men, they hit me and throw me out in the street. Poor kid. No wonder she was unable to show up at Pomeroy's. It took a lot of courage for her to come looking for me, hiding out in the Church and knowing I'd have to pass by there on my way home. I'm not going to bother her anymore tonight with a bunch of questions. While I change my shirt, Adriana goes into the bathroom, takes off her soiled cotton sundress, and washes out the blood. She takes my blood stained button-down shirt from the bedroom and slips it on, while I put ice cubes in a dishtowel for her swollen face. I protest when I see her in my bloody shirt, but she refuses to take it off. Holding the makeshift ice pack to her eye, she watches me prepare a simple dinner of angel hair pasta with prosciutto, peas, and parmigiana Reggiano cheese. I serve it with thick crusted bread, *senza grasso*, gorgonzola cheese, grapes, and a bottle of Chianti. Adriana's split lip causes her trouble eating. She picks at her pasta and drinks several glasses of wine.

After dinner, she lies down on my bed. I cover her up, turn off the light and unplug the phone so its sharp ring won't wake her.

Wandering into the salon I pick up a Tom Clancy novel and stretch out on the sofa. I read about a United States Navy sonar expert trying to home in on a state-of-the-art, Soviet nuclear submarine, so silent, he's barely able to detect its presence, which is where I drift off into the arms of Morpheus.

Early the next morning I'm awakened by the sound of the front door being opened. Stumbling into the hallway in my under shorts, I see Cinzia half inside the door.

"Piero! Thank God! I've been frantic. When you didn't call me I got worried. I rang you all night. Why wouldn't you answer?"

"Oh God, I unplugged the phone."

Just as she mouths the word "Why?" Adriana sleepily emerges from the bedroom.

Seeing her, Cinzia's eyes get big. "Oh!" she exclaims. A look of utter revulsion washes over her face. Glaring at me, she turns, runs out the door and dashes down the stairway.

"Wait!" I shout, chasing after her. "It's not what you think. Please, I can explain."

She races silently down the stairs. I try to follow, but she's too quick for me. "Shit," I yell, hearing the front door open, then slam.

My downstairs neighbor's door flies open. A large, stocky woman holding a broom by its handle appears ready to skewer me. My attire brings her up short and she stares openmouthed. I can hardly blame her. All I'm wearing is my under shorts, a St. George's medal, and a stupid grin.

Muttering *"Buon giorno,"* I stalk back upstairs. Along the way, I curse about what Cinzia must be thinking and all the flowers that I'm going to have to send.

Inside the flat, Adriana sits, cross-legged, on the foyer's parquet floor. She's weeping.

This is definitely not *my* day!

Chapter 14

AT ELEVEN O'CLOCK sharp, I walk into Harry's Bar. Dom's behind the bar, organizing for the noon rush. I slide onto a stool in front of him.

"You don't look too good, Mr. Grant. Is anything wrong?"

What's a bartender for? A confessor! I tell him about my apocalypse beginning with the break-in, Adriana getting beaten up, Cinzia finding her in my flat and fleeing into the early dawn. He's sympathetic, of course. Besides mixing drinks, bartenders are supposed to be sympathetic. Compassion comes with the job. Making sure no one's watching him, Dom mixes me his clandestine cure-all. He calls the formidable-looking drink, which contains a splash from a dozen different liquor bottles, a "Hop, Skip, and go Naked."

"This will pick you up," Mr. Grant.

"If it doesn't throw me across the room first," I remark as I take a sip. Oddly enough, it tastes pretty good. Very good indeed! After a few swallows my spirits improve. I feel a hop coming on, though I'm not quite ready to skip yet. To solve my dilemma, Dom writes down an address for me to give to Adriana. "It's an apartment I have where she can hide out for a while." He winks and I interpret it to mean his wife doesn't know about his crash pad.

"Smashing idea!" I exclaim. After gulping down half my drink, I'm on the mend, getting ridiculously close to joyously skipping, for my flat will be returned to it's former status, single occupancy. I'll make peace with the battleaxe downstairs. And I'll talk my way back into Cinzia's good graces.

"I think you like that drink," comments Dom, noticing it's nearly gone. "Another?"

The drink tastes like another, but I refuse, by saying, "Unless you want to see me naked."

"Not particularly," he laughs. By the way, here's the glass you wanted. Dom reaches under the bar and hands me a plastic bag containing a glass wrapped in a cloth napkin, bearing the Count's monogram.

"That's great, thanks, I exclaim, putting it into my jacket pocket. Now, what is it you wanted to tell me, Dom?"

"I overheard something at the palazzo I'm sure I wasn't supposed to hear. Claudio told me you're an art expert."

"Sort of."

"Then, maybe you can figure out what these guys were talking about and I won't have to get involved."

"Figure what out?"

"What I heard night before last, when I bartended at the Count's."

"Yes."

"Before the guests arrived, I was down in the wine cellar getting the prosecco. While I was standing in the dark reaching around for the light switch, the Count's speedboat driver and one of his bodyguards passed the doorway. They were on their way to the speedboat and they didn't know I was there. The Count's driver was angry about something the bodyguard had said. "What do you mean the Bellini's a fake?" he said, swearing at him. At first, I thought he was talking about the drink we make here which is the only reason I remember the name. But then I got to thinking, why would the Count's speedboat driver get bent out of shape about a drink? Then I recalled when I used to work private parties at the Palazzo Aldrovani how the Archduke's girlfriend, that blond American woman, . . ."

"Moira Dunn."

"Right. She used to warn me not to set the bar up too close to the Bellini, which was a huge oil painting of a Madonna and child. I thought it strange that Nico, the guy who drives the Count's speedboat, would be talking about a famous artist. What could a drug runner possibly know about paintings?"

"Drug runner?"

"Yeah. You didn't hear this from me, Mr. Grant, but he's the one who takes the speedboat out in the lagoon and picks up the Count's drugs."

"Dom, you said Nico questioned the Bellini, and he used the word *fake*, is that right?"

"Absolutely. He said, *falso*, which means a fake."

"Dom, I'll look into this quietly. Not a word to anyone, okay?"

"Sure."

Wow! What a break! It appears the Count may be involved in the Archduke's theft and his men are doing his dirty work. I wonder if they're also involved in Brother Alvise's murder? "Dom, as soon as I get back home, I'll tell Adriana you offered her the use of your apartment. How will she get inside?"

"There's a key under the base of an urn that's full of geraniums. It's on the left side of the stoop."

"Okay. Oh, one more thing, Dom. Can you draw me a map of the inside of the palazzo."

He flinches. "Listen, I can't be involved in this. When I'm working there they watch me constantly. If they find out I helped you I'd not only lose a good paying job, but I'd end up feeding the fishes in the lagoon. Talk with Claudio. Alberto, his fishing buddy, is a building contractor and the Count tried stiffing him. For ten years Alberto worked on that palazzo and when it was time for his final payment the Count refused to pay him. Ask Alberto how he finally got his money," he grinned.

"Okay, I will. Thanks for the help. Tell Claudio I'll be in touch with him." Feeling the affects of Dom's concoction, I slide my glass across the bar. "Sorry, Dom, I can't finish this. If I do, I'll likely get arrested for indecent exposure."

Laughing, Dom removes the glass.

"What do I owe you."

"On the house, Mr. G."

Please, not another new name!

On the way to the flat, I pick up a dozen *tramezzini* for lunch and purchase two dozen red roses. Leaving the roses outside my downstairs neighbor's door, I ring her bell and dash upstairs. Upon entering the apartment, I find that Adriana has left. She's tossed my bloody shirt across a chair in the bedroom. Poor kid, I guess she figured she'd caused me enough trouble.

While I'm sating my snack attack with the *tramezzini*, the doorbell rings. It's Pomeroy and I can tell he's really pissed off. "Open the bloody door," he shouts through the intercom. I hesitate, wondering if I should let him in and figure, what the hell, what else can happen to me today? Undoubtedly, he saw me enter the building and knows I'm here. I push the buzzer to admit him.

Opening my front door, I hear him wheezing and cursing as he ascends the last flight of stairs. Red faced and out of breath, he sticks his head through the open door. "Here's your picture, you swine." He thrusts the package at me like a lance. I snatch it away from him.

"Where's my check?" he snorts. "And where the bloody hell's Adriana?"

His priorities are pretty clear. I tell him, "I have your money and I don't know where Adriana is."

"Bad form," he shouts and charges into the bedroom. "Ah ha! he exclaims. She's been here. Her lipstick is all over your ruddy pillow . . . and I smell her perfume." He holds a pillow to his nose.

"Okay so she spent the night here." "Yesterday evening I found her on the Zattere, beaten to a pulp. One of the Count's goons messed her up pretty bad. I felt sorry for her and let her stay here. And for your further information, Pomeroy, I slept on the fucking couch. Want to check that out too?

"No!"

"Okay, then put that pillow down and bugger off before I feed you to Franco."

"Franco?" He looks alarmed. "Who's Franco?"

"My black widow spider."

"Grant, you're a maniac. Give me my check and I'll be off."

"You bet." Picking up my checkbook, I scrawl one out and hand it to him. "There, now get your Limey ass out of here. I've taken enough shit today to fill in the Grand Canal and turn it into an autobahn."

Giving me a fearful glance, he clomps down the stairs.

From the salon I lean out of the open window and watch him scurry across the campo in the direction of his gallery. Directly in his path a flock of pigeons vie over breadcrumbs. Without thinking, he wades into them. As they scatter, a startled bird excretes a large blob that whitewashes Pomeroy's neck and shoulder. "*Buona fortuna!*" I yell in the Venetian tradition.

He stops and looks up. A scowl crosses his crimson face, as my wishes for "good fortune" reverberate throughout the campo. Flipping me the bird, he turns, and stalks off full of wrath and pigeon poop.

Wiping away tears of laughter, I phone Cinzia, hoping to explain Adriana's presence in the flat. I'm sure once she understands the circumstances, everything will be fine, but she doesn't answer the phone. Early in the evening I try phoning again. This time she answers, but upon hearing my voice, she quickly hangs up. Immediately, I phone again, but she won't answer.

Frustrated, I call the Princess and explain what's happened. I ask her to intercede for me with Cinzia.

"*Allora*, I'll be happy to," she says, "but you must appreciate how this must affect her. It's like seeing her father with one of his little crumpets."

"You mean, strumpets?"

"*Caro*, you're confusing me."

"Sorry. Look I know you're a good fence mender."

"I'll do my best, *caro*. Await my call."

A few minutes later the phone rings. "That's quick." I say, jerking up the receiver. "Irena?"

"I say old chap, cheating on your dazzling wife, are you?"

"Sorry, Colin, I was expecting a call."

"So it would seem," he says dryly. "Are you making any progress or just pissing away our funds? We haven't heard from you in days, not so much as a peep."

"Sorry about that. I'm on to something, Colin. It might well solve any number of thefts."

"I should damn well hope so, considering what you're costing us."

I feel like telling the pompous ass to shove it. He spends more on lunch at Mirabelle than I could dream of spending for two weeks in Venice. Colin lives for his perks, but he's a miser when it comes to anyone else.

"I'm using our flat here, Colin so there's no hotel expense." I still couldn't bring myself to admit that I was merely borrowing Claire's flat and she and I were separated. If I did, he'd saddle up and gallop after her faster than a sheriff's posse.

"Bloody good thing," he huffs. "I don't trust those Guinea hotels, gouging us every chance they get, acting like they expect Lloyd's to pay them reparations for losing Eritrea and World War II."

"That's what I like about you Colin, your objectivity."

"Don't be sarcastic, Peter, It doesn't suit you. Regards to lovely Claire and do stay in touch, won't you?"

I didn't bother responding. I knew he'd already rung off.

It's dark by the time I hear from Irena. She's been on the phone with Cinzia . . . "for hours," she says. She tells me that at first Cinzia had acted cool then later she had admitted she might have overreacted. "She needs space, *caro*. Let her have it. She'll examine her feelings and determine how she feels about you. I'm quite sure she's fond of you. She just doesn't want to be hurt. In the meantime, she'd appreciate it if you would return her Saint George's medal. Put it in an envelope and drop it in her mail box, tomorrow."

"Okay." My heart plummets in my chest like the Titanic. It sounds as though Cinzia never wants to see me again.

Interrupting my dire thoughts, the Princess says, "*Caro*, Cinzia was raised in a broken home by an unhappy woman and although she understands your situation, you upset her by permitting that young woman to stay overnight. She'll get over it and if it's any solace, Peter, Venetian women don't like being ignored for long."

Irena's remark tickles me and we both laugh. I feel better and now more hopeful Cinzia and I will see one another very soon.

"Have you spoken to the Commissario today?"

"No, I've been trying to cope with temperamental women and ticked off Brits. So far, the day's been memorable."

"I am sorry. Luca phoned me this afternoon. He was quite upset. The Questore insisted he travel to Rome to interview the Abbot about Brother Alvise's murder. He asked the Questore to send someone else, but he refused. Luca asked me to tell you not to do anything more until he returns from Rome."

"Did he tell you where I might reach him in Rome?"

"No, he didn't."

"Irena, I met an American woman from New York who used to be the Archduke's paramour. Her name is Moira Dunn. Since her breakup with the Archduke, she's been living in Rome."

"I know her, a blond, very pretty, but plastic-looking."

Count on the Princess to pull no punches. I chuckle to myself.

"Moira's an acquaintance of Cinzia's. She brought her by one afternoon for tea to introduce her to me. She wasn't terribly friendly. She seemed, how shall I say, yes, self-absorbed in her role as the Archduke's companion. What is it you need to know about her?"

"I'm trying to fathom her relationship with Count Benzoni. Twice now, I've seen her in his company. When we were introduced, she took exception to something I said, crossed me off her dance card and passed it on to the Count."

"She's crossed me off too *caro*," laughs the Princess, amused by my reference to the Venetian tradition, where men queue up to sign a lady's dance card at the masked carnival balls.

"I need to find out whatever I can about her. I thought some of your Roman friends might be willing to help us out, provide us some information about what crowd she travels with and whomever it is she dates. I'm trying to determine if she has any connections to the Vatican?"

"Vatican connections? She doesn't seem the type, rather

too narcissistic to worship anyone but herself."

Vitriolic, but probably true. I'm glad I'm Irena's friend, because I'd sure hate to have her as an enemy.

"Do you suspect her of some involvement in the Benedictine's murder?"

"I don't know. There's a strong suggestion of opportunity. Whenever there's been a major art theft she's seems to have been there just before the thefts occurred."

"Let me make a few calls and see what I can find out."

Chapter 15

Dressed for Harry's in a blue shirt, yellow Gucci tie, olive slacks and blue blazer, I enter the salon and say good morning to Franco. He replies by waving one of his forelegs at me. It's nice to be on friendly terms.

Going to the window, I look out at the day. The western sky over Maestre is leaden. However, the clouds don't appear to pose much of a threat of rain. I leave the flat without bothering to take my umbrella.

Crossing the campo, I enter the café across from the Church of Santo Stefano. Standing at the bar, I daydream while enjoying two double espressos. Afterwards, I walk over to the news kiosk for a copy of *Il Gazzettino*. I've given up on *The Herald Tribune*. Whenever I ask for the American paper, they tell me it's already gone. Frankly I don't think they ever carry it. They enjoy baiting me, seeing the disappointment on my face. Screw them, I'll never fall for their little prank again. As I'm about to unfold the Venice paper a commotion in the campo distracts me.

A dozen *Polizia*, armed with sub-machine guns jog into the campo from the direction of the Accademia. They take up positions around my apartment building. While several officers attempt to gain entrance through the street door another officer raises a bullhorn to his mouth and calls out my name. I don't understand what else he says, but clearly the police have come for me.

Alarmed, I shove my folded *Gazzettino* under my arm and join the throng of locals and tourists that hurry through the narrow streets toward Saint Marks Square. My heart's pounds. In spite of it, I try to act normally, like any pedestrian going to work.

In Campo Maurizio I pause outside Cinzia's apartment and scrawl her a note on the outside of the envelope containing her Saint George's medal. The note reads:

"Need your help, police looking for me? — Will phone you later. — Piero."

I drop the note in her mailbox. Feeling panic stricken and faint, I duck into the alley where Cinzia and I first kissed. Why are the police after me? Perspiration trickles down my neck. Taking out my handkerchief, I accidentally drop the newspaper. It falls to the cobbles and flops open. Adriana's face stares up at me from the front page. Above it, assaulting my senses in bold black ink, is that word again, *morto!*

Oh, my God! She's dead!

Shocked, I stagger down the length of the alley with my hand over my mouth. My stomach heaves and at the dead-end I double over and throw up. My roiling stomach refuses to cooperate with my mind until it's purged itself. Finally, I straighten up and lean against the side of a building to catch my breath.

No wonder the police are looking for me. They think I killed Adriana. What am I going to do? Mopping perspiration from my face, I try to compose myself. The police must have talked with Pomeroy and he told them Adriana had been with me. By now they're inside my apartment. They'll find Adriana's lipstick on the pillowcases. They'll smell her perfume. They'll find my shirt with her blood on it and that will cinch it. Now, I'm really bait. Damn! I left the glass with Lili's prints on it back at the flat. *"Que Casino,"* what a mess.

At the head of the alley, I recover my newspaper and try to read the article, but I can't make sense of anything. It's all a blur. I try looking for my name, but it's nowhere in the article. Thank God! I need to find someone who can tell me what the article says. The Concierge at the Gritti knows me. He'll translate.

Watching for policemen, I walk out of the alley and rejoin the morning rush. At Campo Santa Maria del Giglio I leave the mainstream and walk toward the Gritti Palace Hotel with a group of people headed for the ferry that crosses the Grand Canal to *Siestre* Dorsoduro.

By the Gritti, I peel away, push through its revolving glass and brass doors, and enter its pink marbled lobby.

"Gregorio, *buon giorno*," I call out as I step up to his enclosed counter.

He peers over the top of his paper. "Mr. Grant, *buon giorno*." He drops the paper and offers his hand. "Back for a stay?" he asks. He appears delighted to see me. Well he should. On past visits I've generously crossed his palm with millions of lire.

"I'm only in town for the day," I lie.

His failure to ask about *"La Signora"* confirms what I have long suspected, that he was one of Claire's co-conspirators when she walked out of my life. At that time, he'd emphatically denied any knowledge of her whereabouts.

"What's this business in *Gazzettino* about a young lady?"

"A murder," I'm afraid, *una modelo*."

"A model." Now I know for certain the police have already interviewed Pomeroy.

"*Si*," Gregorio continues, "workers found her body in the bottom of a construction barge moored in the Rio del Santissimo. The article says she had been severely beaten and her neck had been broken. Dreadful thing! Such a beautiful young woman." He holds up his paper to show me her picture.

"What a shame," I grimace, trying to control my emotions and my rumbling stomach.

"*Allora,* this sort of publicity, on top of the Benedictine's murder, is very bad for tourism. *Gazzettino's* crime reporter seems only to care about indulging in sensationalism and that's bad, you know? It discourages the tourists from coming to Venice and as you know they are our life's blood."

It's easy to understand Gregorio's concern. He's the practical sort, always worrying about where his next tip is coming from. I slip him twenty thousand lire so he won't feel so threatened.

"*Grazie, Signor* Grant."

"*Prego.*" It doesn't take much to get a smile out Gregorio. Already, I sense he feels his future is a bit more secure.

"Gregorio, I'm going to make a few telephone calls. Would you ask your phone operator to run me a tab. When I finish I'll settle the bill with my credit card."

"*Subito, Signor* Grant."

Going to the lavatory, I rinse my mouth and tidy up my appearance. In the mirror, I'm shocked to meet the owner of a strained and ashen face. The poor fellow! Combing my hair, I speculate about whom to telephone first. The Commissario wins out.

Although he's in Rome, I call his private number and leave a message concerning Adriana's death and my predicament with the police. All I can do is hope he'll call in for his messages, understand my plight and come to the rescue.

Calling the Princess is out of the question. She keeps her phone unplugged until two in the afternoon.

I try Cinzia, but there's still no answer. If she's seen the newspaper and recognizes Adriana, she'll assume I'm the murderer. And if that's the case, she's probably too frightened to answer her phone anyway. If I'm lucky, she spent the night with her mother's and hasn't heard the news yet. Maybe I can make it to Harry's, explain my situation to Harry Cipriani, get him to call Cinzia and tell her what's happened to me.

The only other person I feel I can trust is Umberto, but I don't have his phone number. If I can reach the Vatican Museum my call can be routed through to him. I ask the operator to phone the Vatican.

After a few minutes, the operator says, "Mr. Grant, I have your party on the line."

"Dottore, Peter Grant here."

"Peter, he exclaims, so good to hear from you. Any news to report?"

"Yes, Dottore, the police are after *me*."

"What!" he exclaims.

I explain what's happened. He sounds concerned. "What can I do to help?" he asks.

"Can you please try to reach the Commissario for me and tell him what's happened. He's in Rome, at a Benedictine Abbey. He's seeing the Abbott concerning Brother Alvise's death."

"*Subito*, my boy. Where may I call you back?"

"I'm at the Gritti Palace Hotel, in the lobby. Just ask the operator to put you through to me."

While I await his call, I walk into the bar and order a Coke to settle my stomach. I pay for it with thousands of lire, so many lire in fact I'm sure prescription medicine would be cheaper. Ordinarily, I don't drink soft drinks, but the Coke settles my stomach and makes me feel better.

Returning to the lobby, I see four policemen suddenly burst through the hotel entrance. Hoping they haven't spotted me, I whirl around, stride through the bar, and exit through French doors onto a terrace overlooking the Grand Canal. Off to my right a traghetto bobs at the dock. It's boarding passengers. I sprint down the length of the terrace, vault the railing, and jump down onto the dock. Stepping aboard the ancient gondola, now used to ferry people across the Grand Canal to Dorsoduro, I hand the helmsman sixty lire. The traghetto fare is the only real bargain in Venice. Like the other passengers I stand facing our destination. Only cowards or tourists sit. Legs apart, slightly bent at the knees, I roll with the gondolas motion in the chop of Venice's watery aorta's.

Glancing back at the hotel, I see two policemen emerge onto the terrace. They look up and down, make frustrated gestures with their hands, and go back inside. Whew, narrow escape. I glance down at my watch. It's ten-forty a.m. Oops! Looking down is a no-no. I stumble and nearly fall overboard. The man standing beside me grabs my arm in the nick of time. "*Grazie*," I exclaim.

He gives me a condescending look and motions for me to pay attention. Fixing my eyes on the far shore, I arrive safely in Dorsoduro. *Miracolo!*

Walking through narrow *calli*, past the Guggenheim Museum, then over several arched bridges, I come to the domed Rococo church of Santa Maria de La Salute. In its shadow I take another traghetto and recross the Grand Canal. This time I display the confidence of Washington crossing the Delaware and disembark within sight of Harry's.

As I enter the familiar smoked glass doors, my heart thumps like a pile driver.

"*Buon giorno, Signor Grant,* comé sta?"

"A sixteenth to an eighth, Claudio."

"That doesn't sound good at all." he replies, his smile morphing into a grimace.

"I'm in big trouble, Claudio."

He stops organizing the bar. "Let me go get the boss."

"Wait here, I'll be right back," he says. A few moments later he reappears, trying to catch up to the swiftly approaching Harry Cipriani.

Striding up to me, Harry shakes my hand. "Don't worry, Peter, we'll do what we can to help you."

I explain that the police are looking for me, that they mistakenly think I killed a young woman, and that I need to reach Cinzia. I tell him he's got to persuade her to talk to me, because until Commissario Moretti returns from Rome to straighten matters out, I'm desperate for a place to stay. Going to a telephone beside the bar, he calls Cinzia's number. While I'm waiting, I ask Claudio to give me the telephone number of his fishing buddy, Alberto Capuzzo, the contractor, Dom had told me had done work for Count Benzoni. Writing down Alberto's telephone number he hands it to me and says, "I'll phone Alberto and make certain he tells you whatever you need to know?"

"*Mille grazie.*" As I thank Claudio, I see Harry wave. He beckons for me to join him.

"Cinzia wants to speak with you." He hands me the phone.

"Cinzia, I'm really sorry about what happened yesterday morning."

"Thank you, Piero. I spoke with Irena. She explained the situation to me and I believe you. Harry's told me what's happened. I'll be glad to do whatever I can to help you until the

Commissario returns."

"Thanks. You're a life saver."

"*Prego*, it's nothing. Come over to my apartment as soon as you can."

Wow! Also she called me, "Piero." Grinning, I hand the phone back to Harry.

"*Va bene*," he exclaims and returns my smile. "Now, I'm going to call my cousin and ask her to make sure Luca calls me. He's in Rome you say?"

"Yes. Harry, I can't tell you how grateful I am for your help. You too, Claudio." I shake their hands. Walking out the door, I join the tourists that roam the busy shopping area. Hidden among throngs of people, I work my way through them toward Cinzia's apartment.

As I cross the bridge into Campo San Moise sheets of heavy summer rain cascade down. Ducking under a shop awning, I try to wait out the sudden shower, but two approaching policemen, who appear to be scanning faces, change my mind. Bolting around the nearest corner, I run through the narrow streets with my jacket over my head. At Cinzia's apartment building, I ring her bell and she buzzes me in.

Cinzia stands barefoot in the doorway of her third floor flat waiting for me. She looks lovely wearing a white terry-cloth robe. Her hair, just washed is damp and tousled. She breaks into laughter when she sees my condition, drenched to the skin with my hair plastered to my forehead. She pitches me a beige bath towel she's holding. "Here," she says, "you look half-drowned. Take off your shoes and socks, your jacket and trousers. Then, hand them to me. I can't have you dripping all over my silk Oriental."

"Disrobe in the hallway?"

"Sure, there's nobody around this time of day." She discreetly turns around while I peel off my wet clothing.

Down to a soggy shirt, tie and boxer shorts with her towel draped around my neck, I say the magic word, "*Permesso?*"

"Come in," she laughs. "Look at you! Your hair is as wild as Einstein's."

What does she expect from a vigorous toweling?

As she unfastens my tie our eyes meet. I feel a sudden urge

and for an instant we almost kiss, but the church bell across the campo interrupts, loudly clanging out the noon hour.

"What am I doing?" she says. She lets go of my tie and steps backward.

The ring of the phone breaks an awkward silence. "I'll get it," she says. At her desk she picks the receiver off the cradle. It's a modern replica of an old French phone. "It's for you, Piero. It's the Commissario."

Instantly regretting we hadn't kissed, I take the phone from her hand.

"Peter, I got your message. I spoke with Arrigo not five minutes ago. He told me what happened to you and let me know where I could reach you."

"Are you still in Rome?" I ask.

"Yes. I telephoned my superior, the Questore to try to straighten things out. He informs me that I've been removed from the case. He says the pressure from the Vatican and the Government and all the bad publicity surrounding Brother Alvise's murder has made it imperative that he take over. Worst of all he refuses to accept my explanation about your involvement."

"Why?" I ask.

"He claims to have physical evidence from your apartment that links you to the death of Adriana Fiorucci. He says a witness has told them she stayed with you the night before her death. They have evidence of a sexual encounter and a shirt of yours with bloodstains on it. Pending testing, they are assuming it's her blood."

"It is, Commissario. You knew I was supposed to meet her at Harry's Dolce and she didn't show up. On my way back home I found her in the doorway of a church in Dorsodura. She'd been badly beaten up by the Count's men and she bled all over the front of my shirt."

"Peter, The police also found Brother Alvise's canvas sack in your apartment and that convinces them that you're involved in his murder too."

"That's preposterous. I don't know how it got there. I certainly never saw it, or if I did, I guess I thought it belonged to Claire."

"Then there's the Botticelli they found, they say it's the

original that was stolen from the Palazzo Cini."

"It can't be, Commissario. You saw Umberto unwrap the painting. He and I agreed it was a forgery."

"I know, but the Questore insists the one they have is the original from Palazzo Cini."

"That's impossible. It would take an expert to know the difference between that forgery and the original."

"Additionally, they have notes in your handwriting about a plot to steal the Pala d'Oro from Saint Marks?"

"You and Umberto cooked that scheme up. All I did was make a copy from Umberto's notes."

"I don't recall Umberto discussing the Pala d'Oro with me, but anything's possible, there was so much going on that day."

"He brought it up after you left to return to the Questura."

"Ahh, then that's why I'm vague about it. In any event, the Questore wants you to surrender yourself. He needs to question you in the two murders, the theft of the Botticelli, and the conspiracy to steal the Pala d'Oro. I lied to him and told him I didn't know where you were."

"Thanks, Commissario. Whomever planted Brother Alvise's bag in my apartment must have been the ones who found Adriana while I was meeting Dominick at Harry's bar. They must have taken her away, killed her and then dumped her body. Can't you see Commissario, I'm being set up by Count Benzoni?"

"So it would appear. However, it's my duty to advise you to turn yourself in, Peter."

"Commissario, you know I don't have anything to do with any of this. And besides," I shout in frustration, "it was you and Umberto who talked me into this mess!"

Looking worried, Cinzia comes over to me and puts her arms around me. "Shhhhhh," she whispers, "calm down."

"I'm sorry, Commissario, I . . . I'm upset, but I can't turn myself in. If I do I won't be able to prove my innocence. Dominick, the bartender, overheard the Count's speedboat driver, Nico, talk about the Bellini painting. I'm convinced they were in on the theft and I'll bet the Archduke's painting is hidden somewhere in the Count's palazzo."

"Peter, I must talk with this Dominick fellow."

"Commissario, Dominick's afraid of the Count's men. He won't talk to you."

"Without a statement from him I have no basis for arresting the Count's men," he complains. He sounds irritated.

"I understand, but Commissario, it's important I try to find the Bellini. I have a hunch it may be hidden inside the old chapel. I'm going to meet with the Count's former contractor this afternoon. He's the one who did all his restoration work. He's going to show me detailed plans of the palazzo and the chapel and help me get inside. The Count tried to cheat this fellow out of money he owed and he despises him."

"Peter, I think you're compounding your problems. I advise you not to do this foolish thing. It's too dangerous. As soon as I get back this evening I'll try to reason with the Questore, again. If he refuses to budge from his position, I'll be forced to divulge your whereabouts to him. I must warn you, Peter, the Questore is a very ambitious man. He's anxious to solve this case because of the national attention he'll get and right now he's convinced that you're the prime suspect."

"That's all the more reason not to turn myself in to the police."

"You're flaunting the law, Peter. In spite of what I believe, the evidence the Questore has against you is very compelling."

"How much time can you give me, Commissario?"

"Until tomorrow morning."

"That's not much time."

"It's the best I can offer. If you have to reach me don't call the Questura, leave word with my wife." Giving me his home phone number, he wishes me luck and hangs up.

Glumly, I wrap the towel around my waist and sit down on the sofa. I feel like a man on death row, anticipating the walk to the electric chair. "What am I going to do, Cinzia?"

She bends over and kisses me on the lips. "Don't worry, Piero, I'll help you. I'll go to your apartment and get you some dry clothes and whatever else you need? I've got the keys remember?"

"How could I possibly forget," I reply, giving her a wry grin.

"Don't be a smart ass. If it hadn't been for Irena you'd still be out in the rain or worse and frankly I wouldn't have cared a whit." She looks down her lovely Venetian nose in mock disdain.

"I apologize. How will you get into the apartment with the police around?"

"I'm the building's real estate agent, remember? I have every right to be there. If the police are still lurking around, I'll leave. Otherwise, I'll let myself into the apartment and get your things. My guess is they simply placed a warning sign on your door and left."

I take her hand and pull her down beside me. "You really are something, Cinzia." We embrace and kiss for what seems like ages.

"That's enough, Piero," she says, pushing me away. "You're distracting me. What else do you need beside clothing?"

I tell her. "The most important thing I need is a plastic bag with a drinking glass inside it. It's in the drawer of the foyer table. Be careful with it, Lili's fingerprints are on it."

"What are you going to with her fingerprints?" she asks, looking puzzled.

"Run them through Interpol. I want to know if Lili is who she claims she is and if she's got a criminal record."

"My goodness, I never would have thought of doing that."

"That's what makes me a sleuth."

"All right, Inspector Clouseau, who is this Umberto that you spoke to the Commissario about?"

Cinzia's reference to the bumbling Peter Sellers character cracks me up. When I stop laughing, I tell her. "Umberto Ferculi is the head of the Vatican Museum. He's trying to recover the artifact that Brother Alvise had with him when he was murdered."

"You didn't mention any of this to me."

"I know, I was instructed not to. It was to protect you, but everything's changed now."

"Then you better tell me everything if you want my help."

"All right. Over the past five years there have been a series of art thefts, mostly religious paintings, but other religious objects have also been stolen too, like books, chalices, even an altar. The Commissario's convinced that the thefts are related and I agree with him. When Brother Alvise was murdered the thieves stole the Vatican's holiest treasure."

"What?"

"A nail from the Crucifixion of Christ which is embedded in Murano glass."

"*Madonna!*" exclaims Cinzia. "I never knew such a thing existed."

"Except for a handful of people, no one knows about it."

"I see. That's how Umberto fits in?"

"Right."

"How did you become involved?"

"Formerly, Umberto was a professor of Renaissance art in Rome. He was my mentor and I studied under him for two years. When he learned from the Commissario that I was in Venice working on a case for Lloyd's concerning a theft of paintings from the Palazzo Aldrovani, he asked to see me."

"The Archduke!" she exclaims. "Was it something you said to Moira about one of the Archduke's paintings that made her so angry?"

"Yes, I told her a deliberate lie. She believed that Archduke's Bellini was an original work of art. I told her it wasn't in order to plant a seed of doubt in her mind. I hoped she'd be so upset by it that she'd tell people what I had said. And she did."

"So that's why you two crossed swords. At the time, I didn't understand what had happened."

"That's because you didn't know anything about the Archduke's theft. Moira happens to be a prime suspect."

"Surely you jest."

"Afraid not. The Count, his men, and Lili are also suspects You see Umberto and the Commissario devised a plan where I would act as a lure in an elaborate deception designed to expose the thieves. Your role was to provide me access to an audience where I could plant lies about the authenticity of the Archduke's Bellini. If the thieves thought they might have stolen a fake Bellini, they would likely want to know how come

I knew the painting was a fake. When they checked me out they would discover that I had just made off with a Bottacelli from Palazzo Cini and was preparing to steal the Pala d'Oro from Saint Marks. Chances are they would approach me and the Commissario would then arrest them. The problem is that things have gone terribly amiss and the head of the Questura now believes *I'm* the perpetrator.

"And you used *me*." She looks wounded.

"Yes, but I tried not to put you at risk. I think you know my personal feelings are genuine. I really care about you, Cinzia."

"Dash it all, Piero, you're working for that unspeakable Colin Marshall."

"Yes, but it's only a job. I don't like him any more than you do, particularly after what he's done to you. Anyway I detest him. I know what he'd like to do to Claire."

"I'm not sure I needed to hear that last little gem," she pouts."

"Cinzia, I don't have any hidden agenda. What you see is what you get."

"Piero," She looks me straight in the eye, "I want to believe you. Just don't disappoint me."

"I won't."

"Shall we get on with it then?"

"Sure, but first a kiss?"

"I'd like that," she says, tilting her head up to meet my lips.

Cinzia and I seem to be hooked up to the same generator; lots of current flows through us. We feel it when were kissing. When we surface for air, I ask her, "Do you mind if I ask Claudio's contractor friend to come here?"

"I prefer it. It's not safe for you on the streets."

I telephone Alberto Capuzzo. He's been expecting my call. Claudio has already talked with him. Alberto says he's prepared to help in any way he can. I tell him I need to know the layout of the Count's palazzo and that I'm considering trying to get inside the old chapel. He agrees to bring his blueprints to Cinzia's apartment in the late afternoon.

While I take a shower, Cinzia goes to Claire's flat to get my clothing and the other items I had asked for. With a towel wrapped around my waist I go into the salon to call the Princess, but first I check the clock. It's okay; it's after two o'clock.

"Peter, I'm so happy to hear from you. Has something happened?"

"Yes, Irena. The police are looking for me."

"I knew it," she exclaims. "All those bad dreams I've had."

I explain in detail about the police raid on Claire's apartment, Adriana's murder, and my flight to the Gritti, Harry's and finally Cinzia's. I tell her about my conversation with the Commissario and his removal from the case, the planted evidence to make me look like the perpetrator, and the police accusations.

"Peter, what are you going to do?"

"I don't know exactly, but I'm working on it." I don't want to upset her by telling her that I'm planning to break into Count Benzoni's chapel. Changing the subject, I ask, "Have you had a chance to find out anything about Moira Dunn?"

"Yes, I called an old friend of mine in Rome who was the Gritti Palace's manager when my dear friend Barbara Hutton lived there."

I realize the Princess is about to embark on one of her epic tales. She always identifies friends by telling stories about their lives. She told me the story once, but she's obviously forgotten.

One evening in the 1940's Irena had accepted a dinner invitation from the Gritti's manager. They dined together by candlelight on the terrace overlooking the Grand Canal. During their entree they looked up to see diamond bracelets, sapphire rings, emerald necklaces and ruby earrings rain from the sky and plop into the canal. Abandoning their dinner, Irena and the manager rushed upstairs to the hotel's grandest suite where they pounded on the door. Getting no response, the manager opened the door with his passkey. Rushing out onto the balcony, they found a sobbing Barbara Hutton sitting in a chair beside the balustrade. In one hand she clutched a bottle of Dom Perignon, in the other she held jewels that she had removed from a case on her lap. As Irena and the manager ran to her side, she drunkenly tossed another handful of her baubles over the railing as she wailed that her husband, Cary

Grant, had walked out on their marriage. To console herself she had decided to get drunk and purge her life of all valuable possessions.

The following day the manager hired a professional diver to search the Grand Canal for Barbara Hutton's jewelry, but all they recovered were a few odd pieces. To this day a small fortune still lies in imbedded in the waterway's thick mud.

Hearing the story again reminds me of the morning at the Gritti when Claire walked out on me.

"Irena, that's quite the story, but what did he tell you about Moira Dunn?"

"My friend said he met her at several social functions. She was in the company of Cosimo De Checci, the Italian Minister of Protocol and a financial advisor to the Vatican."

"This is fabulous, Irena. This could be the missing link to Brother Alvise's murder. If you get any more information, please call Cinzia and leave it with her and if she's not here would you leave it on her answering machine?"

"I will. Do you have the crucifix I gave you?"

"I do." I remember it's in the side pocket of the jacket that Cinzia's is bringing me from my flat.

"You know how I worry about you."

With what I'm about to undertake, she has good reason. I can tell she senses it.

As I say goodbye to the Princess, Cinzia walks through the door. She hands me a large plastic garbage bag. Inside are my clothes with the crucifix in my jacket pocket, my running shoes, my Canon thirty-five millimeter pocket camera, several rolls of film, infrared and color, and the glass with Lili's fingerprints on it.

"Any problems?" I ask.

"None at all. As I expected, there was only police tape strung across your door, which warned people to keep out."

"Thanks for the clothes. I'm anxious to get rid of this towel."

"Mind if I watch?" she laughs.

"No." I answer, knowing she's joking. As I start to take off the towel, she blushes and flees into her bedroom.

Later when I'm in my shorts and about to pull on my trousers, I hear, "Nice legs!" I turn to see a lovely brown eye

peeking at me from behind her bedroom door.
 You're the one with the great wheels," I remark.
 "Wheels?"
 "American slang for, legs."
 "Oh, but all Venetian woman have good legs."
 "Not as lovely as yours. Don't you remember me checking them out the other night?
 "*Lupo!*" she shouts and a decorator pillow sails toward my head. Just in time, I duck, but a *chinoiserie* table lamp isn't so fortunate. It tumbles off a table and shatters.

Alberto Capuzzo stands six feet tall with a muscular build and black curly hair. He has rugged features and an engaging smile that displays dimples at both corners of his mouth. From Cinzia's body language and cheery voice, I deduce that she's attracted to him . . . about like an ant to a picnic basket. I can almost hear her mind at work as it mentally fills out marriage papers. I have to admit his good looks make me feel insecure and normally I'm not the jealous type. Fortunately, in spite of his heavy Venetian accent, he speaks English well enough for me to understand him. Otherwise, who knows what intimacies might have been exchanged between Cinzia and Alberto had he spoken only Italian.
 In addition to his roll of plans, Alberto carries a large canvas gym bag, which looks heavy and clanks loudly when he puts it down on the floor.
 "Do you always carry your weight lifting equipment with you?" I ask.
 "*Mi scusi*, I don't understand?" He says, quizzical furrows forming on his brow.
 "He means, what's in the bag?" says Cinzia, beaming at Alberto.
 "Some tools." He shrugs his muscular shoulders. "We talk about them later." He gives Cinzia a dazzling grin. For me there's an uncomfortable pause as they smile at each another.
 "How do you know Claudio?" I interrupt, like a boxing referee stepping in to break up a clinch.
 "*Allora*, we grow up together. I am the godfather of Claudio's first daughter. He seems to swell with pride as says

it. "And he's godfather to my son."

"You're married!" I exclaim, with a smirk.

"Oh yes," says Alberto. His expression turns serious. "My wife and I we have six *bambini*. Like a Pirelli tire, his chest seems to inflate with pride.

"How nice," mutters Cinzia, in a disillusioned tone.

"Yes, *Grazie*. See, I bring all the plans," he says holding up a thick roll of papers.

"Suppose we open them out on the dining table," suggests Cinzia.

"*Perfetto*," exclaims Alberto. He unrolls them. Cinzia brings some books from the salon to keep the sheets flattened out.

"I work for the Count for about ten years. Everything go well until I work on the old church. It was in very bad condition, you know? In three or four more years I think it would have collapsed, but who knows?" He holds out his hands, palms up.

Italians, I've noticed, can't talk without using gestures.

"When I finish the work, the Count, he don't want to pay what he owes me. For him, it's nothing, but for me, you know, it's a fortune. I threaten to sue him to get my money, but he just laugh at me."

"But I'm-a nobody's fool. I tell Claudio about my problem because I respect Claudio. He listen to important people at Arrigo's Bar, you know what I mean? He hears things about people like the Count . . . you understand? Claudio tells me the Count is big time drug user. I suspect this anyway from the funny way his eyes look when I work at his place, so I decide to fix him."

"You what?" I ask.

"Fix him! You know, get even." I look at Cinzia. Her eyes are wide with fascination.

"What did you do?" I ask.

"The Count, he had me build a boat slip for his speedboat on the side canal between the church and the north wing of the palazzo." He flips over several sheets. "Right there," he points. "I pay one of my friends, Paolo, who owns a water taxi to keep his eye on the palazzo. Paolo, he follow the Count's speedboat driver to Chioggia where he watches him meet another boat in the middle of the lagoon. Through his field glasses, Paolo sees the Count's driver exchange lots-a money for drugs. Every six weeks they do the same thing, same place, same time. So the next time the Count's boat is-a ready to go out, Paolo and I sneak up to the palazzo at night. We pour sugar into the speedboat's gas tank and when its engine breaks down in the lagoon, the Count's driver waves to Paolo and me to help him. Paolo he goes alongside like he's going to help, but then he points his shotgun at the Count's driver and he takes all the Count's money. We take off and there's-a nothing the Count can do about the money." he grins.

We all crack up laughing.

"I think this calls for a toast," says Cinzia. She gets a cold bottle of Soave and three glasses. I open it and fill the glasses.

"*Cin-cin*," says Cinzia.

"*Salute*," adds Alberto. We touch glasses and toast Alberto's coup.

"How I can help you?" asks Alberto.

"I'm very suspicious about the Count's chapel, Alberto. Tell me what you know about it."

"As I mention, when I first see the church, I tell the Count it's in such a bad condition that it's cheaper to tear it down than fix it. He insists he wants me to restore it. When I ask him what he plans to do with it, he tells me he wants to close up the windows and doors and put in air conditioner so he can take lessons on the pipe organ, you know, so he won't disturb his neighbors."

"There's a pipe organ?" says Cinzia.

"A very old one, *molto bello, signorina*."

"That's strange," I comment. "The Count told me the building was only used for storage. When did you complete the renovations?"

"Five years ago."

"Interesting," I muse. The art thefts started about that time and the building is air-conditioned. "Alberto, I have to get inside that building. I need you to tell me everything about it, especially how I can gain access."

"I expect something like this," he smiles. For an hour we pour over the plans while Alberto details his reconstruction of the church. When he finishes, I feel I know the building like I'd restored it myself.

"Alberto," all the entrances and windows are bricked up except for two doors into the wings of the palazzo. How am I going to get inside? I don't dare trying to enter through the palazzo. The Count has two nasty looking guard dogs."

"I show you. When we build the boat slip," says Alberto, "we were forced to rebuild part of the Church's foundation wall. Behind it we find an old burial chamber, a vaulted room supported by pillars. It's under the church floor. At high tide the room's full of water but at low tide you can wade through it. Along the side and end walls there are marble burial vaults. At the far end, away from the canal, there's a stone staircase. It rises to a large oblong stone slab in the ceiling. You'll recognize it because there's a small round hole through one end. That stone is set into the Church floor right in back of the altar. Right here," says Alberto, pointing to the church's floor plan. "I don't think anybody's lifted it up in over a hundred years. The Count may not know it's there. The way he treat me when I ask to get paid, I don't tell him nothing about the burial vault. The vault's pillars are in bad shape and one day they will collapse and the chapel floor will fall in. When it does, it will serve him right. Then I will have the last laugh."

"What you're suggesting is that I go through the vault in order to get inside the chapel."

"It's the only way to enter unless you go through the palazzo, which you said was guarded by dogs. Look here," says Alberto, pointing at the plans. "When we built the boat slip we constructed an arched doorway in the Chapel's foundation wall. It allows the water to enter and exit with the tides. The archway is only visible at low tide, but it's big enough for you to fit through."

Cinzia gives us both a look of revulsion and shudders. "It sounds disgusting, all that foul smelling water, sewage, rats, and dead people's remains. Piero, how can you even consider doing this?"

"I don't have any choice, Cinzia. Antonio, how am I going to push up that heavy slab of rock in the floor of the chapel?"

"With a hydraulic jack. I brought one with me. It's in the

bag with a jack handle, a waterproof flash light, a wet suit, booties, and gloves."

I'm impressed. Alberto's thought of everything. "When's the next low tide?" I ask.

"Around midnight, tonight," he grins. "Paolo will take you."

I glance at Cinzia. She's holding both hands to her face. She looks appalled.

Truthfully, so am I.

Chapter 16

Prior to leaving for the Palazzo Benzoni, I call the Commissario and leave word with his wife that I'll be at the Count's chapel after midnight. "Please tell him I'll be at the boat entrance." I have no way of knowing if he'll show up, but his presence will be most welcome if he does. I don't relish being there alone.

At eleven o'clock I pick up Alberto's canvas bag, kiss Cinzia goodbye, and leave to keep my appointment with Paolo. He's waiting for me on the Rio del Santissimo at the far side of Cinzia's campo. A short distance away I see a moored construction barge. I wonder if it's the same one where Adriana's body was found. I say a prayer as we go by it. I can still see her pretty face the morning she first gazed into mine when I had such a terrible hangover. The memory of her makes me sad. I wonder now if I'll ever enjoy Pomeroy's sketch of her. Probably not!

A sliver of moon hangs in the night sky as we enter the Grand Canal and cruise toward the Rialto Bridge. It's eerily quiet and dark on the Grand Canal, save a far off vaporetto and the odd gondola. The city has long been asleep and the dimly lit palazzi stand like two rows of ghostly sentinels as we pass in spectral review.

Nervously, I enter the taxi's darkened cabin, remove my clothing, and slip into Alberto's wet suit. As I pull on the rubber booties and gloves, I feel the boat slow. Shouldering the canvas bag, I step into the cockpit and see the dim facade of Palazzo Benzoni as we round its far corner and enter the narrow canal beside it. Paolo spins the wheel and swings the boat toward the Count's boat slip.

"Get ready," he whispers, throttling back. The water taxi coasts past the speedboat slip and edges along the canal wall behind the chapel.

"Two flashes, a pause, and two flashes when you're ready to leave," instructs Paolo.

"Okay," I reply, climbing on the gunwale.

"Now," he orders.

I step off onto a narrow walkway that separates the chapel wall from the canal. Standing in the chapel's shadow, I wait until the water taxi is out of sight. Then, hugging the wall, I edge forward toward the Count's boat slip. Reaching the corner, I peek around it. Accustomed to the dark, my eyes make out a steel shed mounted on a U shaped wooden dock that protects the Count's speedboat. With its bow facing me, the boat rocks gently against its moorings. Except for an occasional slapping sound made by water sloshing against its hull, it's the only sound I hear. I creep around the corner and enter the shed. Suddenly, a resonating cry startles me. I freeze, then realize it's an echo from the maze of nearby canals, the warning cry of a gondolier. "*Stali!*" he calls as he approaches a blind corner.

"Whew," I exhale. It's incredible how sound carries at night. Lining the chapel wall along the boat dock, I see dark shapes. Digging the flashlight out of the canvas bag, I put my gloved hand over the lens, and flick it on. The muted light reveals a wooden bench in front of a large wooden locker. Two propane tanks and four fuel drums line the wall. Kneeling down on the dock beside the speedboat, I scan the canal wall under the dock with the flashlight. Behind a car tire, used as a bumper, I spot the lancet arched entryway into the chapel's vault. It's only a third submerged.

Clinging to the tire, I lower myself into the dark smelly water. My feet find the doorsill and I perch there while I examine the crypt's interior with the flashlight. In its illumination, I see a decaying, slime covered Gothic chamber with brick, stone, and mortar walls supported by four rows of stone pillars that have begun to crumble. The vault's walls contain niches and in each resides a carved marble or rock sarcophagus, all in a state of ruin. Some gape open, their lids missing, others have dark jagged holes in their sides, signs they have been forcibly broken into and looted for valuables. Swinging the flashlight to my left and right, I see yet more containers that line all the walls.

The spooky scene, with its partially flooded and violated burial receptacles reminds me of the time, as a child, that I had been badly frightened. I had been reading *Dracula*, the part where the vampire crawls up the walls of a castle to get at his victim. A violent thunderstorm unexpectedly arose and my imagination got the better of me. As lightning crackled, thunder crashed, and rain noisily pelted against the windows, the lights suddenly flickered and went out. Leaping out of bed, I dashed to an open window to close it. A flash of lightning, emblazoned the house and a mass of ivy growing up its side looked like a creature climbing up to get me. Throwing my book at it, I slammed down the sash, locked it, and fled into the closet where, huddled in terror, I spent the night too afraid to seek my grandparent's protection.

Holding onto the doorframe, I extend my foot and probe for the floor of the vault. Several inches below the sill, under slippery mud, I find it. Stepping carefully inside the chamber, I wade, thigh deep, toward its middle, sliding my feet forward, one after the other, like a person walking on ice. Mud and garbage dislodged by my feet swirl up around my legs. A dead animal bobs up in my path. Its noxious decaying flesh assaults my nostrils. Trying to avoid it, I slip and nearly fall into the filthy morass. Verging on hyperventilation, I consider turning and fleeing this horrid, vile-smelling vault, but I can't. I have to press on. I must know what's in the chapel above me.

To control my gasping and to dispel the foul odor, I hold my nose and breathe through clenched teeth. I think of Cinzia's jasmine scented perfume. The imagined aroma is a welcome panacea.

Rounding the vault's middle row of pillars, I wade the vault's length toward my objective, a stone stairway that I see at the very end. Ahead of me a high pitched screech echoes through the vault. Caught in the beam of the flashlight a huge beady-eyed rat raises up on its hind legs and stares at me. Its size, nearly as large as a cat, sends shivers through me. Aggressively, it shrieks and bares its teeth. Will it attack? Surely, not by itself. I hear the sounds of others summoned by its cries.

From the canvas duffel, I pull out the jack's crank handle. Seeing it, the rat plunges into the water and swims away. I follow its wake with the flashlight. Reaching the far wall, the rat climbs atop the cracked lid of a sepulchre where it mills about with other large rats. Loudly they protest my intrusion, while around the walls I hear more splashing sounds as even more rats flee their filthy lairs among the dead.

Reaching the slime-covered stairway, I direct the light on the ceiling. Over the stairway I see the outline of the large oblong slab that Antonio had described. The hole, penetrating its thickness, is directly above the last step. Carefully ascending the algae covered steps I make certain no sign of my entry shines into the chapel above. Removing one of my gloves, I shove it into the hole and seal off the light.

On the steps I remove the canvas bag from my shoulder, place it on a step, and take out the jack. I set the jack on the top step several inches below the slab, insert the crank handle, and turn until the shaft gently forces the slab up. I listen for sounds from the chapel and hear only the hum of an air-conditioner. I continue to crank until the opening grows large enough to permit me entry. With my camera and flashlight, I wriggle through the opening on my stomach and enter the chapel.

I breathe in cool air that's tinged with something sweet. Incense. It's a welcome relief from the putrid odor of the vault. Standing up, I turn and quickly sweep the chapel's interior with the flashlight. I see that I have emerged behind the altar at the center of the transept. Unprepared for the sight that greets my eyes, I gasp in astonishment when I see the back of a magnificent, intricately carved wooden altar. Atop it stands a Catalan crucifix. It appears to be the same altar that was stolen in Madrid. Walking around to its front I confirm that it is. A beautiful gold chalice stands in the center of the altar, framed by the Catalan crucifix behind it. I snap several pictures before noticing the carved ivory diptych from England off to one side of the altar. I take another picture. High up on the wall behind the altar hangs a very large painting. I shine the flashlight on it. It's the Archduke's magnificent Bellini. I photograph it, then take another, realizing my hands are shaking with excitement.

As I move the flashlight beam across the altar toward the far wall, something flashes. I see a narrow, tooled, red leather box. Its hinged top lies open. Inside, nestled in purple velvet, lies a spike-like object encased in crystal. My heart threatens to leap out of my chest, *the artifact!* I close its lid and quickly shove it up the sleeve of my borrowed wet suit.

In haste I walk the perimeter of the chapel, following Durer's renderings of the Stations of the Cross. Along the way I take more photographs. On the wall opposite the altar stands a large pipe organ. A thick stack of sheet music lies atop the organ and a program of Bach stands open on its music rack. It appears the instrument has recently been played. I shine the light on the wall beside the organ pipes and discern an outline in the brick. A tall and narrow opening has been recently bricked up. No doubt, it's the passageway for the large paintings that now reside inside the building.

Illuminating the interior wall I see the rest of the stolen art neatly hung as in a museum. I take several photographs before noticing two doors, one at either end of the wall, entrances into each of the palazzo's wings

Turning around, I shine the light toward the center of the chapel. In the middle of the nave stands a massive canopied bed with thick, spiraled posters made of ebony. *How bizarre, a bed in a place of worship?* I walk over to it and shine the light on its tall headboard, which is deeply carved in relief and depicts grotesque-looking Gothic creatures that remind me of Notre Dame's gargoyles. The bed's canopy, drapes, pillow shams, and coverlet are made of rich-looking, black silk brocade with fringed edges The inside of the canopy and the side curtains are lined with a deep red silk, the color of blood. Two gilded torcheres fitted with gas jets stand on either side of the bed. A faint smell of propane lingers in the air. At the foot of the bed stand six lininfold armchairs made of oak their arms carved into hideous gargoyles. The chairs are arranged in a semi-circle as though providing an audience for the bed's occupant. It's the most peculiar sight I have ever seen. Flashing the light toward the altar I expect to find pews but there are none, only two kneeling benches side by side fitted with needlepoint kneeling cushions.

Flashing the light toward the ceiling I see suspended from a thick wooden beam spanning the chapel, a huge wrought iron chandelier so large in circumference that it holds nearly a hundred candles. It is centered over the foot of the bed and the chairs. It has a rope and pulley apparatus that allows it to be raised and lowered or else how would anyone light all those candles? Following the pulley rope with the flashlight beam, I trace it down the middle of the inside wall where it's held in place by a winding device with a toothed crank and handle.

As I snap several pictures of this unusual scene, a reddish glow begins to bathe the chapel's interior, a light reminiscent of a photographer's darkroom.

Panicked by the sudden illumination, I race behind the altar and dive feet first through the opening into the crypt. Slithering down the stairs, I turn over on my stomach and reach for and release the hydraulic jack's lever. Flicking off my flashlight, I wait as noiselessly the slab descends and drops into place as I hear one of the chapel's wooden doors open with a resounding crash.

I realize a heat sensor in the chapel must have detected me. Fortunately Alberto's wet suit had kept my body temperature from setting it off earlier.

For a few fearful moments I huddle on the stairs in total blackness. The dreadful stench of sewage threatens to overcome me, but my fear of the rats propels me down the steps and into the water. Already the tide has risen more than a foot. It now laps at my chest. Leaving behind the jack and the glove I stuffed in the hole, I grab the canvas bag and toss my camera and the artifact into it. As I wade through the filthy water in headlong flight toward the arched entryway I hear growling and barking. The angry mastiffs are just above my head, following me.

Outside the tomb's entrance, I grab the tire and pull myself onto the dock. As I rise to my feet, I hear the sound of pocket change jingle. "Hurry!" urges a familiar voice. "Get to the boat."

Taking the flashlight from the bag, I run to the canal and signal Paolo just as a door in the palazzo bursts open and a spotlight probes the darkness.

Flattened against the chapel wall, I hear the water taxi's engine roar as it races toward me.

Behind me, I hear a cry of alarm and the pounding of two pair of feet on the wooden dock. Silhouetted in a halo of light I see the Commissario turn the corner of the chapel as he races toward me.

Paolo pulls alongside the canal wall, the water taxi's gunwale bumps and scrapes against the concrete.

I hear a heavy thud and a loud "Oomph!" A torch cartwheels into the air and splashes into the canal. As the flashlight sinks with an eerie glow I hear someone gasping for breath. Dashing to the side of the water taxi, I leap into the cockpit and fall against Paolo.

"*Escusi,*" I pant.

A heavy thud comes from the stern where the Commissario has landed in the rear cockpit.

Shoving the throttle forward, Paolo throws the helm over hard starboard and veers into middle of the canal where he races away from the palazzo in a wide arc that carries us into the Grand Canal.

Looking back at the Count's dock, I catch a brief glimpse of a stocky man as he struggles to his feet. Limping, he shouts curses and shakes his fist in the air. It's Nico, the Count's speedboat driver.

As we roar up Grand Canal, throwing a heavy wake behind us, the Palazzo Benzoni suddenly comes ablaze with lights.

"Peter, you'll have to send the Count flowers," teases the Commissario from the doorway to the cabin, . . . "for waking him up!" Disheveled and beaded with perspiration, he enters the cockpit laughing.

Paolo and I join him, but my laughter borders on near hysteria.

"San Toma, *per favore,* Paolo," requests the Commissario. "I need to get some sleep."

"*Va bene,*" replies Paolo, steering the boat toward the far side of the canal. Behind us, The Rialto Bridge grows smaller.

"Commissario, are you okay?" I ask.

"Just exhausted."

"I heard you laughing as you jumped in the boat. What happened back there?"

"That thug who chased us didn't see the wooden bench I pulled across the dock."

"*Accidente!*" I exclaim and we break into laughter again.

"What did you find?" asks the Commissario.

"It's all there, the Bellini, the other paintings, the altar, the diptych, everything, even a four poster bed with chairs arranged around it like some kind of Medieval rite. And I've got the artifact." I reach in the duffel bag and hand it to him. "Here!"

"Madonna!" exclaims the Commissario, taking the case from me. He opens it and looks inside. Paolo throttles back and shines his flashlight on it. Imbedded in the flawless, sparkling crystal is a six-inch long rust-colored spike. "I can hardly believe my eyes," says the Commissario, making the sign of the cross. He's so moved by the sight of the holy object that his eyes become watery. A tear courses down his cheek.

"What is it?" asks Paolo. "A hull spike from a ship?"

The Commissario is too choked with emotion to answer.

"It's a nail from the cross of Christ," I tell Paolo. "*Madre di Dios!*" he says, crossing himself. Staring at the artifact, he asks the Commissario, "May I hold it?"

"*Si, attentamente, per favore.*" The Commissario passes the case to Paolo. Gently cradling the artifact in his callused, rough hands, he tenderly strokes the crystal as though touching the face of a precious infant.

"Incredible," the Commissario exclaims, "The nail from the hand of our savior." He fishes a handkerchief out of his pocket and blows his nose.

"Not exactly, Commissario, more likely, from his wrist.

Although the Crucifixion is usually portrayed with a nail though the palm of the hand, the flesh is much too soft to support a man's weight. Customarily the nail was driven through the wrist."

"I didn't know that," responds the Commissario, "but it makes sense."

Paolo, also choked with emotion, hands the case back to the Commissario. "Grazie," he says, turning back to the wheel. Wiping a hand across his eyes, he pushes the throttle forward and points the boat's bow at San Toma's floating dock.

Following the Commissario into the cabin, I strip off the booties, my remaining glove, and the wet suit. As I dress and put on my running shoes, I say, "thank God you were on that dock or that fellow, Nico, would have had me for sure."

"*Prego*." he smiles. "Now listen, Peter, no more antics. We got lucky tonight, but you're going to have to stay out of sight until I can reason with the Questore. He's intent on arresting you, but this should help," he smiles, holding up the artifact's case. Securing the lid, he pockets it.

"Then he knows about the artifact?"

"Yes, I was forced to tell him. Recovering it will appease the Vatican. And once the Questore get credit for its return, he'll likely turn the case back to me, assuming I let him have all the glory."

"Commissario, that's not right?"

"Of course not, but he'll take credit anyway. As for you Peter, you won't be absolved until we apprehend the real perpetrators."

"We know who they are. The Count and his men."

"Yes I agree, but assuming and proving are very different things. And another thing, I need to obtain from the Dottore his sworn statement that it was he who gave you the Botticelli forgery and the plans to steal the Pala d'Oro."

"The Questore won't take your word?"

"My word doesn't count with him. He's a vain and difficult man."

"*Stupid,* you mean." The Commissario's a lot more charitable than I would be about a boss who doesn't trust my word.

The Commissario gives me a look like there's something

else on his mind.

"What is it?" I ask.

"The young woman, Adriana."

"Yes?"

"When the Coroner examined her body did you know he found out that she was pregnant."

"Oh, Lord!"

"The Questore's convinced you killed Ms. Fiorucci to silence her, so your wife wouldn't find out and also to prevent her from extorting money from you."

"That's absurd. I only knew her for a few days."

"The Questore claims you were in Venice three months ago."

"I don't believe this. Yes, I was here, for two days, but I never laid eyes on Adriana until last week. I suppose that means he's got my passport?"

"Yes, which means you won't be able to flee Italy."

"Goddamn it! Commissario."

"Peter, don't get angry with me. I'm trying to help. I suspect the Count's men waited for you to leave your apartment, broke in, and accidentally discovered *Signorina* Fiorucci. Knowing she could identify them they had to dispose of her. Also they couldn't allow her to interfere with their plan to frame you for Brother Alvise's murder which involved planting his sack in your apartment. They killed her and rigged her death to make it look like you murdered her as well."

I feel sick in the pit of my stomach. "This is a nightmare, Commissario, only it seems to get worse."

"Peter, I'll get to the bottom of this, trust me."

"Yeah," I groan. The last time I heard that expression was a month before Claire left me. "I'll be yours forever, Peter, *trust me*," she had said. Never trust anyone who says "*trust me!*"

"Tomorrow morning, I'm going to take the first flight to Rome and return the artifact to the Vatican. Once it's in their possession I'll get a statement from the Dottore and we'll get this ugly business straightened out. In the meantime, not a word to anyone about the artifact."

"Okay, but what about the Count's chapel and all the stolen art?"

"I'll tell the Questore to order a surveillance team to keep an eye on things. If anyone tries to move anything out they'll be arrested. Otherwise, I'd prefer to wait. Moving precipitously could spoil our chances of apprehending the mastermind of these crimes."

"You mean the Count?"

"Peter, we don't have sufficient evidence to prove he's the culprit."

Feeling the boat slow, I look up and watch it glide alongside San Toma's floating dock.

"Before you go, Commissario, there are a couple of other matters. Princess Irena told me Moira Dunn, the Archduke's old girlfriend, has a new boyfriend. His name is Cosimo De Cheeci. He's the Minister of Protocol and a Vatican advisor. It's possible she could have learned about the artifact from him."

"Fine. I'll check him out."

"What about Moira Dunn's passport?"

"First thing in the morning, I'll tell Roberto, my assistant, to follow up on it."

"San Toma," Paolo calls out.

"Coming," answers the Commissario.

"I have a glass with Lili's fingerprint on it for you."

"Have someone leave it at the Questura with Roberto Chiari. I'll let him know to expect it. And one more thing, Peter, don't worry, I won't tell the Questore I saw you tonight."

"Thanks. I don't know your boss, Commissario, but already I dislike him."

"He's just an ambitious civil servant," shrugs the Commissario.

"Wait, take the film I shot inside the chapel." Opening up my camera, I hand him the film cartridge.

"*Grazie*," I'll have it developed. I've got to get some sleep, Peter. Go back to Ms. Aliverti's and stay there until you hear from me."

"All right."

"Nice work," he says, clapping me on the back. "Try not to

worry too much. *Ciao.*"

Paolo and I watch the Commissario plod into the dark labyrinth of streets. After he disappears, Paolo drives me back to the canal where he'd picked me up. Taking my camera, I leave Alberto's gear on board and walk to Cinzia's apartment building. As I wait for her to let me in, I notice a couple embracing in the doorway of the church across the street. There's something vaguely familiar about the woman, but its dark and I'm too exhausted to pay any attention. After all the filth I've waded through and the tension I've experienced all I want is a hot shower and a good night's sleep.

Cinzia is relieved to see me, but she makes a terrible face. "Phew! Piero, you smell awful."

I lean toward her hoping for a kiss.

"Stay away from me." She recoils. "Into the shower with you. I'm not getting anywhere near to you until you're clean."

Women!

On the way to the bathroom, I hesitate long enough to tell her about the Count's chapel and some of the things I discovered inside. She's wide eyed with fascination. I omit telling her about the artifact since the Commissario prefers that I not talk about it.

"All that art must be worth a fortune?" she says.

"How about a hundred million pounds worth?"

Her eyes get big, but she makes a face and pinches her nose with her fingers.

"That bad, huh?"

"Ghastly."

Spanking clean, I emerge from the bathroom with a bath towel secured around my waist. I find Cinzia sitting in her brass bed. She's covered by a sheet and has her knees drawn up to her chin. The only light in the room is from a thick candle that flickers behind her on the nightstand. It gives off a warm glow that makes Cinzia and her bed look alluring. The fresh scent of vanilla wafts from the candle and mingles with the scent of her perfume.

"Come here," she says, wagging her index finger at me.

I know better than disobey a perfumed woman with seductive eyes. Dropping my towel on the floor, I slip into bed beside her.

She rolls on her side and wraps her arms around me. "I was nearly sick with worry, Piero. I'm so happy you're safe," she murmurs, throwing off the sheet.

I'm about to answer, but the view leaves me speechless.

Curled around Cinzia, I awake suddenly in the early morning hours from a nightmare.

"Piero, what's wrong?"

"The Count bit me," I answer.

"Silly, It's only a bad dream." Rolling over, she hugs me. "Go back to sleep, love."

My dream had seemed so real. I was in Harry's surrounded by rodents dressed as Cardinals. Holding flashlights, they chant in Japanese, gnaw on fried zucchini sticks, and ogle Lili who poses on a barstool with gigantic purple eggplants spilling from the bodice of her gown. Then, from the kitchen, Dominick wheels in Count Benzoni. He sits in a wheelbarrow full of porcini mushrooms while Harry and Claudio applaud. The Count wears a silk jester's costume, painted like a gondola pole, crimson with gold stripes and on his head he wears a Doge's cap. His face is as pale as a cauliflower and his eyes are maraschino cherries. Grinning fiendishly, he leaps up from his mushroom throne and taking a garland of onions, Brussels sprouts, and beets from the basket of a hot air balloon resembling a pigeon with Pomeroy's face, he drapes the garland around my neck. Stepping back to admire his work, he suddenly rushes forward, embraces me and sinks his fangs into my neck.

In the morning when I awake the dream seems so vivid that I involuntarily touch my neck. It feels sore. Quietly I get out of bed, so as not to wake Cinzia. In the bathroom I look at myself in the mirror. There are teeth marks on my neck. Maybe it's only a *hicky?*

Chapter 17

CINZIA AND I laze around in her bed, following the Commissario's orders, staying undercover. I suppose Frette linens qualify. Cinzia and I have the best time, kissing and fooling around. Bodies are such lovely play-toys. I'm enthralled with hers and she seems to be equally entranced by mine. We're enthusiastic, playful and totally uninhibited.

Lying in each other arms after an amorous wrestle, the telephone rings. Cinzia fumbles for it. "*Pronto?*" she answers. Sitting bolt upright, she looks at me and puts her hand to her mouth. "Yes, . . . he's here."

"Who is it?" I whisper.

"Claire."

"Claire?" I sit up beside Cinzia who yawns, flops down on her side, and scrunches up against me. Pulling a pillow over her head, she hides from both conversation and daylight.

"Dog three at last!" shouts Claire. She sounds hostile.

"Woof, woof," I answer.

"Very cute," she says with more than just a tinge of sarcasm. I see you didn't waste any time getting together with my real estate lady."

I couldn't tell if she was mad or jealous, or both. "Come off it, Claire. It was you who suggested I meet her."

"Yes, *meet her*. I never said, *sleep with her*. I only suggested you meet because I felt sorry for you and a little guilty about going away. However, that was before I learned that you're a felon, wanted by the police for two murders and a string of art thefts."

I assume Claire's calling me from Switzerland. "How did you find out? I ask.

"Your picture's plastered across the front page of *Il Gazzettino*. What's gotten into you? When did you start stealing paintings and offing monks and models?"

"My God, Claire, then you're here, in Venice?"

"I'm at my flat with police tape across my front door. The inside looks as though the bora has swirled through it, and there's no TV in my bedroom and Franco, poor thing, is dangling from his web half-starved to death."

Her voice, as icy as liquid nitrogen, sends a shudder through me.

"I suppose," she continues, "you've been so busy with your felonies and fucking that you haven't had a minute to worry about something as trivial as my flat. What an idiot I was to give you my keys. Oh yes, and I found the complaint from my downstairs neighbor that you blasted her out of the building with the stereo. Lastly I found a nude sketch by Pomeroy; is she the one you sent to her eternal reward?"

She doesn't give me a chance to reply.

"From the condition of my bedroom and my missing sheets and pillowcases, I assume you and your art tart had a jolly good romp in *my* bed."

"Claire, I can explain," but I don't try, instead, I get angry. "Hey, aren't you supposed to be in Switzerland," I shout, "until September with your Kraut lover, Prince what's-his-face."

"Hans is not the issue here, Peter."

"Then explain to me why you're back without even letting me know?" I yell.

Cinzia sticks her head out from under the pillow. Scrunching up her face, she sticks her tongue out at me and burrows her head under two pillows.

"I didn't call you," she huffs, "because I was in Monaco visiting Hans' cousins. They're bohemians and they run a grungy pensione on the harbor, hang out with drifters and rail against the Grimaldi family. Hans wouldn't even allow me near the Casino, fearing I might fitter away his precious Deutsche marks. I went anyway, by myself, and ran into Elisio Foscari, the formula one champion. He took pity on me."

"I'll bet he did."

"I flushed Hans like a toilet and yesterday Elisio flew me back here in his Gulfstream."

"Jesus, Claire, now you're running around with a race car driver. Isn't he married?"

"So what. You are too! Obviously, you're using too much Brylcream on your hair and everything's slipped your mind."

Cinzia bounds out of bed, swearing at me in Italian. She grabs a pillow and whaps me over the head with it.

"What was that noise?" asks Claire.

"Pillow talk." Now, listen carefully, Claire. I've been framed. I think I know who's behind all this and I'm going to prove my innocence. I suppose Irena told you where to find me. You must not tell anyone where I am. I'm in real danger and I need time to clear up this mess."

"All right, Peter, but you better make it quick. I'm not allowing you to trash me like you have my flat."

Standing naked at the foot of the bed, Cinzia scowls at me. Balling her hands into fists, she shouts, "*Basta!*"

"I have to hang up, Claire. I'll talk to you later."

Shit! Now I've got two women pissed at me.

Waiting a few moments for her to calm down, I get up, slip on my shirt, and follow Cinzia into the kitchen. She stands at the stove in her terry robe, her back to me as she puts a kettle of water on the burner to boil. Sneaking up behind her, I wrap my arms around her waist and bury my face in her silky hair. "Don't you know a watched pot never boils," I whisper in her ear. You must not be so upset with me."

She twists around in my arms and faces me. Searching the depths of my eyes, she takes my face in her hands and kisses me fiercely. Then, she shoves me away. In an agonized voice she says, "What am I doing with you? *You're married!* I listen to you carry on like a husband, fighting with your wife while I'm lying beside you right after making love. I feel dirty and cheap. And it's my own damn fault getting ass over teakettle over you when I know better." Her eyes get moist and a tear runs down her cheek.

I reach for her. She pushes my hand away and wipes the tear away with her hand. "I'm a big girl; I can take care of myself." Lowering her head, she begins to sob. The teakettle starts to whistle. What a chorus!

Turning the burner off, I hold her in my arms and let her cry her hurt out. I stroke her hair. It smells lovely.

"Cinzia, don't be so hard on yourself. You're the only woman I've had an emotional involvement with since Claire and I separated."

"You sound and act like you're . . . like you're still in love with her," she blubbers.

"I have strong feelings for Claire, but everything's all mixed up. For the longest time I've wanted her back, but she acts so nutty, I just don't know any more. Don't be upset. I haven't met anyone since Claire I like nearly as much as I like you."

Looking up at me with her tear stained face, her hair all askew, she laughs. "Oh, Piero." She hugs me. "I'm sorry about carrying on. I'm feeling vulnerable and I'm having a dreadful time dealing with my guilt."

"Guilt?"

"It's my Catholic morality, my sins, throwing myself at a married man and sleeping with him."

"Isn't that what confession's for?"

"Yes, and I'm going to have to do a lot of penance. And I have another problem, my mother. By tradition, I'm responsible for her. As the youngest daughter, it's my obligation to look after her which pretty much ruins my chance of having a life of my own."

"What about your sister and brother?"

"They have no responsibility for her. My sister, Elenora, is married, she's got children and her life is in Verona. Maximo, my younger brother, is busy learning the family real estate business from father. By law he inherits everything. I'm the one who's stuck. I just can't bear that empty palazzo my mother lives in. It's so unhappy there. Fortunately, managing some of the family properties gives me enough income to afford my own apartment and a little privacy."

"It's not fair that you're responsible for your mother," I protest.

"Well, it may not be fair, but that's the Venetian tradition and there's nothing I can do about it." She buries her head against my chest. "Hold me, Piero."

All at once I'm gazing into mischievous eyes and a beautiful smile. "Piero, since I'm going to have to confess, let's make it worthwhile." Throwing off her robe, Cinzia dashes into the bedroom and flings her lovely body across the bed. "Hurry up," she shouts.

What a kick! Later, I have to reheat the water for tea.

In the shower, I find Cinzia has a penchant for cleanliness. As she lathers my body, I tell her it's next to Godliness. She laughs. "Piero, whatever is going to become of us?"

I start to answer, but she puts a finger across my lips.

"It doesn't matter," she says. "I adore you."

"Me too, but you better stop that." Her other hand is fondling the family jewels.

"Do I have to? You feel so nice."

The phone rings.

Whew! Saved by the bell!

Cinzia ducks out of the shower. Snatching a towel, she answers the phone. It's Moira Dunn. She wants Cinzia to have lunch with her. She says she's going back to Rome and wants to see Cinzia before she leaves. I'm not invited. Naturally, I feel slighted, but I console myself, realizing that one doesn't usually invite a hunted murderer to lunch. It's not good for one's social image. Having me join them would be what the French term a *faux pas*.

When I ask Cinzia if she thinks my picture's been posted on the post office's walls, she gives me a totally blank look. She hasn't a clue what I'm talking about. I guess certain American customs don't make it overseas. I explain the tradition of "most wanted posters" to her. Giving me a serious look she promises she'll stop by the post office to check.

"But you don't have to." I exclaim.

"But I'd like to," she smiles. "I need a nice picture of you for my dresser."

Clever girl! She's got *my* number.

I ask her to find out about Moira's relationship with De Cheeci. "Don't be too obvious," I tell her. "Remember, she's a suspect."

While dressing, I saunter over to the window and look outside. The sky is deep blue and cloudless. It's a gorgeous bright, sunny day and the reflection off the white walls of a church makes me squint. I feel trapped, unable to go out and roam the streets as I enjoy doing. I ache for a *cappuccino,* but I can't take the chance of being seen and apprehended. Being in hiding depresses me. Here I am in the heart of the fabled and extravagant theater of Venice, and like a character in a movie about Mafioso, "I've gone to the mattress." At least I have Cinzia to share my imprisonment.

Cinzia wears a teal-colored silk blouse, a knee length charcoal skirt, and dark hose. All her accessories: belt, pumps, and purse are shiny black alligator. She looks marvelous."Where are you meeting Moira?" I ask.

"The Hotel Monaco."

"Lucky girl."

She plants a soft kiss on my mouth. Her perfume intoxicates me.

"Cinzia, I need a favor."

"What's that?"

I hold up a plastic bag. "It's a glass with Lili's fingerprints on it. Would you drop this off at the Questura? Give it to the Commissario's assistant, Roberto Chiari."

"Sure. I'll take care of it right after lunch."

"Thank you." I start to give her another kiss.

"Careful," she warns. "Don't smear me."

I kiss her on the cheek. As she walks out the door my heart's aflutter. Admiring her lovely long legs, I emit a soft, sexy-sounding wolf whistle.

"Naughty, naughty," she responds, glancing over her shoulder. She gives me a saucy grin and a certain part of her anatomy breaks into a provocative wiggle.

"That shimmy alone is worth twenty Hail Mary's!" I exclaim.

After Cinzia departs, I telephone Claire.

"Well, about time," she complains, "If I'd held my breath any longer you'd be a widower."

"Sorry, I got busy."

"*I'll just bet you did!*"

"Come on Claire, stop the jealousy routine. We're beyond that. Besides what would Mr. Formula One think if he heard you?"

"I've already told him I'm a bitch."

"No comment," I add.

"Peter, Colin Marshall just called here. He says he's 'round the bend' over your headlines in the tabloids."

"Jesus, that's all I need."

"You'd best ring him."

"Did he say anything else."

"Only that he's concerned about me because of your problems. He wants to know if there's anything he can do for me."

"What that bounder wants to do is get into your knickers."

"That's impossible. I never wear any in the summertime?"

"God give me strength," I mutter.

"What was that you said?"

"Nothing, Claire, nothing at all. How's Franco doing?"

"Better, now that he's able to capture bugs again. That was terribly cruel, Peter, shutting all the windows like that."

"So report me to the Society for Prevention of Cruelty to Arachnids."

"Don't be a bore."

"Claire, I'm going to hang up now and call Colin. If you need anything ring me. I'm sequestered here until the Commissario gets back from Rome."

"Who?"

"Police Commissario, Luca Moretti."

"I see."

"Talk to you later, *Ciao*." I hang up feeling irked about her conversation with Colin.

Next, I phone Colin Marshall in London.

"Colin, Peter here."

"Bloody hell, man! What's going on down there? My Venice

underwriter says you're splashed all over the tabloids, wanted for murder and whatnot."

"It's a frame up. I can explain."

"Explain!" he shouts. "You've dragged the good name of Lloyd's into the sewer with your larking about."

"Just a damn second, Colin." I'm really ticked. "I've located the stolen art . . . everything from a half dozen different robberies . . . over a hundred million dollars worth."

"Really?" Instantly, he calms down.

Money talks! "*Really*! It's all here in a Venetian palazzo, which is under police guard as we speak."

"Yes . . . well . . . ahem, perhaps I was a mite hasty."

"To say the least," I respond, not prepared to let him off the hook easily.

"Look old chap, . . . frightfully good work. I'll put a word in upstairs, . . . there should be a hefty bonus coming your way."

"There better be," I warn him. "I've put my life on the line for you chaps."

"I see . . . ahem . . . well, I suppose that's about it . . . ahem . . . perhaps, I should send your lovely wife a little token of our appreciation . . . any thoughts?"

"Yeah. Try Victoria's Secret. She can use some silk panties." I hear a strangling sound on the line. I purposely omit saying goodbye and simply hang up before he can. Leaping out of my chair, I give the wall a high five. "YES! Way to go Doge Three!"

For want of something better to do, I walk around Cinzia's apartment admiring her taste in antiques and fabrics. She has a pretty apartment richly appointed with family possessions, silver, china, books, pictures, and nick-knacks. I even peek inside the medicine cabinet looking for a nail file. You can tell a lot about a person from their medicine cabinet and Cinzia passes with flying colors. It's as neat as a pin and there's no trace of tranquilizers or sleeping pills. Good sign. I pilfer an emery board.

When Cinzia walks through the door after her lunch with Moira, I'm on the sofa filing my nails.

She does an amused double take.

"How'd it go, *bella?*" I ask her.

"I'm beautiful?"

"Sexy too. And you do a mean shimmy." I stand up and embrace her.

"I missed you, Piero." She looks tenderly at me and we kiss.

Breaking away, she sighs deeply. "If this is the kind of treatment a lady gets when she returns home, I may go out to lunch every day," she teases. "What are you looking so smug about?"

I grin at her. "I just verbally tarred and feathered an obnoxious Englishman."

"Colin?"

"Yep."

"Bully for you. I hope you really gave it to him."

"I did."

"My hero." She kisses me with passion. "You're going to be very upset with me."

"Why?"

"The glass you gave me to take to the Questura. I dropped my purse and it smashed. It was an accident and I'm sorry."

"Don't worry about it." The disappointment on my face gives me away.

She hugs me. "Please don't be upset with me."

"Okay, I won't. How was lunch?"

"Lunch was delightful," she says, tossing her purse on the sofa. She sits down beside it. "Moira's always so chic. She has a lot to say, although she tends to be a bit . . . "

"Outspoken," I interrupt.

"Very, though I must admit, she's nobody's fool and she's up on all the dirt. After listening to her, I don't share your feelings about her being involved with the Count in any art thefts."

"Why?"

"Well, her new paramour, De Cheeci, is a financial advisor to the Vatican. He doesn't know and doesn't care a whit about art and antiquities. He's only interested in making millions in the stock market."

"Then the two of them have something in common. Moira loves spending other peoples money."

"I guess she'll have the chance, he's moved her into his apartment. Anyway, Moira told me that last night she received a phone call at the Gritti around one thirty in the morning. Whoever it was, listened to her voice and then quietly hung the phone up, but not before she heard a clock chiming in the background. She recognized the clock by its distinctive sound. She said it was a French case clock on the *piano noble* of the Count's palazzo, right outside Lili's bedroom. Why would someone from the palazzo call to check on Moira unless they suspected she might have been involved in the break in?"

"That is curious."

"She said the Count phoned her this morning and told her he'd been up most of the night. He said a burglar had tried to get into the palazzo and that his speedboat driver had been injured chasing away the intruder."

"That doesn't exonerate Moira. What if she fabricated the story to try to throw us off her trail?"

"I don't think so. My intuition tells me she's sincere. I asked her why she risks her reputation being around the Count. She says she could care less what the Venetians think about her and that the Count was the only Venetian who remained friendly after she stopped seeing the Archduke. She told me everyone else treated her like refuse they leave outdoors for the trash collector. She feels sorry for the Count and confirms that he's dying of AIDS.

"I didn't realize Moira was such a champion of the debauched."

"I don't think that's the reason. Moira's a rebel. She's not particularly judgmental and she likes to champion underdogs. And listen to this! Moira thinks the Count's going to marry Lili."

"What!"

"Exactly my reaction. But think about it for a minute. She's been the Count's hostess and housekeeper for the past six years. All that time she's lived in his palazzo and he's become dependant on her, especially now that he's dying. He's got her to look after him and manage things while he's still alive. Moira say's the Count is the last of the Benzoni's and he hasn't any heirs."

"What a windfall that would be for Lili. No wonder she's hung in there. Nevertheless, I'm skeptical about Moira. She could still be involved. Judging from her nasal twang and her coarse speech I'm willing to bet she's from a really tough background in some Mid-Western City. Though she looks pretty terrific on the exterior, I think on the inside she's a cool calculating broad."

"Piero, that's a terrible thing to say."

"But probably true. Did she have any comment about me?"

"She told me your statement about the Bellini being a fake was so outrageous that it made her furious. She said she knew the painting was genuine. She was also aware that it had been stolen. The Archduke, shaken by its theft, called her and told her even though he wasn't supposed to."

"Now, I understand her reaction. She thought I was trying to con her."

"Exactly. She didn't know what to make of you and she's still wary. She told me that she saw you at the Count's palazzo one evening, that you stayed awhile, then left before dinner. She said she gave you a wide berth."

"I laugh. "That's an understatement. She avoided me like I was a plague doctor. I'm sure she's happy the police are after me."

"Actually, she was more concerned about me. She asked if I'd been out with you after that night at Antonio's."

"What did you tell her?"

"I told her you were a one night stand."

"You didn't?"

"Of course not. I told her you were just a social obligation," she teases, sticking me in the ribs with an index finger.

"Hey, don't do that. I'm ticklish. It's true, I was an arranged date. Listen, getting back to something you mentioned, you said you and Lili were once friends, right?"

"Yes, until about five years ago. When I first met her she seemed very nice. She was married to a French diplomat named, Jacques Poirel. He was a tall handsome man, rugged features and salt and pepper hair. He'd fought with the French

Foreign Legion in Indo-China and had been wounded. He walked with a limp and he was a quiet attentive man. Frankly I found him extremely attractive. As I recall, he was a military attache and he and Lili traveled extensively. It occurred to me he was perhaps more than just an ordinary diplomat?"

"You mean an intelligence officer?"

"Exactly. At any rate, I heard rumors from friends that Lili had been having numerous affairs. Her behavior upset me so I dropped her as a friend. When her husband found out about her infidelity he divorced her and left Italy."

"Hmmmm. Do you recall anything about her background?"

"Not much. She never talked about her childhood or her parents except to say that she ran away from home at age sixteen and lived in Rome. I never asked her any questions. She was reluctant to talk about her past."

"Did she have any brothers or sisters?"

"She mentioned once that she had a brother, much older, whom she hardly ever saw. Apparently he left home while she was still a child."

"Do you recall her maiden name?"

Pausing to search her memory, Cinzia replies, "She may have told me once, but if she did, I don't recall it."

"Do you know how to reach Lili's ex husband?"

Absently, Cinzia chews on her lower lip. "Mmmmm. After he left Italy, I believe he returned to France. That was so long ago, I wouldn't know where to begin to try to find him, maybe the French Embassy in Rome might know his whereabouts."

"If he was an intelligence agent the authorities might not be cooperative. I think I'll ask the Princess. She's sure to know someone in Rome who may have come in contact with Lili. Look what she dug up on Moira."

"About De Cheeci," laughs Cinzia. "Did Irena mention to you that *he's* married."

"No, but with Moira, some things never change."

Around three in the afternoon I telephone the Princess.

"Thank God," exclaims Irena. "I'm so relieved to hear from you. I had visions of you on the Bridge of Sighs, glimpsing your last look at freedom before being shut up in stygian darkness in the Doge's dungeon."

"It's not that bad, *yet*," I assure her. "But it will be if the police find out where I am." I fill her in on my hair-raising visit to the Count's chapel where I'd located the stolen art. "The Commissario is going to Rome tomorrow morning. He's planning to visit Cosimo De Cheeci, then get a statement from Umberto Ferculi to absolve me of the theft charges."

"Good," she replies.

I ask her about Lili Poirel.

"Oh, Peter," she sighs heavily, "not that dreadful woman?"

"I need to find out everything I can about her, her maiden name, her background, things like that. Do you know anyone who might have known her when she lived in Rome?"

"Have you asked Cinzia? She was friend's with Lili until she found out Lili had an affair with her father."

"I have, but she doesn't recall much."

"I'll see what I can do."

"You're an angel!"

"No, *caro*, just a Princess. Now, how is everything between you and Cinzia?"

"*Perfecto*," I reply, wondering why Cinzia hadn't mentioned her father's affair with Lili, then, I suppose it's an embarrassment to talk about it.

"I'm so glad. She's such a lovely intelligent woman and I'm so fond of her. Give her my love."

"With pleasure."

"Where shall I call you if I find out anything."

"Here, at Cinzia's"

"Oh!"

On her cherubic face, I can just picture Cupid's smile.

About eight o'clock in the evening Claire telephones. Cinzia answers the phone and hands it to me. She gives me an apprehensive look.

"Hi, what's up?" I ask.

"Peter, There's someone here who wants to talk to you." Her voice quavers and she sounds frightened.

"Claire, are you all right?" I glance at Cinzia who's listening to us, an expectant look on her face.

"No, I'm not. There's a problem."

"What kind of —"

Claire lets out a startled cry and I hear the angry voice of a woman who has just jerked the phone from her hand.

"Listen carefully," says the woman. "You have something that belongs to me. And I have something that belongs to you." Her voice is menacing. "You will bring me the object you took from the chapel and your wife will not be harmed. Otherwise, she will end up like that *puta*, Adriana Fiorucci."

Putting my hand over the mouthpiece, I whisper to Cinzia, "I think it's Lili. She's taken Claire hostage. She wants me to bring her something that I took from the chapel?"

"Are you sure it's Lili?"

"I'm pretty sure. Listen in." Cinzia leans close to me. We share the receiver.

"Where are you calling from?" I ask.

"Your wife's flat. Bring the object over here, now!" Cinzia nods her head up and down. Silently, she mouths the words. "It's her."

"Listen, I can't go out in the streets in daylight. I'll be arrested if I'm seen," I say, stalling for time.

"*Allora*, then have Cinzia bring it to me."

"She's just left," I lie. I'm not endangering Cinzia's life. How the hell does she know I'm the one who took the artifact? Suddenly, it hits me, the woman embracing the man in the church doorway. Lili! It was her bushy hair that looked familiar.

"Look, In an hour, it'll be dark. I'll come over then, okay?"

"Come alone. If I see the police or anyone with you, your wife will die."

"Just don't harm her. I'll be there. I promise."

She hangs up.

Looking stricken, Cinzia rushes into my arms. "Piero, what are we going to do?"

Chapter 18

Having Claire held hostage by Lili forces me to tell Cinzia about the artifact. We locate an oblong red box that holds several long strands of Cinzia's pearls. She dumps them out and hands me the box. It's nearly the same size as the one that had held the artifact, but without the gold tooling. And it's just large enough to contain a small crystal bud vase that sits on Cinzia's night table. Ripping off a piece of brown kraft paper from a grocery bag, I twist it and shape it into a makeshift spike, which I insert inside the vase. I ask Cinzia if she has any purple silk. She goes to her closet, strips the lining out of one of her jackets, cuts it to fit the inside of the box and glues it in place.

The makeshift artifact looks convincing, at least good enough to fool anyone at first glance.

I ask Cinzia if she has a pistol.

"Whatever for?" she replies, giving me a contemptuous look. I forget that Venetians refuse to admit that crime exists in their city. "Piero, I want you to call the police."

"Cinzia, you know I can't. They'll arrest me. And if I don't show up that woman will kill Claire."

"I'm scared, Piero. Then at least, let me go with you," she begs.

"No. That's out of the question. It's too dangerous and

you heard what she said, that she'll kill Claire if anyone but me shows up."

"Then, let me call the police once you've gotten there."

"No. No police! I can't take the chance. If Lili sees them she's liable to kill Claire and me. I have to handle this my way."

"Piero, What are you going to do?"

"I don't know. I'll think of something." As I put on my jacket, I try to reassure her.

She throws herself into my arms, holds me tight, then turns, and runs into her bedroom. A theatrical exit, I muse as I let myself out. I put the jewel box in my inside jacket pocket. Patting my side pocket I make certain that I have the Princess' crucifix. Then I head down the stairs.

It's night when I step outside Cinzia's apartment building. The campo teems with strollers and people returning home from work. Walking rapidly and watching for policemen, I knife through the pedestrians and arrive in Campo Santo Stefano without incident. As I approach Claire's building, I look up. From a salon window I see Lily. She watches me, her face in shadow under her frizzy mass of hair.

Letting myself in the front door, I walk a measured pace up the stairs. At each landing, I pause to catch my breath before climbing to the next level. I don't want to be winded when I enter the flat.

Finding the front door ajar, I push it open, and walk into a dark foyer. Following a light from the salon, I enter and find Claire bound hand and foot to a chair with a gag in her mouth. She stares at me with wide pleading eyes. I step toward her. She squirms, makes muffled sounds, and rolls her eyes at me.

Her warning comes too late.

From behind, Lili seizes my right arm in a judo hold and twists it violently. Tumbling head over heel I crash against a bookcase. The impact knocks the breath out of me. Gasping, I look up and see Lili stride toward me. She holds a pistol in her hand. As she stoops down to retrieve the box that has fallen from my jacket pocket, I see Franco dangling from a single gossamer thread a foot above Lili's head. Dislodged from his web by the impact of my body against the bookcase, he frantically tries to arrest his fall.

Lili picks up the box, a feral grin on her face, stands up, and aims her pistol at me. As she's about to pull the trigger, Franco drops down in front of her face, his web line tangled in her hair.

Shrieking, she slaps at Franco.

Seeing her approaching hand Franco jumps onto Lili's cheek, darts under her jaw, and bites her in the neck. Horrified, she drops the pistol, which clatters to the floor as her hands go to her neck. Lili's eyes bulge and she cries out in pain. Staggering backward she crashes against a Venetian commode. Her knees crumple and she sits down hard on the floor, her legs splayed apart. I see a stunned beseeching look in her eyes, which turns to sheer desperation. Her eyelids begin to flutter, her jaw drops open and from her mouth comes a strangled plea for help.

It's too late. Her body begins to shudder and convulse as Franco's poison takes effect.

On my feet now, I glance at Claire. Wide-eyed, she gapes at Lili, transfixed by her convulsions. Kicking the gun away, I rush to Claire and free her as Lili gasps for breath. Her hands fall from her throat and land limply in her lap.

Franco's crushed body tumbles out of Lili's hands, rolls off her leg and drops to the floor. Slowly his long black spindly legs curl over the red hourglass on his abdomen, and he lies motionless.

Lili's breathing turn shallow and labored. Her chest expands in one great heave and, like air rushing out of a balloon, she expels a long sigh. Her eyes roll back into her head and slowly she pitches over onto her side. On her neck are two red puncture wounds where Franco's fangs have fatally pierced the carotid artery.

"Ouch!" exclaims Claire as I yank the last bit of duct tape from her lips.

"You all right?" I ask.

"Damn it, Peter, I've never been so frightened in my life. She was going to kill us, wasn't she?" Her voice is hoarse, quavering. She rubs the chafe marks on her wrists and ankles.

"No doubt about it. She would have claimed she had to

kill us in self-defense, and she'd probably have gotten away with it."

"But why would she want to kill us, Peter?"

"To cover up her involvement in the murder of the model and the Benedictine monk."

"Is she dead, Peter?"

I walk over to her and touch the inside of her wrist. "I can't feel any pulse, Claire. If I remember correctly, Black widow spider venom attacks the central nervous system. It must have shut down her ability to breathe."

"And Franco?"

"Dead too I'm afraid."

"Oh, Peter, look at poor little Franco. He's all curled up."

I thought Claire would burst into tears, but she just clenched her fists and looked distraught. All at once her expression changes as though something has just dawned on her. Looking at me with her soft green eyes, she innocently asks. "Gosh, Peter, what if Franco had bitten me?"

"Francesca, Claire. Franco was actually a female black widow spider."

"Franco was a girl spider?" She looks astonished.

"When I saw the red hour glass I was reminded that it's only the females that have it. They're much bigger than male black widows and they carry a large amount of venom. Males are tiny. The female usually eats the male after they mate."

"That's disgusting!"

"Hell of a way to end a romance."

"Peter, we have to give Franco . . . I mean, Francesca, a burial. After all she saved our lives."

"I'll get a match box from the kitchen."

"Before you do, will you check again to make certain that awful woman's really dead."

"Sure." Bending over Lili, I pull back the collar of her shirt and feel for a pulse. There's none. I see something else. On her shoulder is a tatoo.

"She's dead all right. Look at this, Claire." I pull Lili's shirt back, exposing her tatoo.

"A devil's face!" exclaims Claire. "How odd. What do you suppose it means?"

"I have no idea, Claire."

"What was it she wanted from you?"

"That," I said, pointing to the red box on the floor. Its lid had flopped open during the melee, exposing the fake nail stuck inside Cinzia's crystal bud vase.

"What is it?" she asks, her eyebrows arching in bewilderment.

"It's a facsimile of a nail set in crystal. The real nail, a priceless relic taken from the Crucifixion of Christ and encased in Murano crystal, was stolen from the murdered Benedictine monk. I found the artifact last night when I broke into Count Benzoni's chapel. Lili wanted it back. She didn't know I had already given the real one to the Commissario." I told her how Cinzia and I had rigged up the fake one, hoping to fool Lili.

"But . . . but," stammers Claire, "How did Lili know you had this thing?"

"She made an educated guess that I'd taken it. She and the Count framed me for the murders of Brother Alvise and Adriana Fiorucci. Knowing I was on the loose they suspected that I might be hiding out with Cinzia Aliverti. After they discovered the artifact missing from the chapel, Lili staked out Cinzia's building. When she saw me leave the water taxi at two in the morning and enter Cinzia's building, she knew I was the one who had the artifact."

"I don't understand all this?" she says.

"Look, I'll explain later. Right now we better get out of here before someone comes looking for Lili. Besides, I can't let the police find me here. In my situation the police would never accept my explanation of how she died?"

"I can't look at her anymore, Peter." Claire puts her arms around me and hugs me. "Thank you," she murmurs. "I knew you'd come and rescue me."

"I'm glad you're okay." I tell her. It feels good having her in my arms again, all the old familiar scents, her hair, her body lotion and her perfume. I can't do this. "Come on, Claire, get your things. We'll have to stay at Cinzia's until we get this mess sorted out."

"Oh, terrific!" she exclaims, "Your wife and your lover in

the same apartment."

"Claire, if you'd rather, I'll leave you here with Lili's body?"

"No, no, I'm coming." She dashes into the bedroom, muttering, "Poor Francesca."

Using a kitchen spatula, I drop Francesca's little balled up body into an empty matchbox and slide the lid closed. I pick up the artifact replica and slip it inside my jacket. Putting the matchbox inside a plastic bag, I hand to Claire.

She tenderly tucks it inside a pocket of her garment bag, looks at me sorrowfully, puts her arms around my neck, and breaks into tears. "I loved him so."

"Her!"

"Whatever," she sobs.

Before leaving the apartment, I telephone Cinzia.

"It's me, Piero. I'm okay and so is Claire."

"*Madonna*, I'm so relieved," she sighs.

"Cinzia, Lili's dead, killed by a black widow spider. We're getting out of here this second. Give us ten minutes, then phone the police and tell them there's a dead woman in Claire's apartment."

"What are you going to do now?"

"Claire and I are on our way to your flat."

"*Madonna!*"

Picking up Claire's garment bag and cosmetic case, I escort her out the flat's front door. I don't bother to lock it, no sense forcing the police to break it down.

On the way to Cinzia's we see a pair of constabulary approaching. Stepping into a narrow ally I hide my identity in Claire's embrace.

"Hurry, kiss me," I tell her.

She complies.

The patrolmen grin at us, make racy comments known only to Italians, and walk on. Kissing Claire is eerily familiar, those lovely soft, full lips. I'm reluctant to stop. Afterward, I feel guilty and wonder if Cinzia will notice any traces of Claire's lipstick on me.

Seeing me with Claire has its affect on Cinzia. When we

arrive, her greeting is reserved and formal. The idea of Claire moving into her apartment unnerves her. She's quiet, tense and wary, as if she expects Claire to run off with her jewelry or . . . worse, *me*. I feel the tension and try to ease it by opening a bottle of prosecco I find in Cinzia's refrigerator.

"I phoned the police, says Cinzia. They wanted to know who was calling, but I hung up."

"Thanks." I reply, pouring three glasses of prosecco.

Before long we've consumed the whole bottle and the nervousness abates. Actually, I soon have Claire and Cinzia laughing. I tell them about Pomeroy being whitewashed by the pigeon and about the dozens of flowers I had to buy Claire's neighbor because of the noise from the stereo. The awkwardness between the two women vanishes when Cinzia announces that Claire will be sleeping with her and I'll be alone on the sofa.

"Poor DOG Three," laughs Claire, giving Cinzia a hug.

"DOG Three?" says Cinzia, her expression one of curiosity. "It's just a pet name." Claire replies.

The phone rings. Cinzia picks it up.

"It's the Princess. For you Dog Three," she says, grinning as she hands me the receiver.

"Irena, I take it you have some news for me?"

"*Si, caro.*" She tells me.

"Holy mackerel!" I shout.

"Peter, you mustn't yell in my ear," she protests.

"Sorry Irena. Why didn't I think of that?"

"I remembered that Lili got married here. As I've warned you that's bad luck. Never marry in Venice. At any rate, I telephoned City Hall and had someone look up her marriage license in the municipal registry."

"Good Lord, then she must be related to Umberto. I've got to warn the Commissario before he gets to him." I look at Claire and Cinzia. They're perched on the edge of the sofa, riveted on my conversation with the Princess.

I put my hand over the receiver. "Lili's maiden name is Ferculi. She was born in Frascati, near Rome."

"Listen, Irena, let me get back to you. I have to reach the Commissario right away. I'm very grateful for the information." "*Prego, caro,*" she exclaims, happily. "*Ciao.*"

As I hang up I picture her elfin smile as she claps her plump hands together, applauding her own cleverness.

Claire and Cinzia are both on their feet, talking at once, bombarding me with questions. "Wait, wait," I interrupt, "I have to call the Commissario."

I call his home number. There's no answer and I'm in a near state of panic, fearful that I won't be able to reach him. I have Cinzia call the Questura and ask for Commissario Moretti. They tell her he's away from the city and can't be reached, but she can leave a message.

"But it's a family emergency." she insists.

"Sorry, police policy, we can't help you." They hang up.

The girls look at me expectantly, awaiting an explanation. "Irena told me Lili and the Count took out a marriage license. I've got to reach the Commissario before he meets Umberto. There's only one thing for me to do. I'll have to chance taking the night train to Rome. "It's absolutely critical." I exclaim. They both look at me like I've lost it.

"Are you mad?" asks Claire.

"You'll be arrested. The train stations will be swarming with police!" exclaims Cinzia.

"Not if you get me a ticket and I board the train in disguise."

"In disguise?" they chorus.

"What kind of disguise?" asks Cinzia.

"Dressed like a woman?" It's the only thing I can think of.

Despite the seriousness of the situation, they fall all over each other in gales of laughter. There's little left for me to do but join them, so we all howl together.

To the rest of the world, Claire and Cinzia look like two doting nieces escorting their tall eccentric aunt to the railroad station. I wear a long black flowered dress, a large straw hat with a plastic flower stuck on it and a beige knit shawl. I carry a purse and a small Fendi overnight bag. I don't look too bad, perhaps a tad forlorn, owing to a gaping hole in the pantyhose I borrowed from Claire. I had poked my finger through the right knee, trying to pull them on. Cinzia's low heels are too tight. They hurt my feet and cause me to walk with a shuffle. Through my pain, I wonder, how in God's name women manage to walk in spiked heels? I can't wait to get on the train and kick these pumps off before I end up with corns. Suddenly it becomes clear to me why Claire used to surreptitiously slip off her heels at restaurants, movies and the opera.

I sit in the waiting room, while Cinzia buys me a train ticket. I ponder removing Cinzia's pumps, but the vision of not being able to get them back on dissuades me. In a vision, I picture myself holding my pumps in my hand as I pad along the concrete concourse in my stocking feet like some danced out debutante. A policeman takes a close look, sees through my disguise and busts me on the spot. Off to the dungeons I go. Best just to bear the pain and smile, I decide, ending my little fantasy.

Cinzia thrusts a ticket at me. I take it from her and we hurry off toward the train.

"Slow down, my feet hurt," I complain.

Claire looks knowingly at Cinzia. They exchange glances and snicker.

"Now you know how it feels to be a woman," Claire comments.

"How did I know you were going to say that?" I reply, wobbling along between them.

"Don't forget to validate your ticket in the machine," Cinzia reminds me. I'm glad she reminds me. The pain has made me forgetful. Stopping, I insert one end of the ticket in the machine. "Thwap!" It time stamps and dates my ticket.

We encounter the first class coaches at the beginning of the platform. Fortunately, mine is the second one from the end. No way I could have walked another car length. We climb aboard and find my first class compartment.

Slumping into my seat, I groan with relief and kick off the offending pumps. Cinzia and Claire break up laughing. Claire fishes in her purse and holds a compact in front of my face. I see that my hat is crooked and my lipstick is smeared.

"I look like a street walker," I remark.

"You look priceless," says Claire. "I wish we had a camera."

"Thank God, you don't!" I genuflect in gratitude. "You better get off this train unless you intend to accompany me to Rome?"

"Were going. Be careful, Piero," advises Cinzia. She blows me a kiss. I guess she doesn't want to mess up my makeup.

Exiting the compartment, they leave the train. I move to the window seat and watch them stop and search the windows until they find me. They point and wave. As I wave back, I notice they both appear worried.

While punching my ticket, the conductor stares at me. He has the most peculiar look on his face and checks my ticket twice. It's obvious, he wonders what a disreputable-looking transvestite with torn hose is doing in first class. Heading for the next compartment, he shakes his head in disbelief. Once he's gone, I stretch out across three seats and fall asleep.

Shortly before arriving in Rome I awake and take Cinzia's overnight case into the lavatory. With water and cold cream I transform myself back into a man. "*Ecco!*" What a relief! Well, at least I've learned something. Impersonating a woman is a lot of work and it's also painful. Good thing I didn't have my period.

Storing the overnight case in a locker at Rome's Stazione Termini, I realize I haven't eaten anything since yesterday. Famished, I step up to a coffee bar and have a *cappuccino* and three Parma ham and egg *tramezzini*. With my stomach gurgling approval, I walk out of the station and get into a taxi. "Take me to Vatican City, please." I tell the driver. He speeds off into traffic, the tires squealing and smoking in protest. Good thing I didn't tell him, "step on it!" or we'd be airborne.

The usual summertime haze hangs over the city like a soggy bath towel and the car's air conditioning is off. I ask the driver to turn it on. He shrugs, waves a hand in the air, and shouts, "*finito!*"

"So's *The Herald Tribune*," I mutter, rolling down the window. Warm humid air flies into my face along with a wide variety of insects, road grit, and smog, which is occasionally tinged with certain foul aromas, one of which I'm certain emanates from the front seat.

Darting and weaving, we barrel through the early Rome rush hour traffic like a contestant in the Italian Gran Prix. I'm convinced every Rome cab driver believes he's Mario Andretti and his Fiat is a powerful formula one Ferrari. The driver terrifies me as he races by other vehicles, but I know if I protest he's only going to utter a sardonic laugh and mash the accelerator to the floorboards.

Watching the city rocket by unnerves me. Closing my eyes, I hang on for dear life and pray. It seems the appropriate thing to do since we're either going to zoom into the great hereafter or arrive in Vatican City. As we carom across a bridge over the Tiber, I open my eyes. I gasp as the cab careens wildly into Vatican City. Fortunately, the taxi's brakes take hold and we screech to a halt in Saint Peter's Square, which isn't square at all, it's round!

Getting out of the taxi, I gratefully heap a mound of lire in the driver's outstretched hand. His tobacco stained teeth, exposed by a grin redolent of garlic tells me he's satisfied with my exorbitant tip.

So I over-tipped, so what. I'm delighted to be alive. Feeling shaken like a martini, I turn my gaze to my namesake, the Basilica of Saint Peter. In appreciation for my safe deliverance, I contemplate lighting a candle within its vaulted echoing walls, but upon checking my watch, I see that it's already past eight o'clock. Some other time, I vow and hurry to the Vatican's main entrance.

I know that Umberto's office is in a modern building called the Pinacoteca which displays beautiful works of art formerly "liberated" by Napoleon and later returned. It's important I head off the Commissario before he gets there.

Striding a long distance beside Vatican City's outer wall, I finally come to the Museum Gate. There, I find a convenient spot to stand and watch people assemble for the nine o'clock opening. Already a long line has formed, typical of the summertime tourist crush. I scan the crowd, but the Commissario is not in the queue.

By nine-thirty the haze has burned off. The heat, like a celestial blowtorch, becomes intense and the air, heavy with humidity, threatens to suffocate me. To escape, I get in line, buy my ticket and wait inside the entrance where there's shade. Within minutes, the familiar face of the Commissario appears. Threading his way through the crowd, he mops his face with his handkerchief and does a double take when he spots me approaching him.

"Peter, what are you doing here?" he exclaims.

"I'll explain in a minute. Buy your ticket first."

"Not necessary, official business," he says flashing his police identity card.

"Thank God, I found you before you got to Umberto. I'm convinced he's mixed up in this nasty business."

The Commissario looks at me with astonishment.

"Let me explain. Last night Lily Poirel took Claire hostage in an effort to get back the artifact which she presumed I had."

"How did she know?"

"While you and I made our escape along the Grand Canal, Lili guessed that the logical person to break into the chapel and remove the artifact was me. She figured I might be hiding out at Cinzia's so she hurried there and staked out Cinzia's building. When she saw Paolo drop me off she knew I was the intruder."

"Why didn't she confront you?" asks the Commissario.

"I don't know, perhaps she thought it was too risky."

"You're right, that's a heavily traveled campo. How did she know your wife was back in Venice?"

"I've wondered about that myself, but there's a logical answer. One of the Count's men must have noticed the apartment lights the night Claire returned and reported seeing her. Lili figured the best way to get the artifact back was to take Claire hostage. She forced Claire to phone me at Cinzia's to lure me into a trap. Once she recovered the artifact she planned to kill us."

"But you didn't have the real artifact."

"I know, but Lili didn't know that. Cinzia and I fabricated a fake artifact. I took the fake to Claire's flat in the hope that it would fool Lili into releasing Claire. Of course I didn't realize she intended to kill us. I got into a struggle with her she wound up dead."

"You killed her?"

"No, no, not me. Claire's pet black widow spider killed her."

"A black widow spider, you say?" He frowns at me in utter disbelief.

"I swear it, Commissario. The spider dropped on her and bit her in the carotid artery. Its venom paralyzed her and she stopped breathing."

"*Mama mia!*" exclaims the Commissario. "Did you report her death to the Questura?"

"I had Cinzia call."

"*Va bene.*"

"And there's more. I asked the Princess to find out everything she could about Lili Poirel. She uncovered evidence that Lili was born in Frascati. Her birth name is Ferculi."

"I believe the Dottore's told me that's where he's from."

"Then Lili must be related to Umberto."

"Well, well." Says the Commissario, making excited gestures with his hands. "We'll find out soon enough."

"When the Princess told me about Lili, I tried to reach you to stop you from going to see Umberto. Your home phone wouldn't answer and the Questura wouldn't tell us where we could reach you."

"They're not permitted to give out any information. Fortunately, I wasn't able to see the Dottore yesterday. Say, how did you manage to elude the entire Italian police force?"

"A disguise."

"What kind of disguise?"

"I dressed as a woman."

The Commissario bursts into gales of laughter. "I would have enjoyed seeing that."

"Yeah, I looked pretty ridiculous." I feel heat rise up my neck and spread across my face.

"Don't be embarrassed," he says, giving my flushing cheek a good-natured pinch.

"Don't do that!" I push his hand away.

"*Scusate,*" he says. "I'm glad you found me." A random thought suddenly commands the Commissario's attention. Taking me by the arm, he starts walking. "Come with me," he says, urgently.

Flashing his police identity to a guard, we enter the museum and take off down a long caramel-colored marble hallway. For a large man the Commissario moves quickly. From the rear his fast paced walk and rotund shape reminds me of "The Great One," Jackie Gleason. I have difficulty catching up to him.

"Where are we going?" I ask.

"To see a old friend, Father Colabella."

"Who's he?"

"A Jesuit priest. He's the Vatican's psychologist. He deals with their personnel and I want to find out what he can tell us about the Dottore."

"Like who are his siblings?"

"That plus I'd like to know if he's still in Vatican City, which I seriously doubt."

Chapter 19

THE COMMISSARIO and I find Father Colabella in his office. He's sitting behind a large mahogany desk upon which sit stacks of documents arranged in meticulously ordered piles. I notice his finely sharpened pencils all face in the same direction. I do a psychological analysis. These are trademarks of an anal retentive perfectionist.

Father Colabella, a gaunt, starkly handsome priest, is attired in a black cassock. He appears to be in his late forties. His thick wavy hair has gone prematurely white and as he rises to greet us I'm struck by his height, well over six feet. He has steely blue eyes that seem intelligent beyond his years. As he greets me and I feel as though I have been assimilated and processed, much the way a computer devours data and stores it for its future use. I doubt that little escapes this priest's penetrating gaze. He speaks with a voice that is refined, measured, and terse, a scholar who disdains interruption and is accustomed to being heard. Despite his formidable appearance, I sense that he's not without humor and compassion, which fine wrinkles at the corner of his eyes and a gentle manner suggest. "What a pleasant surprise," he exclaims, warmly embracing the Commissario. "It's been at least three years, Luca, has it not?"

"More like five, Father. I'd like you to meet an American friend, Peter Grant. He's an art expert who is working on this case with me."

"I'm pleased to meet you, Peter," he replies. He gives me a firm, handshake. "Please, won't you have a seat?"

"Yes, thank you, Father," I respond. The Commissario and I face Father Colabella across his desk. He sits in a high-backed black leather swivel chair with his elbows resting on its arms. He presses his fingertips together so that they form a vee that acts as a support for his chin. He leans slightly forward and looks at us intently. "Now, how may I help you?"

"This is a delicate matter, Father," says the Commissario.

"How so?"

"Because it involves a Vatican employee, Dottore Umberto Ferculi. The authorities, Mr. Grant, and myself all appear to have been duped by him."

"In what respect, Luca? "You know you can rely on my discretion. I assume this is matter is confidential."

"Highly confidential."

I watch the Commissario with interest as he mentally organizes what he's about to say into a logical sequence of events.

"I've been investigating a series of crimes, Father. Without exception, they all appear to be related and all involve the theft of valuable religious works of art. Most recently these crimes have resulted in two deaths, the most notable being the Benedictine monk, Brother Alvise, who was murdered in Venice for the religious artifact he was transporting for the Vatican."

"Ah, I don't mean to interrupt, Luca, but all of us in the Vatican have heard rumors about this artifact though we haven't officially been told about it. Yesterday afternoon I heard that it had been recovered."

"It was, Father. Mr. Grant located it and yesterday morning I returned it to the Papal secretary. I must tell you, that as we speak, Mr. Grant is technically a fugitive. Though, I know he's innocent of any crimes, he has not yet been officially absolved of blame in connection with the murders I mentioned. Your museum director, Umberto Ferculi, it appears, orchestrated a plan, which Mr. Grant agreed to undertake, with my urging. This plan was a clever ruse conceived by him to implicate Mr. Grant. Initially, even I was fooled into believing Mr.

Grant might have been the perpetrator. Fortunately though, Mr. Grant, acting boldly on his own initiative, located the stolen art objects and brought to light some of the suspects. His efforts led to the recovery of the artifact and I now believe your museum director is the master-mind behind these crimes."

"I see," replies the priest. His only reaction is a slightly raised left eyebrow,

"There is also a woman involved. Her name is Lili Poirel, nee Lili Ferculi. We believe that she's related to the Dottore's, perhaps a younger sister, but we need to confirm this with you."

"Luca, I'll be pleased to help. Why don't we have a look at the Dottore's employment dossier? Please excuse me while I get it," he says, rising from his chair.

"Of course, Father. May I use your telephone to phone my office in Venice."

"Certainly, give the operator the number you want to call. I'll be right back."

I get up from my chair and walk to the window while the Commissario calls the Questura. The priest has a serene view across Vatican Park with its large expanses of verdant lawns, its prolific flower gardens, and its stately shade trees that cast hazy shadows across emerald green grass. All around the park's perimeter stand an assortment of tall gray buildings. Formidable and mute they encircle this luscious Eden in the same manner in which the colorful and highly visible Swiss guards protect the Holy Father.

"Peter," calls the Commissario, interrupting my reverie.

I turn and walk back to my chair. "Yes?"

"My assistant, Roberto has examined *Signorina* Dunn's passport. There's nothing of any substance to link her to the thefts. I'm going to ask him to run a routine background check on Lili Ferculi."

"Good idea," I reply.

"Peter, Roberto wants to know what happened to the glass you wanted examined for fingerprints."

"It was accidentally broken. Can't you take prints directly from her corpse.

"Unfortunately, we no longer have the body."

"You can't be serious?"

"*Scusi*, but the Coroner reported that Lili's body was stolen from the morgue sometime during the night."

"What!" The news stuns me.

The Commissario speaks to his assistant for a few seconds then hangs up.

"Gentlemen," says Father Colabella, striding into his office. Waving a thin manila folder at us, he returns to his chair. "What would you like to know?" He opens the folder and directs his gaze at the Commissario.

"Umberto Ferculi's birthplace, father?"

He scans the first page. "Frascati."

"Any designation of next of kin?" asks the Commissario.

"Yes, a sister, Lili Poirel and a Venice address."

"*Grazie*, Father."

Father Colabella's eyes move from the folder to the Commissario's smiling face. "Now, I suppose you'd like to know where Umberto is?"

"Please," responds the Commissario.

"I'll call his office at the museum and see if the staff knows his whereabouts. First, let me notify our head of security."

"Go right ahead, Father," says the Commissario.

We're not surprised to learn that Umberto has disappeared, but we are astounded to learn that after the Commissario returned the artifact, the Dottore took possession of it and once more it's missing.

Chapter 20

EMBARRASSED by the loss of the artifact and the disappearance of its trusted museum director, the Holy See decides that Father Colabella will accompany us back to Venice to try to help locate Umberto and attempt to recover of the artifact.

"Commissario," I ask, who tipped off the Dottore to the artifact's return."

"The Papal Secretary," interposes Father Colabella. I expect they wanted him to examine its condition. After all, he was involved in the investigation and conservation process."

"Its reappearance at the Vatican must have come as quite a shock to the Dottore," I comment.

"I expect it did." remarks the Commissario. "I doubt Lili told her brother that it had been removed from the chapel."

"That makes sense. She expected to recover it from me before he found out it was gone."

"Commissario, what exactly does Umberto plan to do with the artifact?" asks Father Colabella.

"I suspect he plans to ransom it to the Vatican," deadpans the Commissario. "Because of its priceless significance, he figures the Vatican will pay most anything to get back. The other art-works in the chapel are too well known to sell, so the artifact is the only object of real value that he has."

"What shall we do?" inquires Father Colabella.

"Fly to Venice. It's obvious the Dottore has gone there. Who else would steal his sister's body from the morgue? I've alerted my men to look out for him and I've doubled security around the Count's palazzo."

Climbing into a Fiat sedan assigned to Father Colabella, a Vatican chauffeur drives us to Rome's Ciampino Airport. At the Commissario's urging, I tell the priest about my involvement in the case. He seems particularly fascinated by the Count's chapel, how I got inside and what I found, stolen artworks, the hideous looking bed with its strange grouping of chairs, and the artifact. He laughs when I tell him how the Commissario had let me know he was waiting for me in the pitch dark outside the chapel, by jingling his pocket change.

"Yes, and it's a good thing I was there, Father. If I hadn't sent the Count's speedboat driver tumbling headlong over a bench, Peter wouldn't be here to tell you this story."

"That's for sure, Father. The Commissario saved my . . . ah, butt!" I tell the priest about Lili taking my estranged wife hostage, my rescue attempt and Lili's bizarre death from the venom of a black widow spider. As I'm talking to him, I realize I'm still troubled about how Lili knew Claire had returned to Venice. A strange thought keeps gnawing at my mind, but because of its implications, I'm reluctant to dwell on it. Then there's Lili's tattoo, which I can't seem to get out of my mind either. "Commissario, did I mention to you that Claire and I found a devil's face tattooed on Lili's shoulder?"

"No"

"Sorry. I guess in all the excitement it slipped my mind."

"I doubt it's significant. Many people have tattoos these days." The Commissario seems disinterested.

"What is the motivation for tattoos, father? You're a psychologist."

"They're generally expressions of individualism, nonconformity, or protest. Many are symbols of loyalty to particular groups, street gangs, cults, and military or para- military organizations. Others are simply reminders of a personal experience or a caprice. Tattoos are a very ancient and primitive art form."

"What do you suppose was the significance of Lili's tattoo? The face of the devil was quite malevolent looking."

"I doubt it's important to the case." The Commissario gives me a blase look.

I change the subject. "By the way, Commissario, what did you do with the film I gave you? I'll need copies of the photographs for Lloyd's."

"I have it, but so far I haven't had an opportunity to get it developed."

"Film?" says the priest.

"Pictures I took inside the Count's chapel, Father."

"Speaking of the Count's chapel would you have any objection if I accompany you inside?"

"No problem, Father."

"Thank you," he replies, lapsing into silence. He stares through the tinted glass window at the countryside whizzing past.

I wonder what's on his mind. I had intended to ask the Commissario about his visit with Cosimo De Cheeci, but there's really no point. Moira's passport has alleviated my suspicions. I suppose she could be accused of gold digging, but that's for Cosimo De Cheeci to worry about. I have quite enough on *my* plate.

After landing at Venice's tiny Marco Polo Airport, the Commissario commandeers a cellular phone from the nearest policeman. While he talks to the Questura, I excuse myself from Father Colabella and use a public phone to ring up Cinzia. I want her and Claire to know I'm back in Venice, and most importantly, I want to warn them not to leave the apartment until I get there.

"I'm glad you're safe. I can't wait to see you!" Cinzia gushes.

I hear the excitement in her voice, but it seems forced, oddly insincere. "I'll be there as soon as I can. It's still not safe for you and Claire to leave the apartment. Umberto Ferculi has fled the Vatican and we believe he's in Venice. I'm worried he might come looking for Claire if he finds out Lili died in her flat. If anything occurs that's at all suspicious phone the police right away."

"Okay. How long will it be before you get here?"

"I don't know. The Commissario may insist I go to the Questura with him."

"You haven't heard?"

"Heard what?"

"The Questore was just on television! He announced that a man had turned himself in and confessed to the murders."

"You mean, I'm off the hook?"

"I think so," she replies. Glancing up, I see the Commissario. He walks rapidly toward me. Father Colabella trails him. The Commissario has a big grin on his face and he keeps on giving me a thumb's up sign.

"Cinzia, sorry. I've got to go. I'll be there as soon as I can, *Ciao*."

I hang up the phone and that strange gnawing feeling tugs at my gut. Something's not right.

Embracing me, the Commissario gives me a bear hug. "You're a free man, Peter. No more dresses," he roars with laughter. "Let's go. The police launch is on its way to pick us up."

"Oh, no," I moan. Cinzia's cosmetics case. "I forgot and left it in a locker at the train station in Rome."

"Need your lipstick?" The Commissario chuckles. "Give me the locker key. I'll send for it."

"*Grazie*." I hand him the key.

"*Prego*." He pockets it. We walk through the baggage claim area, exit the terminal and walk onto the pier. Much to my chagrin, the Commissario regales the priest about how I disguised myself as a woman to avoid arrest.

Racing across the lagoon in the police launch toward the isles of Venice, which resemble a far off Disneyland, the Commissario tells us about his phone conversation with his assistant, Roberto.

"Peter, the reason you're no longer a suspect is that one of the Count's bodyguards fled the palazzo after Lili's disappearance and has turned himself in. He told Roberto he believed that the entire scheme, which Lili orchestrated, was unraveling. He told Roberto he didn't want to spend the rest of his life in prison. And by the way, Maria Grazia Lili Ferculi does have a police record. Roman authorities arrested her on numerous occasions for petty theft, solicitation for purposes of prostitution, and possession of narcotics. She and her Sicilian pimp, Niclolo Castelvetrano, served two and a half years in prison on narcotics charges."

"The Count's speedboat driver?" I ask, rubbing my arm, still sore from Lili twisting it and flipping me across Claire's salon.

"Yes," replies the Commissario. "The bodyguard claims that Nico and the other bodyguard were the ones who accosted Brother Alvise. He said the monk resisted then tried to run away, but he tripped, fell against one of the gondola posts and knocked himself unconscious. When the assailants tried rolling him over to remove his sack, he accidentally slipped into the canal and drowned."

"Accident! In the United States if someone dies in the commission of a felony, it's first degree murder."

"Yes, but in Italy we leave charges to the discretion of the Public Prosecutor. In this case I doubt he'll be sympathetic to any lesser charge than life in prison. The bodyguard also admitted that after the monk's death, Lili concocted the idea of framing Peter for the crime."

"Along with Umberto's help," interposes the priest.

"Undoubtedly. The bodyguard says he never heard of Umberto Ferculi. He maintains their orders came directly from Lili."

"What's Count Benzoni's role in all this?" I ask.

"The bodyguard told Roberto the Count wasn't involved and that he had no knowledge of the thefts. He said it was his job to keep the Count from interfering and to keep him out of the chapel. The mastiffs you assumed were the Count's dogs are actually Lili's. She trained them to attack anyone who tried to enter the chapel without her."

Remembering the savage noises the dogs made in the chapel as I escaped through the vault sends chills up my spine.

"So," says Father Colabella, "after the plans to rob Brother Alvise had gone tragically wrong, they told Lili. She immediately conferred with her brother and they devised a scheme to lay the blame on Peter."

"Correct," says the Commissario.

I continue, "So when Umberto learned that I was in Venice in connection with the theft of the Bellini painting, a theft he'd arranged, he went to the Commissario and in his official capacity, sold the Commissario on his plan to uncover the Brother Alvise's murderer and recover the artifact. But in truth, it was a clever scheme to make me scapegoat. Isn't that right, Commissario?"

"Precisely."

"The perfect double cross. And to think that all these years I admired and respected him. Now, it's clear to me why he waited for you to leave Claire's apartment before he made me copy down the plan to steal the Pala D'Oro."

"I'm sorry, Peter, I didn't know."

"Forget about it. Umberto duped both of us. Did the bodyguard say anything to your assistant about breaking into Claire's flat?"

"Yes, he admitted they had been there twice, the first time when you were at the Count's palazzo . . ."

"When they tore up the place and stole Claire's TV."

"Right." The mention of Claire's TV causes the Commissario to smile. "The second occurrence took place the morning you left to meet with Dominick at Harry's Bar. Unexpectedly, they found Adriana inside the flat. Because she could identify them, they had to kill her. Nico smothered her with a pillow, broke her neck, and stuffed her body inside a large zippered bag, which they had used to transport the real Botticelli painting to the flat. They planted Brother Alvise's sack in plain sight and substituted the Palazzo's Cini's Botticelli for the fake one. After dark, Nico carried the young woman's body to the construction barge and dumped it. An old woman living above the canal heard noises, looked out the window, saw the body, and summoned police."

"They did a damn good job of making me look like the murderer. What do you suppose became of the fake Botticelli?"

"Good question, Peter. I suspect they probably hid it somewhere in your wife's flat." Pulling out his notebook, the Commissario scrawls himself a note.

"Commissario," I interrupt. "It's important we find out who leased the Count's chapel."

"Excellent suggestion, Peter, but Roberto's already got that information. He talked to the Count this morning." The Commissario fishes in his jacket for his notebook as the shadow of the vaulted Rialto Bridge suddenly plunges the launch into semi-darkness, the Commissario retrieves it from his jacket pocket. Thumbing through the pages, he says, "Yes, here it is. It's a corporation, EMCA, Cie."

"Who's the owner?"

"I don't know. Roberto's checking it out. First, we're stopping by the Questura and then we're going to Palazzo Benzoni. "Will you be joining us?

"Yes, but I have to check up on Claire and Cinzia. What time shall I be there."

"Three o'clock.

"That's fine, Commissario."

"Where can we drop you, Peter?"

"Santa Maria del Giglio," I reply.

"*Va bene*," says the Commissario, dropping the book back in his pocket.

Leaving the launch, I walk toward Cinzia's, my eyes cast down on shiny cobbles polished by centuries of footsteps, the narrow windings of Venice that separate faded pastel walls, poxed by crumbling plaster and brick. Deeply lost in thought, my mind swirls to near overload as it fits together jumbled pieces of information. Suddenly, the shards fall into place and I behold a mosaic inlaid with betrayal. Its impact sinks into my very fiber like the fangs of a lion. Its crafter's name . . . *Cinzia*!

Chapter 21

I HAVE NEVER been very good at verbal confrontations. In fact, I usually do whatever I can to avoid them. Some people delight in face-offs. Not me! I'm a lover not a fighter. While growing up I was taught to suppress my emotions, particularly anger. So when I get upset, I usually retreat to my Martian cave, lose myself in trivia, and emerge later rather than sooner. My opponent gets no satisfaction, which can be irritating. I have observed first hand that inhabitants of Venus are usually adversely affected by this conduct. On rare occasions when contest is unavoidable I rely on biting sarcasm as a weapon. Mine can be withering, which Claire can attest to. Afterward, though, I'm usually quick to apologize, but forgiving is one thing and forgetting another.

Too late I came to realize that Claire's memory was long and my Martian traits had built up her resentment to the breaking point and had caused her to bolt.

I have no idea how Cinzia will react to my confronting her. I have no experience with her emotions other than her most endearing ones. The others are hidden beneath the *bauto tabarro*, or cloak and mask of incognito. The Princess was right, everything in Venice is a façade and its citizens still indulge in the ancient Italian art of intrigue.

Opening her apartment door to my knock, Cinzia sees an

unexpected look upon my face. It both surprises and repells her. Silently, she stands aside as I enter.

"Piero, she blurts out, I'm so glad—"

I interrupt before she can finish her sentence or embrace me.

"Where's Claire?" I ask.

"She went back to her flat to get an address book. I told her you said she shouldn't go out until you got here, but she said it was imperative that she phone someone."

"Damn," That's not very smart. I pick up the phone and call Claire's flat, but there's no answer.

"She's probably on her way back," says Cinzia, sitting down on the sofa. She sits stiffly and looks up at me. Apprehension shows in her face.

"What happened in Rome?" she asks, forcing a smile.

"It's what's happened here that I'm worried about, Cinzia."

"What do you mean?" Her body tenses.

"You set me up, didn't you?"

"No, Peter, I . . ."

"There's no use denying it, Cinzia. I know what you did and why you did it."

Anger flashes in her eyes. "I don't have to listen to you."

"Would you rather I phone the Commissario. Perhaps you'd rather explain to him instead."

"Her shoulders sag. She looks down at her hands, wrings her fingers, and mutters, "no."

"I thought as much. At first I thought it odd that you omitted telling me about Lili and your father having an affair."

She glances up. "How did you . . ."

"Irena. The more I thought about it, the more it disturbed me, particularly when I couldn't figure out how Lili found out Claire was in Venice. But now it's painfully obvious. You told her."

"I did not. How can you make such dreadful accusation?"

"Because you've made it easy for me. Cinzia, tell me about EMAC, Cie. Don't those initials stand for Elonora, Maxim, and Cinzia Aliverti? Isn't that your family company? And didn't that same company lease Count Benzoni's Chapel?"

Cinzia stares at me, aghast. Her face turns ashen.

"You discovered that your father had leased the Count's chapel and you correctly assumed he had done so at Lili's behest. They were having an affair at the time. You found out she was using the building for illegal purposes and you decided to investigate. One day you saw a load of paintings being carried inside and you suspected they'd been stolen. That's when you knew you'd found yourself a permanent ticket out of Venice, away from your philandering father, your self-pitying mother, and your suffocating existence with little money and even less hope for a future."

Leaning forward, Cinzia covers her face with her hands and begins to whimper. "How can you say these things?" she cries. "I thought you loved me . . . It's not true . . . It's not."

"I'm not feeling sympathetic, Cinzia." I pace back and forth in front of her. "You delved into Lili's background, found out about her sordid past, and decided to use it against her. That's called blackmail, Cinzia. If Count Benzoni had found out he was harboring a convicted criminal who had brought along Nico, her former pimp, he would have thrown her out in the street. You stood to get a big slice of the pie when the stolen art was finally ransomed to Lloyd's. And you of all people knew they'd pay to recover the stolen art with no questions asked? I'm sure, if I ask, Colin Marshall he'll remember your interest in their art theft claims. I'll bet you know exactly what's inside that chapel and how much it's all worth."

"Peter," she sobs. "Stop it . . . stop . . . please," she implores, tears cascading down her cheeks. "I'm sorry. Everything got out of control. Nobody was supposed to get hurt. I got so frightened."

"Yeah, everything came apart after Brother Alvise's murder. You never thought you'd be mixed up in anything like that so you played along with me while I eluded the police, got inside the chapel, and found the artifact the monk carried. It didn't take a rocket scientist for Lili to figure out I was the one who took it. She knew for sure when she saw me enter this building at two o'clock that morning. When did she get to you? Before or after you met with Moira?"

"Before," she gasps between sobs.

"That's what I thought. You didn't want her coming after

me in your apartment, so you told her Claire was back and if she took Claire hostage I'd be forced to go there, didn't you?"

"Yes . . . I'm so ashamed," she cries out.

"And you told her about the glass that I gave you and she watched you smash it, right?"

"Yes, yes." Barely audible, she asks, "What are you going to do to me?"

"Nothing, Cinzia. I'm just going to leave."

"Oh, Piero, please forgive me . . . I didn't mean to hurt you and Claire." She reaches out to me and starts to get up.

"Don't," I shout at her.

She throws herself across the sofa and bursts into sobs.

Turning away from her, I walk toward the door. On the foyer table lies a reminder of our efforts, the makeshift artifact, still nestled in its oblong, red leather box.

Chapter 22

HEARTSICK and suddenly weary, I walk out of Cinzia's building, take a deep breath, and head toward Campo Santo Stefano. I look up to see the sky clouded over. A dull haze lingers over the city. It produces a strange silvery light, not bright, but dull like pewter, a color as somber as I feel.

Half way to Claire's flat I spot her standing atop the hump of a graceful curved bridge. A curly, dark haired gondolier in a red and white striped shirt flirts with her. The seafaring Casanova tries to coax her into his shiny black gondola that bobs in the canal beneath the bridge. It's obvious from his mannerisms what's on his mind.

Spying me, she shouts, "Peter!" Breaking away, she rushes down the steps of the bridge and flings her arms around me. I stand unyielding and stiff, wooden as a cigar store Indian.

"Peter, what's wrong?" she asks, gazing into my pained face. "You look as though someone died."

"She might as well have." I remark, my eyes tearing.

"Cinzia?"

"Yeah." It's all I can do to keep myself from crying.

She takes my arm. "Come on, Peter, let's go back to the flat and talk about it."

It takes a half dozen tissues and an hour to explain everything to Claire. She's sympathetic. She's also surprisingly charitable about Cinzia's behavior. "I think she's desperately unhappy. I know how it feels and she's had nearly half a lifetime of it. I know you're hurting, Peter, but don't be too harsh on her."

"If you say so, I won't. How come you left Cinzia's apartment?"

"Cinzia got very nervous. It made me terribly uncomfortable. I made up an excuse and left for a while. It's a good thing I did."

"I guess." I get up from the davenport and walk around the salon. "Claire, I've got to meet the Commissario and Father Colabella at Palazzo Benzoni at three. I don't want you staying here. It's not safe right now. Will you do me a big favor?"

"What's that?"

"Take a water taxi to the Giudecca and stay with the Princess until we find Umberto Ferculi. It'll make me feel better if I know you're with her."

"Sure. Do you mind if I tell the Princess you went to Rome in drag?" she grins.

"You'll make me the laughing stock of Venice."

"I'll tell her to keep it to herself."

"Ha, fat chance."

Claire looks absently at the ceiling above my head. "What's that brown thing in Francesca's web?"

"What!" I look up alarmed. Staring at the spider web I see a small pear shaped object in the far corner of the web. Little black specks are crawling on it.

"My God! I exclaim, baby spiders."

"Baby spiders?" Claire jumps up and joins me.

"Yes, that's an egg sac. See, there must be dozen little ones crawling around."

"Francesca's babies," shouts Claire. She jumps up and down.

"I'm so excited."

"Hey, stop that . . . your neighbor downstairs . . . I'll have to buy more flowers."

After the Princess agrees to look after Claire, I hail her a water taxi and send her off to the Giudecca then I board a vaporetto, which takes me to the Rialto Bridge. Walking from the Rialto to the Count's palazzo, I realize that I have on my jacket with the Princess' crucifix in my right hand pocket. Good, I'll return it to her when I pick up Claire.

The Comissario, Father Colabella and a dozen heavily armed police officers in battle dress and helmets await me. The area is cordoned off to spectators who have gathered to gawk. The Commissario waves me through a metal barricade and a web of yellow tape that would have made Francesca jealous.

"Why all the firepower?" I ask the Commissario.

"My men reported gunshots from inside. We'll stand away from the front entrance while they secure the building."

"What about the Count?"

The Commissario flashes his cellular phone. "I tried calling. No one answers, but there's organ music coming from the chapel."

"Really?"

"I heard it too, Peter," says the priest. "Bach. It sounds like one of his dirges."

"Umberto's a classical pianist," I tell them. "I haven't a clue if he plays the organ."

"We'll soon find out. All ready, men?" the Commissario cries out to his officers.

"Do they know about those two big mastiffs inside?"

"You two with the riot guns, go in first. Watch for two attack dogs."

Three burly men rush the entrance with a hand carried battering ram that resembles a torpedo with handles. Four assaults send sharp bangs echoing across the canal and finally succeed in splintering one side of the massive entrance door. Forcing it open with pry bars, the advance team slips inside with the classic moves of men trained in military operations. A burst of gunfire erupts from inside, followed by a yelp then quiet.

Shouts resound from inside the palazzo until they reach the man at the door who also shouts."

"What are they saying?"

"That the entry's clear," says the Commissario, motioning

us forward. "Let's go."

I follow Father Colabella and the Comissario inside. It looks the same as the first time I visited the Count except on the marble floor, in a widening pool of blood, lies one of the mastiffs, a black and brown brute, its head blown half off. The gory sight sickens me and I turn away.

I hear the sounds of the swat team as they move behind the staircase, fanning left and right, four men each side, going down the corridors, banging open doors, shouting, pointing their weapons, as they move along the parallel wings leading to the cloisters and the chapel.

"We'll wait here until they've secured both wings," advises the Commissario. Behind us eight more heavily armed men enter the palazzo and move up the marble stairway to the *piano noble*. They follow the same pattern as the others. I'm a bystander, oddly out of place, captivated and yet scared all at once. My heart races, pumping adrenaline and suddenly there are loud cries from the floor above from the *piano nobile*. I can't understand anything they yell, except, "*morto*." It's that awful word again.

The Commissario bounds up the stairs with Father Colabella hard on his heels. I follow, afraid of being left behind. The second dog lies dead in the doorway to the salon. I heard no shots. Perhaps that was what the Commissario's men heard earlier.

Inside, staining the parquet crimson, lies the Count, his body twisted grotesquely in death, shredded flesh gaping from his thigh and his where his throat has been ripped out. The priest bends down, obscuring my view and halting the bile that's risen in the back of my throat. I swallow hard, and gasp hoarsely to Father Colabella, "Watch the blood, Father, he had AIDS."

"*Grazie*," says the priest, praying over the Count in melodious tones of Latin. The Commissario puts his hand on my shoulder, "You all right?" he asks.

"I will be if I don't look."

"Go out in the hallway, open one of the French doors and get some fresh air. He sounds clinical as though bloody, mangled bodies are an every day occurrence. I trot across the terrazzo hallway and jerk open one of the doors. A breeze brushes against my face, erasing the smell of death and replacing it with the pungent, syrupy fragrance of wisteria laced with the attar of roses. Stepping out on a narrow balcony I breathe deeply and gaze down at the serenity of the garden below. I hear it's fountain gurgle and splash, I hear the chatter and flitting of sparrows, and very faintly, I hear the swell of an organ in the chapel beyond. Save the voices from the salon, the only other sound is the product of my imagination. From the gaping jaws of the fountain's ferocious-looking winged lion, I seem to hear a deep guttural snarl.

Following three members of the swat team, we move along the long ground floor corridor of the left wing, the one that abuts the canal and leads to an entrance into the chapel. At intervals along its stucco passageway stand suits of armor. On the walls between these vacant medieval warriors, hang the tools of warfare, pikes, broadswords and lances, maces, longbows, and arrows, and daggers, rapiers, and crossbows.

Midway down the corridor, there's an open door. It leads to the cloister and beyond its columnar arches, the garden. At the hallway's terminus we see an archway and set into it a thick oak door that opens into the chapel. We wait as our escort goes forward to take up their positions. They throw open the door, which hits the wall with a resounding thud.

Music and light flood the corridor. The three guards with their deadly assault weapons become shimmering silhouettes against the soft glow of candlelight.

We walk up behind them. They stand frozen, their automatic rifles trained on a solitary figure, who sways to the ebb and flow of sound as his fingers caress yellowed ivory tiles and his feet dance on wooden pedals. He pays no attention to the intrusion. He focuses only on the music, a candle lit manuscript propped on its stand above the keyboard, and the sound of a powerful refrain that issues forth from towering steel organ tubes. The exquisite and powerful refrain of Bach's cantata *Wachet auf, ruft uns die Stimme*, "Awake a Voice is Calling" reverberates throughout the chapel. The cantata, a parable about five wise men and five foolish virgins who go forth to meet the bridegroom, has some meaning for Dr. Umberto

Ferculi, but as yet, we are not privy to it.

Oblivious to the soldiers and the weapons trained on him, Umberto plays on. Finally, as the music reaches the crescendo of its finale, the Commissario begins to applaud. "Bravo!" he shouts "Bravo! Bravo!"

Spellbound, I watch Umberto. Smiling, he turns toward us, stands, and with perspiration beading his face and staining his shirt, he inclines his head forward. Then moving his arms in unison, he makes a graceful and sweeping, theatrical bow.

"Magnificent, Dottore!" exclaims the Commissario. "I had no idea you could play so beautifully."

"Thank you, Luca. I had planned to play for Lili's wedding to the Count, but alas, as you know, it is not to be." Ignoring the heavily armed men and their guns, he walks toward the huge Gothic bed in the center of the chapel. Over it hangs the massive iron chandelier that shimmers and glows with light from a hundred candles. And standing on each side of the bed are the gas torcheres, aflame with wisps of black smoke trailing upward.

"Stand down." the Commissario orders the armed men. "He's harmless."

I whisper, "Don't you mean, deranged?"

The Commissario hears me, but he ignores me. "Dottore, we must ask you to come with us."

"In a moment, Luca. First, I'd like to show you something." We follow Umberto and on the bed we find Lili's body, naked and decomposing. It lies atop the coverlet. Her mouth is pulled back in a hideous grin and her hair is a great tangled nest resembling rusted steel wool. Already her pale body is horribly discolored and a rank stench that rises from her putrefying flesh overwhelms me. Gagging, I put my hand to my nose and mouth, avert my eyes, and back away from the bizarre sight.

"My beautiful sister, Luca," laments Umberto, his voice breaking. "Like our noble ancestors, we were planning to gather around the marriage bed to witness the consummation of her marriage to the Count."

"Yes, I'm terribly sorry, Dottore." The commissario grimaces.

"I see you brought Father Colabella, perhaps he—"

"Of course," the priest interrupts, humoring the tortured Umberto.

While he prays over Lili's corpse, I walk toward the altar. Behind it, on the wall in semi-darkness, hangs the magnificent Bellini. It's *déjà vu*. The diptych sits on the right side of the altar, in the center, the Catalan crucifix with the graceful gold chalice standing in front of it and on the left side lies the artifact's oblong red box. Its leather appears stained. Reflected in the candlelight is a silvery trail of water droplets that make a path across the altar.

That's odd. Condensation from the air-conditioning ducts? My thought is interrupted by an urgent cry from the doorway.

"Commissario?"

I turn to see the Commissario beckon me to follow him. Abandoning the altar, I turn to accompany him. Umberto kneels by the bed praying alongside the priest.

Another armed officer has joined the three who stand guard at the door.

"Yes?" says the Commissario as he approaches.

"Sir, it's about the other bodyguard. We flushed him out of hiding in a crawl space on the third floor. He's been handcuffed and taken outside, but we're unable to find any trace of the speedboat driver.

"I'm certain he's hiding somewhere in the palazzo. Take my men and go back over the kitchen, the storerooms, and the wine cellar. These old palazzi have hidden passages. Look for them and find him."

"Yes sir, *subito*." He leaves with our three guards following him.

"Commissario, you'll be happy to know the artifact is sitting on the altar."

"Good, I'll tell Father Colabella to retrieve it."

"All of the artwork seems to be here, but I'll make certain by walking around the chapel to check."

"Do that." He pats me on the shoulder and walks back to Umberto and Father Colabella. I hear, "*In Nomine Patris et Filii et Spiritus Sancti, Amen.*" Then, having completed his unction, Father Colabella stands up and confers with the Commissario. Shortly thereafter I see him walk toward the altar to recover the artifact.

As I skirt the inside perimeter of the Chapel taking a mental inventory of the paintings, I momentarily lose sight of Father Colabella. Walking toward the organ, along the wall that connects to the palazzo, I catch a glimpse of him moving in my direction along the opposite wall. He looks like a specter in his dark cassock. An occasional glint of illumination, a reflection of light from the silver crucifix that hangs from his neck reminds me he's human. He follows the Durer etchings of the Stations of the Cross. I stop in the shadow of the organ and watch him as he whispers his prayers and kisses his crucifix before moving on to the next work. At the last etching he turns and walks toward me.

Suddenly a dark figure emerges from behind the other side of the organ. Stealthy and quick as a commando, he seizes Father Colabella from behind and wrests the artifact from his grasp.

Unseen, I melt into the shadows and wait.

As the assailant forces the priest toward the open doorway into the palazzo I see that his captor is Nico. He has one hand across the priest's mouth and in the other is a sawed off shotgun that he's stuck into the priest's back to prods him toward the exit. Unaware of what's happening, the Commissario has his back toward us as he talks and gestures to Umberto.

Reaching in my pocket, I extract Irena's crucifix. A weapon!

As Nico and his captive walk past me, I grasp the crucifix like a pistol, step quietly out of the darkness, jab its blunt end into Nico's back and shout, "Drop the gun, Nico."

The Commissario whirls around and raises his pistol.

Nico grunts, releases the priest and throws down the shotgun. As it hits the floor, it discharges with a deafening roar followed by a loud clang as the projectile from the gun smashes into the wall mounted pulley mechanism for the chandelier.

Twisting around, Father Colabella seizes Nico in a headlock. I pin Nico's arms and we wrestle him to the floor. The Commissario dives on top of us and we hear the sound of glass shattering.

The artifact!

Something on the pulley snaps off and clangs to the floor. The pulley's crank handle rotates. Spinning like a propeller it sends rope flying off its cylinder and the massive chandelier plummets. Falling through the canopy, it splinters the bedposts and collapses the bed onto the floor. Crushed beneath its immense weight are Lili's corpse, Umberto, the arrangement of chairs and the torcheres. Flames from the candles and the torcheres ignite the bed covers, turning the rubble into a flaming pyre.

Sticking his pistol in Nico's face, the Commissario forces the cursing Nico to lie on the floor while he snaps handcuffs on his wrists.

"Fire!" I yell as the rubble becomes an inferno.

Father Colabella leaps to his feet. Bending over he picks up the red leather box that lies among pebbles of smashed crystal. His knowing eyes meet mine. We're horrified.

From the altar comes a piercing, scream that echoes above the sound of crackling flames and a dreadful cracking noise that sends a tremor rumbling across the chapel floor like an ice floe about to break up.

"*Madonna! Aiuto . . . Aiuto!*"

That voice?

"It's Cinzia!" I shout, running toward the altar.

Underneath my feet I feel the floor begin to sag. As I dart away to the side of the chapel, the floor implodes sending burning rubble, the chandelier and the bodies of Lili and Umberto in a great cascade into the putrid waters of the vault below the chapel. A great cloud of steam billows into the chapel as I race behind the altar.

Through the smoke and steam I see a stone slab lifted up from the floor by a jackscrew. And behind it, huddled against the back of the altar is a pathetic looking figure in sneakers, jeans, and a sweater. Soaked to the skin, covered in sewage, and screaming in terror is Cinzia. She stares at me through fear filled feral eyes. In her hands she clutches to her breast a dark red leather box, its fine gold tooling barely visible.

Chapter 23

CINZIA CAN'T SPEAK, nor will she permit anyone but Father Colabella to touch her. In deep shock, she allows him to carry her in his arms to the water ambulance that the Commissario has summoned to carry her to the hospital. After she's gone the Commissario takes me aside in the front entrance to the palazzo. "Peter," he says, "I don't know what's going on between you and Signorina Aliverti or how she managed to get inside the chapel and frankly, I don't think I want to know. Since we have Brother Alvise's murderers and we've got possession of the artifact, I'm satisfied. No more speculation, we'll just leave things as they are?"

"Fair enough," I reply. "Would you mind calling the Princess on your cell phone. Claire's with her and I have to arrange to pick her up."

"We'll run you out there in the launch," he offers.

"Thanks."

"*Prego.*" He phones Irena and she insists we come for tea. Her invitation is a comic relief. The Commissario accepts and after hanging up breaks into hysterical laughter, admitting that his growling, empty stomach compelled him to accept.

"After all this you're able to eat," I marvel.

"*Allora*, case closed," he smiles.

When Father Colabella, the Commissario and I arrive on

the Giudecca, the Princess is prepared. Radiant in a deep purple caftan that effectively displays her emeralds, she greets us as though she's been expecting royalty. Her tiny apartment shimmers with gleaming silver platters that are heaped with tea sandwiches, smoked salmon, pastries, and cookies. An ice bucket holds chilled prosecco and on her inlaid coffee table, surrounded by Vieux Paris china and Niello flatware, sits her silver samovar filled with hot tea. Standing by to assist are two white-gloved waiters borrowed from Harry's Dolce.

Acting as lady in waiting, Claire smiles, gives proper greetings and leads us to the recamier for our audience with the Princess. It amuses me how Irena snatches the priest away and compels him to sit beside her like a King Charles Spaniel. Turning her attention to him, she dismisses the Commissario and me with a regal wave of her hand. The Commissario helps himself to smoked salmon while I join Claire who gives me a sexy little wink and tells me I can expect a warmer greeting from her later. I'm not exactly certain what she means, but it sounds promising.

After a while I walk over to the Princess, reach behind her and hang her silver crucifix in its accustomed place on her wall.

"Was it useful, *caro*?" she inquires, her eyebrows arched.

"More than you'll ever know," I reply, smiling at Father Colabella.

"I'm elated!" she exclaims with a merry laugh.

"Actually, it saved *my* life," says Father Colabella.

"How lovely," she comments then changes the subject. "Peter, Claire tells me you and Cinzia had a little spat. I trust it's nothing serious."

"Nothing a dozen roses and Lloyd's reward money won't fix."

"I thought surely you'd bring her to tea."

"As Father Colabella can attest she had quite an ordeal," I reply.

"The Commissario said if it hadn't been for Cinzia, we might not have recovered the artifact. Is that correct, Father?"

"Yes, Princess. Cinzia is a brave young woman."

Excusing myself, I rejoin Claire and the Commissario.

Left to our own devices, we quaff and nibble, and discuss trivia. Mutely attesting to our appetites is the disappearance of a generous quantity of food and drink. Catching murderers is a real calorie burner.

We look on as Father Colabella shows the Princess the artifact enshrined in its protective covering of Murano glass. Totally enraptured, she looks any second as if she might swoon. "Oh, my!" she gasps, "A nail from the hand of the crucified Christ. Why it's extraordinary," she says, running her chubby fingers lovingly over the glass."

"Yes, it is," replies the priest.

"And to think it's survived for almost two thousand years. *Allora*, Father, Isn't it interesting how good and evil vie with one another to see which will lead us through the streets of life? When I was a young girl, I was taught to be wary of people and never to trust anyone until I knew their true identity. But how can one be sure? Take Dottore Ferculi for example. Who would have dreamed he would have been consumed with such greed?"

"Certainly not the Vatican," replies Father Collabella. "He managed to deceive all of us."

"Do you think he was truly evil?"

"That's hard for me to say. Peter knew him better than I did. Perhaps we should ask his opinion?"

"Peter," calls Father Colabella.

"Yes, Father."

"The Princess just asked me whether Umberto Ferculi was an evil man. What's your view?"

"I think so. When that huge chandelier was falling, about to snuff out his life, I saw the most diabolical smile on his face. I don't think I'll ever forget his expression. In fact, it reminded me of the face I found tattooed on Lili's shoulder."

"The face of the devil!" Irena exclaims.

"Yes. How did you know?"

"Ha!" she says with an ingenious smirk. "That's easy. The Dottore's name, Ferculi, is the anagram for Lucifer."

Chapter 24

When the Commissario drops Claire and me off at the Rio San Vidal, he gives me a parting embrace, Venetian style. It makes me feel like family. "Peter," he says, jingling his change, "Don't be a stranger."

"I won't," I laugh.

As the Commissario heads down the Grand Canal for home we wave goodbye. I purposely avoid looking across the Rio San Vidal at the palazzo where Cinzia's mother lives. I don't approve of selfish mothers with agendas for screwing up their daughters.

Walking back to Claire's building, I spot a package lying on the entrance hall floor. It's addressed to Mrs. Peter Grant. I pick it up and notice it's postmarked from London.

"Who's it for?" asks Claire.

"For me," I lie, terrified of its contents. That pervert, Colin Marshall, took me seriously and there's no telling what kind of risque undergarments he's bought Claire. No way she's getting *this* package.

"Mandy's Intimates, Knightsbridge?" she questions, glancing at the sticker on the outside of the package. "I suppose it's racy lingerie for Cinzia?"

"Yeah," I reply, turning crimson.

"Peter, do you love her?"

"I thought I did, but I was never *in love* with her like I am with you."

"Right answer." Entwining her arms around my neck like a python, she trains her sparkling peridot eyes on me and plants a lovely soft kiss on my mouth. Her body feels warm and inviting. "I heard you tell the Princess that you're giving the reward money to Cinzia," she murmurs in my ear. "That's a lovely gesture. I'm beginning to think you appreciate women after all, Dog three."

"Woof! Woof!" I reply.

"You're adorable!" Nuzzling my neck, she nibbles on my ear lobe, and whispers, "I might learn to love you again. No promises, you understand, but for now, why don't you just take me upstairs and we'll play."

"Backgammon?"

"Afterward, maybe."

Printed in the United States
3992